THE

Space

BETWEEN

Trees

KATIE WILLIAMS

THE *Space*

BETWEEN

Trees

THE Space BETWEEN

Trees

By Katie Williams

chronicle books · san francisco

Library of Congress Cataloging-in-Publication Data available.
ISBN 978-0-8118-7175-4

Book design by Natalie Davis.
Typeset in Adobe Jenson, Norwich, and Berthold Akzidenz Grotesk.

Manufactured by C&C Offset, Longgang, Shenzhen, China, in March 2010.

1 3 5 7 9 10 8 6 4 2

This product conforms to CPSIA 2008.

Chronicle Books LLC
680 Second Street, San Francisco, California 94107

www.chroniclekids.com

To my parents

Chapter ONE

I'M IN HOKEPE WOODS this morning, like I am every Sunday, delivering papers and keeping an eye out for Jonah Luks. It's early when I drive into the neighborhood, so everyone's still sleeping. Me, I'm wide awake to see all those Hokepe houses cast in blue like the light in a movie theater after the credits have gone up and out. The streets are real quiet, too, not even one lone dog-walker yanking his pup away from something it wants to sniff. I pull Mom's car to the curb where Jonah always parks his truck. No truck, though—too early for Jonah Luks. When I step out of the car, my breath puffs in front of me like some strange language I'm speaking. It's early March and the snow is finally off the ground, but not the frost yet, and this early, it's chilly out. I try to sink into it—my couple hours in the cold—and drag my satchel from the backseat, lifting the strap over my head.

The paper route is something I've had since I was eleven. Eleven-year-olds aren't expected to stick with things, but I've stuck with this, and now I'm sixteen and the oldest paper carrier on the list by about three years. The only girl, too. This doesn't embarrass me. I like the job. Anyway, it's better than dripping medicine into some neighbor kid's ear or getting my arms sticky scooping ice cream out of a tub. The beauty of a paper route is this: You put a paper on a doormat. Done.

Also, I like the Hokepe houses. They have these details to them—windowpanes tinted green like they've been made from pop-bottle glass, brass sundials that cast spiky shadows, bunches of clematis so thick it looks like you could stick your hands in them and climb straight up a wall, stained-wood porches, peaked windows, speckled bricks—all the good stuff. They're worlds different from the houses Mom and I rent, like the one we have now, with its screen doors sagging like a body's pressed against them, the shag carpets hopping with fleas, and someone's greasy head stain on the wall above my bed. Now, it's not like you'd call the Hokepe houses mansions—they aren't big or showy enough for that—it's more that everything has been thought about and put in its right place, and so when you step up to one of their doors, you kind of feel like you've been considered and put in your right place, too.

Hokepe isn't that large a neighborhood, but almost every house orders a Sunday paper. It usually takes me two hours to finish my paper route. I like to do the blocks in the middle of the neighborhood first and save the ones on the edges—the ones surrounded by the woods—for later. But today I must be walking slower than usual because I'm only halfway done with the middle houses when I notice that the sun has gotten its hairline up over the ground, which means that it's time to catch Jonah Luks. Jonah must be slow this morning, too, because when I get back to the place where he parks, his truck still isn't there. So I drag out the next few deliveries, rearranging the contents of my satchel, straightening any askew doormats, and setting both feet on each porch step. A few minutes later, I hear

Jonah's old engine rattle, so I run back to the house next to where he'll park and pretend I'm just coming down its front walk, even though I already delivered a paper there half an hour ago. Jonah pulls into his usual spot along the curb, and I can see that salt and rust have turned the bottom of his doors into lace. When he gets out, he pats the side of the truck, like it's done a good job getting him there, which I guess it has.

I call out, and Jonah raises a hand. No one looks as good raising a hand as Jonah does. I don't know why that is. Maybe it's something to do with the angle of his palm or the torque of his wrist. When Jonah waves, he looks like he could be hailing his golden retriever or his old, doting grandmother or his college roommate (though probably not the last one, since Jonah dropped out of college two years ago).

I am, of course, none of these. But I pretend to be as important as each of them as I wave back—in fact, more important than all of them added up together. Jonah lets his hand drop and gets so busy rummaging in the bed of his truck that I'm able to walk all the way over to him without him even noticing me. When I tap him on the shoulder, he jumps.

"Boo," I say.

"Boo, you," he says.

"You're late. Did you have a late night? Did you stay out and party? Did you drink until the sun came up?"

He frowns and returns his attention to his truck. The words *Jefferson Wildlife Control*, stenciled on its side, are peeling a little at their feet. I push the bottom of one of the *l*s down, but it rolls back up again. Jonah is trying to get out his sled, but it's stuck, the prow of it jutting up out of the truck bed, the stern trapped under some junk. He has so much trash in his truck it's like he was raised by raccoons.

"It's like you were raised by raccoons," I say.

He doesn't answer.

I watch him work at it, and while he does, I look him over—the shadow on his jaw, the curl of his nostril, and the underbrush of his eyebrow. I think, *He is assembled so correctly.*

"I know something you don't." I dance a little on the spot; he doesn't look. "I know what you'll get today."

"Get?" He squints.

"Out in the woods. What animals you'll get."

"Oh, yeah? What?"

"Rabbits."

"Yeah?" He finally yanks the sled out with an ugly metallic sound. "Rabbits, plural?"

"Barely plural. Just two." I lean against his truck and take the sled's pull-cord with my finger. The cord is stained gray from all the grime on Jonah's hands. Sometimes I try to hold the same thing he's holding but in a different place—like, just now, Jonah has the end of the sled and I have its cord. This makes it almost like we're touching each other. Jonah drops the sled.

"Is rabbit the minimum?" I ask.

"Minimum?"

"Size-wise, I mean. If you see something smaller, do you still have to pick it up? What about a frog? Would you have to pick up a dead frog?"

"I guess," he says.

"What about a snail? A beetle? A potato bug?"

I keep on talking while he moves things around in his truck bed. Every once in a while, he grunts or says "yep." He doesn't seem to be paying much attention to me. Jonah is unflappable—so unflappable that sometimes I want to shake him just to hear if anything inside rattles. I set my satchel of papers onto his sled and pull the thing a few yards down the street. The sled's bottom scrapes against the asphalt, leaving a line of red paint behind me.

"Oops," I say.

Jonah stops with his business in the truck and looks at me out of the corner of his eye.

"I need that."

I smile and keep pulling it. "No, you don't. I told you. You're only going to find two rabbits today. They're little. You can put one under each arm."

He walks over, lifts my satchel from the sled, and threads the rope out from between my fingers. His hands are the swollen and chapped type, the kind that remind you more of tools than of body parts. I wonder what my hand feels like to him. Sweaty and twitchy, I suspect, like some dying animal he'd pick up out in the woods. I've tried to test it out before, what my hands would feel like to someone else, but it's no good holding the damn things myself. The sled skips back to the truck after Jonah. I follow and lean against the side of the truck just next to where he is.

"What'll you give me?" I ask.

"Give you?" His back is to me. He pulls out a pair of work gloves and tosses them on the ground by his feet.

"Knowledge is power. I told you about the rabbits. What'll you give me?"

He thinks a second. "Rabbit soup."

This is the thing about Jonah. You assume he's barely paying attention, and then he zings you. *Rabbit soup.* I like this, and I call it after him as he takes his sled and walks off between the houses and then into the woods. "Ha! Rabbit soup!" He raises a hand without turning around and then disappears in the trees.

Already I'm examining our conversation in my head, pulling out a sentence or two to keep for myself, fixing up the rest. In my mind, I picture the line of Jonah's shoulders, replay the fall of his voice, and memorize the lift of his eyebrows. I'll be reporting the encounter on Monday, after all, and I have to figure out exactly how it should be told.

I sit with these girls in the cafeteria—pastel sweaters, home-packed lunches, unpierced earlobes, and unbreached hymens. Be assured: These girls and I aren't friends. I don't have any friends. This doesn't bother me much. Most of the time I can be on my own—during classes, in the halls, on weekends—but in the cafeteria, I've got to sit somewhere. These pastel girls always have open seats at their table, so, a few months ago, I sat down in one, and no one told me to leave. I sat down in one again the next day and watched them unwrap their PB&Js, lay out their carrot sticks, poke straws into their juice boxes, and never look at me, not even once. I trucked through my food, chewing and swallowing to the rhythm of their conversations, which they had in sort of a whisper. That's when I started calling them the Whisperers, just to myself, though, because who else was there to talk to?

One day, after a week of sitting there, when I'd balled up the ends of my lunch and gotten up to go, one of the Whisperers said, "Bye, Evie." I turned around, but I didn't know which one of them had said it; I only knew a few of their names—some Jennys and a Kier. "Bye," I said to all of them. And even though we wouldn't be friends, it was nice to exchange hellos and good-byes. It wasn't like we had anything more than that to say to each other. But then, the next day when I sat down at their table, wouldn't you know it, they were talking about Jonah Luks.

It turned out that a number of the Whisperers lived in Hokepe Woods, and they'd seen Jonah tromping out to the trees, his sled bobbing after him like some loyal beagle. Jonah is "older," has broad shoulders, and has a bit of red in his hair; this is more than enough to build a crush on. The Whisperers, I soon discovered, talk about Jonah all the time. They murmur, squirm, and, if one of them says something even a little bit sexual, squeal.

"That guy?" I said that lunch a few months ago. Back then, I'd never talked to Jonah, but I'd seen him on my route. "I know him." Suddenly they were blinking at me, and I felt like I'd turned on the lights in a roomful of mice. "Evie," one of them breathed, and then they were all squeaking my name.

At first, talking to Jonah was a game and winning it meant that I came to lunch with a new Jonah story for the Whisperers. I don't think it was their friendship I wanted so much as their attention. No, more than that, I wanted something to happen; I wanted something to happen *to me*. And to make something happen with some college-dropout laborer guy, rusty truck and muddy work boots included, was . . . well . . . better than nothing happening at all.

The Sunday after I found out that the Whisperers were obsessed with Jonah Luks, I found his truck and waited by it until I spotted him coming out of the woods at the edge of the neighborhood, at which point I dumped all my newspapers onto the ground in front of me. This was something I'd seen a woman in a movie do once with the contents of her purse, and it seemed like a good strategy until I'd actually done it. I hadn't thought about the moment after the dumping when I'd have to stand there with papers piled up to my ankles, feeling as stupid as possible. I bent down and tried to shovel the papers back into my satchel as quick as I could, but Jonah got there before I was done. And, the thing is, the trick from the movie *worked*. Jonah knelt down next to me and started picking up papers without a word, like it was simply the next task on his to-do list. And me, I knelt next to him and pretended that I wasn't watching his hands grab those papers, his palms blackening with ink. His hands were much larger than mine, much larger than you'd think, even, judging from his own wrists—it was like they really belonged to another, bigger person.

When we'd gotten all the papers in the bag, I stuck out my own little hand and said, "Hi, I'm Evie," which nearly took all my breath and definitely all my nerve.

When Jonah said his name back, he smiled a little, not to me really, but more to himself. And I got the feeling he'd known all along that I'd dumped the papers out just so he'd help me pick them up.

"Sorry about the ink," I said. He looked puzzled until I showed him my palms, all smudgy gray, too. "On your hands."

"Better than possum blood," he answered.

I screwed up my face and said, "*Possum blood?*" And that was the first time I made Jonah Luks laugh.

Every Sunday after that, I'd wait and catch Jonah coming out of the woods. I'd circle around him and his sled, chattering at him so that he wouldn't have a chance to tell me to go away. With no one else to talk to, I found that I had a lot saved up to say, and poor Jonah got most of it.

During these near-monologues of mine, I'd pick out a little something to build on. Maybe he'd say a few words or move his hand—now, this was valuable material to be remembered, reworked, and relayed to the Whisperers during lunch. One time, I told this story about how Jonah reached past me to grab a length of rope, and I told it like he was trying to hold my hand but then was too shy to do it after all so he pretended like he was just getting the rope. And the so-called Whisperers? They *shrieked* when I told them that story. People at other tables looked over at us, they were so loud.

Jonah's job is to get rid of the animal carcasses in the woods around Hokepe Woods so that the people who live there won't stumble upon, say, a dead deer when they take a walk through the trees behind their house. He gets a deer every couple of weeks, and smaller stuff—rabbits and woodchucks and such—almost every time.

No one knows where all these deer are from. The woods only go back a couple miles so there shouldn't be so many of them, but somehow the deer keep coming—cropping the neighbors' gardens, bedeviling their dogs, launching themselves in front of their teenagers' cars. In fact, Jonah told me about how last summer a deer jumped over the back fence of one of the houses and landed right splash in some family's swimming pool, and during their little girl's birthday party, too. Luckily, at that moment, all the kids were inside doing presents, and not in the pool, like they'd been earlier. I can imagine it—the splash, the kids running to the back windows just in time to see the deer surface and kick up a foam, its black eyes bright, before their mothers led them away. The fathers claimed that the deer, a full-grown buck, had tossed its head, and they couldn't get close enough to pull it out. One of them managed to lasso its antlers and nearly got yanked in with it. By the time they called Jonah, the deer had put its head down and sunk to the bottom. When Jonah got there, he asked them why they didn't drain the pool. They hadn't thought of that, they said.

After he goes into the woods, Jonah usually walks among the trees nearest to the houses because the dead animals there are the ones people are most likely to find and complain about. If I listen hard, I can hear the sound of his sled runners on the ground, and I can walk along at his pace, both of us working our way around the edge of the neighborhood, him through the trees, me on the sidewalk. When I get to a house where I have to deliver a paper, I go do it and then hurry back to catch up with the sound of Jonah's sled. When Jonah stops to take a look at something or tie his boot or pull out a smoke or whatever he does, I wait on my side until the sled sound starts up again. Then I keep walking with him.

On this morning, I deliver papers for about half an hour, walking along with the sound of Jonah's sled. But then, after coming back from one of the houses, I can't hear the sled runners anymore. I jog up a block to see if Jonah has gotten ahead of me, and then I walk back slowly, listening. Nothing. I decide that Jonah must've walked deeper into the trees where I can't hear his sled anymore, so I turn away from the woods and go deeper into the neighborhood, because I still have half the houses in the middle left to do.

It takes me about an hour to finish in there, and by the time I'm done, the sun has made it over the horizon and is cutting right through the houses, lighting up their rooms, waking up their people. I pass some smug joggers, a boy pulling on a jowly dog, and a lady in her bathrobe standing barefoot in the middle of her front lawn. Each of these people waves at me, which is a funny thing that's true about delivering newspapers: Everyone waves as if they like you. I still have all the rest of the border houses to finish, and I'm thinking and hoping that I might run into Jonah again. In fact, I'm walking along, listening so hard for the sound of Jonah's sled that I almost miss Jonah himself standing right there on the front porch of my next house.

Jonah has told me before that he isn't allowed to talk to the residents of Hokepe Woods. In fact, his boss, Mr. Jefferson, has very particular rules about this. That Jonah is not allowed to speak to residents is the first and most important rule. If a resident speaks to Jonah, however, Jonah must wave back, not nod or say good morning—he's got to wave. This second rule hasn't been tested out yet, though, because none of the people who live in Hokepe Woods have ever even said "Hi" to Jonah. "They don't want to think about me," he told me, one of his longest sentences to date.

So, anyway, there I am on the sidewalk, and there's Jonah up on the porch, where he's definitely not supposed to be, pink-eared, sled-less, with his hand raised to knock. Jonah doesn't knock, though; instead he kind of pauses with his fist in the air like he hears someone coming to answer. Without even thinking about it, I back into the yard of the house next door and crouch down in its front garden. It's a small plot, covered in cedar chips and planted with shrubs. The shrubs offer some kind of place to hide, even though I'm pretty sure that my forehead is sticking out over their fuzzy tops. The cedar chips poke at my hands, and a little ant crawls across my knuckles. None of it is too comfortable, really, and I don't know how much longer I can squat there, so thank God when the door of that house swings open. The only problem is that where I'm crouching, I can't see who's answered it. Jonah starts talking, but he's too far away for me to hear what he's saying. Then, he disappears inside, which I'm sure is against all of Mr. Jefferson's rules.

Well, I sit around in that garden for nearly fifteen more minutes, which I count off on my watch one after the next, like papers delivered to porches. The house Jonah has gone into is the only modern one on the block—a stack of a house—and the windows are all tinted dark, so I couldn't peek in even if I had the courage to. Sure, it crosses my mind that Jonah is having sex with the woman in that house. On my paper route, I see dozens of Hokepe Woods' divorcees trussed up in shiny jogging suits and skinny headbands, speed-walking themselves into successful and fulfilling futures. They're the only ones who don't wave at me, because they've got their eyes set in the distance, like they're looking for the next thing. Jonah could be their next thing.

I think about how I'm going to explain Jonah's affair with a divorcee to the Whisperers Monday at lunch. How can I spin it? What words can I use? I finally decide that I can't tell them anything because I don't know how to say it, and they wouldn't know how to understand it either. The Whisperers think that Jonah and I are in love with each other. And maybe that's okay after all because we were in love—no, *are* in love—in the story I've been telling. And the story hasn't changed, no matter what's happening in the house.

I settle on down among the shrubs, telling myself how everything is just fine, but soon enough my throat begins to ache. And after a second, I've got my face pressed into my arm and I'm crying. And it's not so good, with the ants and all. They start crawling from my arm onto my face, and I don't even care enough to brush them off. In fact, I want them there because they make the whole thing worse with their tickling feet, and I can sort of convince myself that I'm crying about the ants instead of about Jonah. I'm crying about those ants.

When the sirens start up, I stop outright crying and settle for sniffling so that I can hear them better. I expect them to fade off like sirens usually do, but instead they get louder, which means that they're coming my way. Then I can see them—two police cars and an ambulance, all three wailing.

Suddenly everything that was still a second ago is moving—the houses, too. Their curtains flick open, and people start to peek out; they try to stand far enough back so that no one will see them looking.

The emergency cars stop in front of the house that Jonah went into, and Jonah is out on the porch with an old lady (I mean, *ancient* old) at his side. The idea of Jonah's affair slips away, along with all the words I could have used to explain it.

Jonah shakes hands with the officers, who are up on the porch now, and then everyone—the officers, the old woman, me behind the bush—is looking at Jonah, waiting for what's next. Jonah presses his fist to his mouth like a drain stopper. We wait and wait, and just when it seems like he's never going to talk at all, he lifts his head and does. The officers listen and take notes in those tiny notebooks that they have. One of them says something, which causes Jonah to step off the porch and walk around the side of the house. Most of the officers and the ambulance workers follow him, all except one, who disappears back inside with the old lady.

I wait there in the garden for about half an hour. My papers aren't delivered and I have to keep pulling my sleeves down over my hands to keep the cold from stinging them, but I tell myself that there are things more important than newspapers and hands. Another couple of cars pull up, and more men get out of them. These men aren't in uniforms, but I can tell that they're police. They say a few things into their radios and troop back into the woods after Jonah and the others.

I wait some more. Every once in a while, one of the neighbors wanders out onto his lawn and stands there swaying for a second before losing his nerve and going back inside. But no one comes out onto the front lawn that I'm hiding in, and no one bothers me in my garden; in fact, no one even sees me except for one young police-man who just happens to glance my way as he walks by. He stops and stares as if he doesn't think I'm really there. He's all freckled, and it looks funny, the combination of freckles and uniform, like he's just a kid dressing up as a policeman and not a real cop at all. For a second, I'm afraid that he might order me to go away. But when I raise a hand and wave at him, he waves back, a little mystified, and then walks on.

Most of the policemen have been going into the woods along the far side of the house from where I'm hidden, so to me, they appear and disappear like actors walking on- and offstage. To pass the time, I give them stage names: White Mustache, Likes His Hat, and Little Ears. I realize that Jonah must have found something in the woods. I suppose I even know what he's found.

Then Jonah reappears, and I'm struck by him, really struck—like a clock, like a lightning rod, like oil or gold or a glass jaw. I'm struck by the shiny hood of his coat up around his neck, by his hands in his pockets, by his silence, by the familiarity of him. He's a comfort in that moment. In my story or outside of it, I know Jonah Luks.

So I stand up without thinking about all the cops around, without thinking that I probably shouldn't. My satchel swings into my legs and almost knocks me flat over. I step out of the garden. Jonah stops talking and looks over at me, and the officer with him stops, too. The officer sees me and squints.

"You, girl!" he calls.

But before he can say anything else, the body is between us. Two ambulance workers are bringing it out of the woods right past me. They have it on a stretcher, but they can't roll the wheels on the grass, so they carry the whole thing a few inches off the ground. And it must be heavy, since each of them is straining from the effort. They stare at each other as they walk so as to make their steps even, and it's like they're two musicians playing a duet, keeping time with the music.

Now, when I say that they're carrying a body, I don't really mean "a body." I mean, the body is there, of course, but it's covered up: zipped in a bag and then covered again with a green sheet. But none of that keeps it from being a body. I know—all of us there know—it's a body. Everyone goes sort of quiet as it passes. The groups of police in the yard lift their heads and stop talking to each other; the neighbors all pull their curtains wide open, not caring anymore who sees them looking. And as for me, I'm picturing myself inside that bag. I can't help it. All of a sudden, in my imagination, I'm in there with the smell of something factory-made and the tug of rubber on the back of my neck; I'm seeing the bag's zipper from the wrong side, all the teeth backward.

Then, the body is gone. The stretcher has passed me by, and now all I'm staring at is one of the ambulance workers' acrylic shirts and the back of his uneven haircut. Jonah is still there on the other side of the yard, looking across at me without any expression on his face at all.

I think, right then, that I could run to him and bury my face in his coat. I think about how it would probably smell like dead deer and sweat and the back of his truck. He'd probably put his arms around me if I cried, at a time like this he would; he'd have to. I think of the different words I could use when I retell it later to the Whisperers: *He hugged me. He embraced me. He took me in his arms.* We're across the yard, staring at each other. His eyes are shiny, and he opens his mouth to say something.

And maybe in someone else's story, I run to him. Maybe he fixes his arms tight around me so that they move in and out with my breaths; maybe he murmurs a few quick words right into my ear and I nod at their truth. But in this story—in my story—I turn. I run away. There's the sound of the stretcher sliding into the ambulance. There's the weight of my satchel as it slaps the backs of my legs. There's the flicker of curtains falling closed as I run past pretty houses, and more pretty houses. There's the voice of Jonah calling out, "Evie!" And even as I run away, I take note that it's the first time he's ever said my name.

Chapter TWO

I RUN FOR A WHILE, but I'm not that good a runner. Also my satchel keeps slamming into my legs. So after a few blocks, I slow down to a walk and pick up the satchel, carrying it like a baby up against my chest. I look back a few times, hoping maybe to see Jonah jogging after me, arms ready to take me in, or else an officer snapping open his handcuffs, adjusting them to fit my wrists. No one's following me, though, and I make it back to Mom's car all by myself.

Jonah's truck is still there, parked in front of me. I glance into the truck bed as I walk by: a mess of tools and rope, a few torn plastic sheets—all of it dusted with these little twists of fur. I feel exhilarated by what I've seen, by the run, and yet guilty, too; after all, someone has died. And it's this mix of giddy and guilty, this feeling that none of the rules apply, that urges me to step up to the truck bed and stick my hand down in the mess. I could take something of Jonah's, I think, something little that he wouldn't miss. Something I could hold in my hand.

I feel around in all that junk, rough with rust and grime, until my hand wraps around some sort of metal handle. It feels right, like the handle was waiting there for someone to grab on to it. I think about how maybe Jonah had killed that poor dead guy and this will be evidence I can hide for him. I picture myself on the witness stand, lips pressed tight. *Young lady*, the judge booms. And when my fantasy disappears, I realize that I'm still holding on to the handle of the thing in the truck, so what is there to do but pull it out?

⟡

When I stick my key in the door back at home, it turns too easily. The door's already unlocked—a sure sign that Mom's waiting for me. She leaves it open if I'm not home when I say I'll be, like I've forgotten my key and will be locked out, even though she knows I've never forgotten my key, not even once. Sometimes in these rental houses, though, the deadbolt is so old that trying to unlock an open door makes my key get stuck, and I have to stand on the porch and jimmy the key until I give up and ring the bell. Then Mom takes her time getting to the door, finally whipping it open with a little sigh, like, *Oh, it's you.*

Sure enough, Mom is right there on the couch, waiting for me. Her feet are tucked under her and the colored ad insert from the newspaper is spread out on the coffee table. She runs her hands over the insert like she could actually touch the people printed there; her finger hits the shoulder of a boy in a polo shirt, then swipes the breasts of a woman wearing bright lipstick.

She's heard me come into the room—I'm sure she has—but waits a minute before she looks up—she likes her poses and pauses, Mom does. Sometimes she'll stop in the middle of saying something just to watch her own hand as it gestures, and you can see her admiring it, as if her hand is some creature independent of herself—some moth or sparrow—as if she's not the one moving it around.

Mom grew up beautiful. Now, some beautiful people let their beauty just lie there on them, like a coat of sweat on their face, but Mom, she manages hers. She orders her beauty into shape like a squad of soldiers or a page of math problems. So when she finally decides to look up at me, her face is all set, her beauty ready to salute. She smiles a big smile and scratches the cushion next to her.

"Sit down," she says. "Right here."

This is not so good. I'd expected that she'd snap at me for getting back later than usual so that I could snap back at her and go hide in my room. I want an excuse to be away. I want to lie down somewhere quiet, flat and still, and think about that body. Instead, I sit on the couch cushion next to her. She hasn't put her makeup on yet, and her face looks blank without the features drawn on it, her eyelashes silvery, the tip of her nose pink as if she has a cold. I can see the pores on her nose, like seeds on a strawberry, an imperfection that she wouldn't normally allow to be seen.

"Did you deliver your papers?" she asks.

There are a dozen papers still in my satchel in the trunk of her car and, beneath the satchel, the object I pulled from Jonah's truck. It has teeth on it, I discovered, glancing at it as I drove home. It's a trap of some kind, the size of a large book, cold and heavy. I stowed it with the thought that I could do something with it later, hide it or return it or bury it unsprung.

"Of course," I say.

"It took you a while." She says this like it's just a little something to say, but then she doesn't say anything else after it, like it *wasn't* just a little something to say but a question and now she's waiting for my answer. I try to think of what she might want me to admit. Maybe someone called her (The cop who yelled at me? A neighbor? Jonah Luks himself?) and told her that I had been spying on the police. Maybe someone had seen me swipe the trap.

"I guess it did take me a while," I say, because now is not the time to confess to anything. "Did you need the car?"

"No, no . . . ," she says. "It's just . . . when I woke up, you weren't here." She flips through the advertisements. "Did you meet one of your friends?"

"Yeah, sure. At six on Sunday morning. We went to the mall and bought prom dresses. Then there was this slumber party—"

"Well, I don't know. Someone who really wanted to see you might get up early."

Even though I barely ever leave the house for anything that isn't work or school, Mom keeps thinking that I have all these friends. Of course, *she* had a ton of friends when she was my age, and she still talks about them all the time—these Betsys and Carols and Pams. She doesn't ever talk about how they are *now*—some grotty house-wives or dog-groomers or something—but how they were then, hanging out and pulling pranks and throwing parties.

This idea that I have friends is so important to Mom that some-times I help her out—like, I'll repeat something funny that Angela Harper said in chem, not including the fact that she'd said it to Rachel Birch, not to me. There's a price for this, though, because for weeks Angela's name will ring through the house. "How's Angela?" "Did Angela think the test was hard?" "Did Angela like your hair-cut?" And I shrug and mutter my *maybe*s and my *I don't know*s, until, embarrassed by the idea that Angela Harper might somehow dis-cover that my mother thinks she's my best friend, I tell Mom that

Angela and I don't hang out anymore and I mention a new name for her to latch on to.

"Maybe a boy?" Mom is saying.

"Maybe a boy what?"

"Maybe you met a boy. A boy who's a friend."

"Mom. *No*. God." I put my hands over my face and look at out between my fingers. "Why would you say that?"

"You were late." She shrugs and hikes her bare feet up onto the coffee table, and for an instant it seems like she hasn't thought about the movement before she's made it, but then she course-corrects her legs into something more graceful. "That's why I was late when I was your age."

"Yeah," I say, not saying the rest—that she was pretty, that boys wanted to meet up with her, that this is not my situation. You might think that I feel bad about how I'm not as pretty as my mom. The truth is, I've never felt bad about it at all; in fact, I'm happy about it. See, Mom would have a hard time if I were pretty *and* young. She can handle one of these things but not both of them.

"I woke up, and you weren't here," she repeats, and this time it's almost like a child has said it. *I woke up, and you weren't here.* She looks down at her toes, wiggles them. She's waiting for me to say something, and I finally figure out what it is.

"I'm really sorry."

And suddenly everything is all right. Mom sits back. She tucks her hair behind her ears and beams.

"Don't apologize, silly." She makes a perfect fist and bops me on the nose. "I have waffles."

I follow her into the kitchen.

It feels weird eating the waffles, something about their sponginess, their sweetness. I think for a second about the body, how that guy won't eat any more waffles, not ever. Won't eat anything ever again. I chew and swallow.

After dishes, I hide in my room and wait for Mom to get in the shower. Then I sneak out to the car for my satchel. Back in my room, I pull the trap out to look at. It's a mouth, an arc of teeth with springs at each end. Right now, the trap is closed. I touch my pinkie to one of the springs and feel the coil of it, and how much potential there is in that coil, how it controls the stretch and the snap-shut. It's about the length of my forearm, and I wonder what it's meant to catch. Deer? Wolves? Bears? Though, of course, there are no wolves or bears in the trees around Hokepe Woods, or at least I don't think that there are. I hold the trap where I think Jonah probably held it, on the edges of its smile. It's cold and heavy in my lap. But there's nothing you can really do with a trap unless you're going to set it, so I end up hiding it behind some shoe boxes under my bed.

The rest of the day I read a book, finish an essay for school, and come out every once in a while to turn on the TV, pretending like I'm bored. I can't find anything about the body—no late-breaking news or special reports—just the regular basketball games and Sunday movies. The afternoon has this high, white light to it, cold enough to keep the frost on the ground so that everything is hard and crackly. It's one of those days that looks like a photograph, and you almost feel like you can't step out into it or you'll ruin the picture.

So I stay inside, and every now and then, I think about the body. What do I think about it? Not much. Mostly that I've seen it, just the fact of seeing it, which is like the tickle of the ants across my cheeks. I think about Jonah, too—if he went back to the police station, if he's in trouble, if he's saying my name to himself right now. Mostly, I think about how I'll have something to talk to him about next Sunday.

Mom and I watch the news with dinner. I wait for it. I wait all the way through the weather report (cold, sunny) and the human-interest bit (a goat that can sort poker chips), and still there's nothing about the body, nothing about Hokepe Woods. After dinner, the phone rings and Mom takes it. I don't think anything of the call, not even when she shouts to me from the living room. This is not unusual, her shouting. When something on the TV strikes her as amusing, she yells my name, even though by the time I get there the punch line has been delivered or the exotic bird has flown away.

When I get to the living room tonight, though, the TV is off, reflecting back tiny, shadowy replicas of ourselves in its dead eye. Mom is on the couch, sitting with perfect posture, her legs angled to one side and her toes pointing in the exact same direction, like she is the quivering needle on a compass. Mom has made the box of Kleenex from the bathroom and two glasses of water into an unlikely centerpiece on the coffee table. She scratches the couch cushion next to her. I sit down.

She looks regal that way, sitting with her back straight and her face serious, like someone with underskirts and an official title. I know she'll wait to talk until I say, "What is it?" She likes to be asked for things.

"What is it?" I say.

"I've had a phone call."

I look at the Kleenex box. "Is it Dad?" I say, before thinking better of it. Mom's serious expression wrinkles into something more annoyed.

"Of course not. It was Veronica from work."

"So?"

Mom touches a hand, quickly, to the bridge of her nose, and I notice that her posture is brittle like crackled paint, like you could chip little bits off of her.

"Is Veronica okay?"

"It's Elizabeth McCabe," Mom spits out.

This all takes a minute for me to think about, because it's not really an answer to my question and, besides, no one's called Elizabeth McCabe *Elizabeth* for years.

"You mean Zabet?" I say. "Zabet McCabe?"

Mom grabs the Kleenex box and sets it in her lap, and her hands float over its white tuft. "This is bad news, Evie." And when she says this, her posture relaxes and her hands drop down onto her knees, and we both breathe in once and then out together, like we've planned it. Then Mom says, "Elizabeth—Zabet—she's passed away."

I wait for a second so that I can recheck the words, their meanings. "That's terrible," I finally say, because what else am I supposed to say? News like this is, at first, just news.

I ask if it was a car accident. Last year, two kids from my school died that way. Principal Capp planted two trees out in front of the school, one for each kid. We had this joke around school that the two kids who died had been secretly buried under those trees, their bodies fertilizing them. This past winter, though, the trees started dying from some disease that had crawled under their bark. The school had practically a hundred exterminators come out to look at them, but not one was able to figure out what was wrong, much less fix it. No one makes that joke anymore about the dead kids being buried there.

Mom tells me that Zabet didn't die in a car accident. But then when I ask how she did die, Mom gets this funny look on her face, an awkward look, a secret-telling sort of look, and I realize she doesn't have a pose ready for whatever is in her head. She licks her lips (which she's always telling me not to do because it chaps them) and tucks her hair behind her ears. "She was killed by someone. A person."

"Like murder?" I say, and it sounds so silly, something people say through red lipstick with a dramatic gesture upstage—*Murder!*—that I accidentally grin.

"What on earth is funny?" Mom looks appalled.

Now, of course it's not funny; of course it's terrible. Sometimes that's when I grin, though, when something is terrible. I don't know why. It's like my mouth is attached to one of those board-game spinners, and it spins all the way around the possible shapes it could make, only to land on the exact wrong one.

"How?" I say.

"How was she killed?" Mom frowns. "By a person. I told you that. She was murdered."

"No, but how did the person do it?"

Mom wrinkles her nose. "I don't know."

"You didn't ask?"

"Well." Mom looks at me, then away. "Veronica didn't have so many details. She'd heard from her sister-in-law, who . . . well, I don't know how *she* knew. I think she was hit on the head? Elizabeth, not Veronica's sister-in-law. Veronica thought that might be it: head trauma. They found her out in the woods near one of those neighborhoods."

This is it, the information I've been waiting for all day, coming not from the nightly news but, improbably, from Veronica at my mother's office. And there's that body bag again marching through my head, left to right like the words in a sentence. I really don't put it together until that moment: that I saw a body, that *Zabet* was the body. I'd sort of assumed it was a man in the bag, some homeless man or amateur hunter; you know, some dumb stranger who had done something risky or stupid or unlucky. But then I remember how all the policemen got real silent when they carried that bag by. And I realize that they must have known that it was a girl in there. I picture myself hiding in those bushes, how when I'd popped up, they had all stared at me like I was a ghost, a ghost girl.

"I saw her," I say, before thinking that I probably shouldn't say this, not to Mom, anyway.

Mom has her hand on her own throat. She's all questions. "You saw who? When? What do you mean? Elizabeth McCabe?"

"Last week," I say. "At school." It's like a reflex, this lie, to protect Mom, to protect myself from Mom's upset, and I don't even think much about telling it. I think about Zabet's locker instead.

I can picture exactly where it is, in what locker bank, in what hall, all that. They paint the lockers different colors, and Zabet has an orange one. I don't know why I think about a dumb thing like that right now. There's nothing special about Zabet's locker. It's a locker. We all have one. But I start wondering what they'll do about it, that locker, if the kids on either side of it will want to move to new lockers, if the school will assign the locker to someone else next year, if the kid who has it the next year will know that it was Zabet's, and if he does, how long it'll take—how many years, how many kids—until no one remembers that it used to be hers.

"Was she raped?" I ask. Mom takes her hand off of my shoulder and moves the Kleenex box back onto the table. She nudges a glass of water toward me, but she doesn't say anything, so I ask again. "Was she raped?"

Mom looks up at me, real quick, and I know then that she heard me the first time. "Why on earth would you ask a question like that?" She pulls the glass away from me like I'm not allowed to have water anymore.

"I don't . . ." I smile again, despite myself. "I don't know." And I don't. I had wondered, that was all. It seemed important.

Mom stares at me for a minute. Then she says in her airy voice, "We don't need to know every last detail, do we?" She lifts the glasses and carries them out of the room, again very grand, with her duchess walk. I hear her pour the water out and start to wash the glasses, even though neither of us had drunk a sip from them. I follow her to the kitchen and stand in the doorway. I try to think of something else to say that can cover up the last thing that I'd said.

"It's weird to think about," I say. Mom keeps on scrubbing at those glasses.

And it *is* weird to think about. It seems like there should have been a warning or something. Like how your throat feels heavy so you know that you're going to get a cold the next day—some warning like that. I try to remember Zabet back when we were kids, to remember if I could see it on her, some hint of her death, some odd glow or ancient prophecy, some bird cawing at her strangely. I don't remember anything like that, though. I only remember that she liked the red flavors of jam but hated the orange or purple ones, that she refused to let anyone cut her fingernails and they'd grow long and tear off sometimes when we'd play. But those were hardly omens.

"There were two of you," Mom says over the sound of the water in the sink. "You were two little girls."

"Mom?" I say. "Hey, Mom?" She's crying now, so she won't turn around. She doesn't like how it makes her face all pink and puffy. I watch her shoulders for a minute; she has the clean glass in her hand. Then she lifts the glass up, and we both look at it for a second, the light from the kitchen shining through it, before she sets it down in the dish rack. Then she lifts the second glass and holds it under the light just the same. It's so pretty the way she does this—just how she means it to be.

Chapter THREE

I DON'T KNOW WHAT TO EXPECT when I get to school the next morning. Rows of girls in black dresses, maybe. A huge photograph of Zabet with flowers and candles in the main hall. A choir. A preacher. A psychologist. When I get there, though, it's just school. All the kids are hanging out in packs. The boys' jaws are pink from their dull razors. The girls have blow-dried their hair to make it shiny and straight. They smell like breakfast and sleep and the closets at home that they keep their coats in. They slam their lockers, bump into each other on purpose, and yawn their cereal breath.

I walk through the halls and listen for someone to say her name: *Zabet*. No one's talking about her, though. No one knows what happened. What's more, there's no one I can tell. I feel like if I began to speak, it would be in a foreign language, one that I couldn't even recognize myself. Maybe it wouldn't be a language of words. Maybe if I opened my mouth, thimbles and postage stamps and spools of dental floss would drop from my tongue.

I begged Mom to let me borrow her car this morning. I wanted to drive past Jonah's house. True, I don't exactly know where Jonah's house is, but I thought that if I drove around the rental houses near the college, I might spot his truck. If his truck were out front, it'd mean that he was okay, that he wasn't in jail. I can't imagine what it was like, seeing her dead like that. But that's not true; I can imagine *exactly* what it was like. I can imagine it twelve different ways, twenty different ways, seventy. In fact, I sort of wish I had seen it—the body—so that I could hold just one picture in my head.

Mom wouldn't let me take the car, though, and so the only thing I could do for Jonah was call Jefferson Wildlife Control. I looked up the number in the phone book and thought of a good cover story to tell Jonah's boss if he answered.

"There's an animal," I said to myself as the line rang. "There's an animal in my backyard. . . ." The answering machine picked up. I didn't leave a message.

In the halls at school, I look around for Hadley Smith, Zabet's best friend. She will definitely know about what happened. Hadley's not at her locker, though. Not at Zabet's locker, either. She's probably at home, I decide, or maybe over at Zabet's house, being a comfort to the family. Both the Smiths and the McCabes live in Hokepe Woods, a few blocks away from each other. In fact, both of their houses are on my paper route. I never got to Zabet's house on Sunday; her family's paper is still in my room, in my satchel, under the bed.

I picture Hadley on the McCabes' couch, her tough face shrinking in on itself in grief, the same way a peach does when you let it soften. *You knew her better than anyone*, Mrs. McCabe might say. And then Mr. McCabe would touch her arm and murmur, *You're like a daughter to us now*. Hadley should nod then, a single tear slipping down her cheek and into the scar on her chin. Then she should take each of their hands in her own. I hope she knows what to do in a situation like this.

In homeroom, Mr. Denby is arranging about a billion stacks of paper on his desk, neatening up the edges. I'm the first one there. I'm always the first one there. I take a seat over by the plants. Mr. Denby has got dozens of them; the whole windowsill is leafy. Sometimes, when kids are bored in class, they poke holes in the leaves or tear off pieces of them. I used to do it, too, until one day, before class, Mr. Denby walked over and lifted up one of the tortured leaves and stared at it for about a whole minute. After that, I left the plants alone.

I put my head down on the desk. I didn't sleep much last night. It was like I lay down in that little crawlspace between awake and asleep, almost dreaming, then almost waking, then almost dreaming again.

It's not that I was grieving or anything, though of course I thought about Zabet. In fact, I tried to conjure up each of my memories of her, give each of them a turn in my mind. I thought about how bossy Zabet was, like whenever we had to choose something—pieces for a board game, snacks after school, clothes for dress up—she'd say, "I will have . . ." and then, whatever one she wanted most, she'd grab it.

But I also couldn't help thinking about how Zabet had died. I couldn't help thinking about the murderer, who he was, where he was, why he'd picked her and not some other person. In fact, I couldn't think about Zabet without thinking about him. It's like the two of them were mixed up together in my head, and that seemed unfair somehow—not to me really, but to Zabet.

Mr. Denby looks up from his papers and then blinks like he's a little surprised to see me there. "Good morning, Evie," he says. And, right when he says it, I realize that *he* knows about Zabet. Of course he does; all the teachers probably do.

So I say, "Mr. Denby, I know, too."

He blinks. "You know what?"

"I know about—" But I can't seem to say it right out like that; it feels like it'd be against the rules, like I'd be swearing or something. "I know about . . . *you know*."

"I don't." Mr. Denby tilts his head about halfway around, like he's going to wind it right off of his neck.

"About the thing?"

"Thing? Be precise, Evie."

"The thing you probably have to tell us when class starts?"

He's quiet for a second, and he gets that look like he's trying to decide just how to answer me, which, to be truthful, is a look that I get from teachers quite a lot. Finally, he makes a decision and points over his shoulder. "Actually, it'll come over the loudspeaker." Then, "How do you know about that?"

"I was there."

"You were . . . ? No, no," he says. "We must be thinking of different happenings."

Before I can tell him that we're not, that we're thinking of the same exact happening, a few kids wander in, looking around like they're lost, even though this is the same homeroom that they come to every day. Then the bell buzzes, and all the rest of the class bursts in. Mr. Denby takes roll. After he's done, he glances back at the loudspeaker, which beeps the second he looks at it.

"Mr. D, you're psychic!" someone says.

A few people laugh, but Mr. Denby spits out this harsh "shh!" and everyone looks around at each other, stunned and mock hurt, because usually Mr. Denby is very nice to us, even when we destroy his plants.

It's Principal Capp on the loudspeaker. Instead of his typical "Good morning, Chippewa braves!" he says, "Greetings, Chippewa students, staff, and faculty," and you can tell by his voice that, whatever he's saying, he's reading it off a piece of paper. "I am deeply saddened to report that we have lost one of our own. Elizabeth McCabe passed away early Sunday morning."

"God," someone says.

They all know now, I think. *It's not just me*. And this makes me feel both better and worse.

Principal Capp goes on to talk about the counseling office and the nature of tragedies and transportation to the memorial service on Friday. Almost everybody's looking at the speaker, and the ones who aren't are looking at Mr. Denby. Then, with another beep and a zip of static, the announcement is over.

People start whispering then, and I can hear the word *How? How? How?* all around the room. *How did she die?* In the back of the room, Chelsea Snyder's face has become pink and slick and snotty, and the girls around her pat her back or shoulders or wherever they can find a little untended patch of her.

"Dude," I hear one of the boys call in a low voice. "That's fucked up. How do you think it happened?" Then a group of them starts talking about times they almost died but didn't, eliciting quiet laughter and oaths of "shiiit." I look from one group to the other, not sure if I fit in with the criers or the taletellers or anyone.

The girl in the desk next to me turns. Her name is Nora Whitaker, and she hasn't spoken to me all semester. Now she says, "I don't even know who that girl is," like that settles it. Then she cocks her head and reconsiders. "Did you know her?"

"Yeah," I say.

"You *did*? Were you, like, friends?"

"Not really. When we were kids."

"Oh." She seems disappointed.

"I mean, we were pretty good friends back then."

"Yeah? You must be sad, then. Are you sad? Should I stop talking to you because you're sad?"

"No. You can talk."

Two other girls have joined Chelsea Snyder in her tears. They've formed a pinwheel shape, facing in, foreheads pressed together and arms around each other's backs. I wonder if I should be crying, too, but I feel dry, tapped. I hear Tyler James say, " . . . unconscious for about four hours." Mr. Denby walks up and down the rows, peering over our shoulders, just like he does when he assigns us a group worksheet.

"So, what was she like?" Nora asks. She's wearing a little floral kerchief over her hair. She keeps adjusting it, half an inch back and forth on her head. All her tiny features are arranged at the center of her face. There are some types of pretty that I would never want to be.

"She was . . ." I don't want to say *nice*. Saying *nice* seems terrible, a throwaway line for the back of someone's yearbook. "Well, she hangs—hung—around with Hadley Smith and them."

"Oh." Nora wrinkles her nose. No one much likes Hadley Smith. "Wait. Zabet McCabe. Is she that one girl?" She doesn't elaborate.

"Maybe," I say.

"Yeah." She nods decisively. "I think I know her."

We're quiet for a second. The pinwheel in the back has started to sing something in soft, quavering voices. Nora glances at them and then sighs. I can't tell if her sigh is sad or derisive or bored. I feel a sweep of anger against Nora Whitaker and, at the same time, a duty to make sure that, in the face of Zabet's death, she is something (anything!) other than bored.

"There was this one time," I say.

She looks round. "Yeah?"

"There was this time when Zabet and I—we were maybe eight or nine—and we were at the arboretum for a field trip."

"I went there," Nora breathes as if this is an amazing coincidence, when really every elementary school takes a field trip to the arboretum every fall.

"So we were at that one part in the nature center—maybe you remember—where this lady takes an owl pellet and dissects it? Well, she was really good at it, the lady was. She had these tweezers, and she just dug into the thing. She set all the fluff and weird stuff on one side, and every once in a while, she'd find a little bone and set it on this velvet cloth. After a couple of minutes, she has a bunch of little bones on the cloth, and she starts putting them in an order, and it makes—"

"A mouse," Nora says.

"Right. A mouse skeleton. So the mouse is finally finished, and Zabet turns to me, and she says—"

I pause.

"Yeah?" Nora says. She leans forward.

"Zabet looks at the skeleton and says, 'It's all in there.'"

Nora blinks. "Then what?"

But there isn't more to the story. That's the end of it.

Chapter FOUR

OVER THE NEXT COUPLE OF DAYS, everybody talks about Zabet and the murder. During roll call, the teachers stare pointedly at each of us like we might cry at the sound of our own names. Some girls do cry, and other girls scoff at them for being fakers and drama queens. In the hall, some kids trade made-up details about the autopsy or guesses about who the killer might be; some kids lean on each other's shoulders and sigh, *It's so sad*, and, *I just can't believe it*.

The news crews come around a few times, but Principal Capp makes them stay off school property. When we walk out of the building after sixth period, the reporters are lined up across the street in camera-ready peacoats and scarves, waving us over. Some kids go. Mom and I see them on the news while we eat dinner. They all say the same things: *She was so nice. It's a tragedy*.

The newscasters tell us that, though forensic evidence proves that Zabet was killed in the woods and not dumped there, no one knows for sure what happened that night. All anyone knows is that Zabet said good night to her mother around eleven on Saturday and went upstairs to bed. There were no signs, they report, of a break-in, so the current theory is that she snuck out, maybe just to take a walk.

No one even knew she was gone. Zabet's mother thought she was still asleep in her room when the police knocked on the front door Sunday morning to bring news of her death. This means that I knew Zabet was dead, or at least that *someone* was dead, before her mother did, which gives me the creeps.

Rumors fly that the police are at the school, using Capp's office to question kids. I never see any police officers, though I guess it might be part of their job *not* to be seen. Whenever anyone gets a note to see the principal, no one makes the soft joking call of *Ooaaahhh, you're in trouble* anymore. I wait for my name to be called but never hear it. What did I see, anyway? Nothing they didn't see. A body pulled out of the woods.

The Whisperers don't know that I used to know Zabet, and I don't tell them. They don't guess that I was there when the body was found or that Jonah was the one who found it. They think of Hokepe Woods as their neighborhood, not mine. They whisper about how the body was only a few yards from their houses and maybe, if they'd only looked, they could have witnessed the murder from their bedroom windows. They have hypotheses about who the killer is: the college kid who runs his own lawn-mowing business; Larry Smalley, who tried to commit suicide last year (maybe because he was in love with Zabet, they surmise); a friend of one of the Whisperers' brothers, who stares at them a second too long when they're over for a slumber party in their pajamas.

"It didn't have to be Zabet who got murdered. It could have been any of us," one of them whispers, and another one flicks her on the arm. "Don't even say that out loud."

At home, Mom keeps checking to see if I have a temperature. Her hand flies out as I walk down the hall, when I sit on the couch, when I do homework at the kitchen table, slapping onto my forehead without warning. After a few seconds holding it there, she always says, "You feel a little warm."

I keep calling Jefferson Wildlife Control, and I keep getting the answering machine. Finally, I make up an excuse to take Mom's car and drive to the address listed in the phone book. It ends up being Mr. Jefferson's home, which is gabled and white and doesn't look like it'd have anything to do with animal carcasses. I drive past a few different times, whenever Mom sends me on an errand, but I never see Jonah's rusty old truck or Jonah himself. On the news, the anchors say words like *murder investigation* and *manhunt* and *suspects*, but they never mention Jonah, so as far as I can tell, he is free.

I still can't fall asleep that night. I can't turn on the light, either, or Mom will see it under the door. I think about Zabet a lot. *Zabet's dead*, I tell myself. *Zabet was murdered and raped*. I keep saying it, even though it makes me feel nothing.

I think about when I first knew Zabet. We were eight. My dad had just moved out, saying he'd come back soon to visit, which he did, a few times. Once, for my tenth birthday, he took me to this pizza place with a playground for little kids. Even though I was way too old for the indoor playground, he seemed to expect that I'd play on it, so I did, crawling through the tunnels with the smaller kids, who stared at me. I felt hot with shame. That was his last visit, and for a long time I wondered if maybe he was as embarrassed as I was. Mom claims that she has a phone number for him if we ever need to call. But I've never seen it.

When Dad left, I was supposed to be sad about it. I put my head down on my desk in class and sighed so loud that the teacher sent a note home. I knew I was supposed to act like this, that everyone expected it. Really, it was okay having him gone. Mom was happy again. She would order takeout and wear lipstick and talk with her hands. She had to get a full-time job, so she hired Zabet's mother to watch me for a few hours after school.

Zabet was Elizabeth back then. (It wasn't until middle school that Hadley Smith convinced her to cut four letters from her name.) Our elementary school was divided into bussers and walkers. The walkers lived in the new neighborhoods, which were close to the schools. Bussers lived in apartments or rented houses farther out. The walkers were wealthy, and the bussers were poor, and if you think little kids don't notice stuff like that, then you're wrong. We knew whose clothes were hand-me-downs, whose sneakers were off-brand, and whose names were on the free list that the lunch lady kept taped next to the register.

Under the normal order of things, Zabet was a walker and I was a busser. But Mom met Mrs. McCabe at a PTA meeting, and Mrs. McCabe, perhaps seeing an opportunity for charity, offered to watch me until Mom got off work, which meant that I got to walk home with Zabet and a few other walkers after school. That first day, I waited for them in the coat room after the bell. They hitched their backpacks up and re-knotted their laces. I stared at their legs as we strode forward, making sure to place my feet just like they did. Hokepe Woods was in the final stages of being built back then, so a few of the houses were still under construction. Zabet and I used to tunnel through them on our way home, sliding between stud beams or patting the shiny panels of insulation.

Zabet was a whole head taller than me, with sturdy legs and the starts of breasts. Around her I was embarrassed by my littleness. But I also felt quick in my thoughts and words, and it seemed that maybe this quickness came from my littleness, too. Zabet would believe anything I told her. Even if later I told her that I'd only been joking before, she'd still believe whatever I'd said first, and I'd have to keep reminding her that it was a lie. I don't mean that she was stupid; she wasn't. She got herself lost in stuff was all—stories. This made it great fun to tell her things—true things, false things, fabulous things—just to see her face glaze over and her mouth fall open.

I told her this one story (and this was a true one) about how a few weeks before my dad left, he and Mom were arguing in the kitchen. I don't really remember what the argument was about—just something—but Mom got so angry that she started pulling on her own hair. Dad was standing by the dish rack, and I saw him look over at it a few times. Then his hand twitched, and he'd grabbed a colander out of the rack and thrown it at Mom. It was only plastic, though, so it just bounced off of her chest to the floor. But he already had another thing coming right at her—a metal ladle. Well, Mom reached up and caught it, just before it hit her, the handle less than an inch from her pretty nose. She stared at the ladle for a second, and he stared too, like they couldn't believe it was there in her hand.

Zabet loved this story. She had me tell it about twenty times, and she'd correct me if I described something even a little bit different than the time before. For a while, we'd steal the colander and ladle out of her kitchen and act out the scene in the woods behind her house. She always insisted on being my mom so that she could catch the ladle in midair. "Quick eyes!" we'd yell, instead of "think fast" or "heads up."

Every once in a while, Zabet would leave her hands at her sides and let the ladle hit her. Then she'd rub her face and say, "Yeah, that hurt."

One time, I threw the ladle harder—much harder—than I ever had before. I don't remember if I planned to throw it like that or if it just came out of my hand that way. Later I'd think that maybe I had meant to throw it hard because Zabet was so gullible, so willing to take whatever I threw. I didn't even yell "quick eyes!" that time. I just watched the ladle spin, handle over scoop, a baton of silver, and waited to see if this would be one of the times that Zabet let it hit her in the face. She kept her hands down at her sides; she was staring at me. My breath rose up high in my chest and my stomach lurched, but still I didn't call out a warning. At the last second, Zabet reached up, caught the ladle, and held it shining in the air.

Chapter FIVE

HADLEY SMITH is back at her locker on Thursday morning. While she was gone, I had tried to imagine what she would look like when she came back. I'd pictured her in a long black dress with a ragged, old hem that dragged on the floor or maybe all her clothes mismatched like she'd put them on without even looking at them. But instead she's in the ratty, gray fisherman's sweater and jeans that she always wears. She's got girls on either side of her, leaning on the locker bank, staring up at her solemnly, expectantly, like cats waiting for a treat.

Hadley and her friends are the so-called bad girls. They're not really that bad, though. It's just that all the other kids at Chippewa High are so well behaved that these girls look bad by comparison. They steal lip gloss, skip pep rallies, talk back to teachers, cut in line, and maybe some of them have had sex—only maybe, though. The other girls at school are scared of them, and the boys ignore them, except for the few that don't.

There are rumors about them, especially Hadley—that she carries mace in her boot, that she goes to college parties, that she's having an affair with a married man, that she's having an affair with a teacher, that Capp wants to expel her but her dad threatened to sue the school. I saw her smack a girl on the back of the neck once, hard. And another time I heard her call the vice principal by his first name. It was strange to think that Zabet was her best friend—Zabet, so gullible, so malleable.

Hadley slams her locker door, and the girls leaning next to it flinch. She says something quick and breaks out of their circle. A couple of them start to follow her, but then fall back into meaningful looks like they don't dare. Hadley's walking right toward me, her face screwed up in a snarl that makes me want to fall back, too. But I stay where I am, and when she gets close, I say, "Hadley."

She blows right past.

I find her again in the cafeteria. She's in the a la carte line by herself. The boy behind her keeps looking at her and then looking away. Kids at the tables are doing the same thing. In school, even if you don't know someone's name, you know who her best friend is. Everyone knows that Hadley Smith was Zabet McCabe's best friend or, rather, that the girl with the scar on her chin was best friends with the girl who was murdered.

I think about how if Hadley hadn't moved here, then it might have still been me, and not her, who was Zabet's best friend, me everyone would be staring at now. And Zabet would still be Elizabeth. And maybe if she'd still been Elizabeth, then she wouldn't have died. Maybe the two of us would have been together that night, having a sleepover, and she wouldn't have been out in the woods by herself. Or maybe we both would have been out there in the woods together, and I would've been the one who was killed.

Zabet and I hadn't been friends for a long time, if we ever were. When I was starting middle school, Mom decided I was old enough to take the bus home and stay by myself. I told her I wasn't and begged her to still let me go to the McCabes', but this baffled her; she didn't think I liked being babysat. Besides, we'd relied on the kindness of the McCabes for long enough. So she had a talk with Mrs. McCabe, ending the arrangement, and I returned grudgingly to the bus circle.

Zabet invited me over a few times after that. But I was too embarrassed to invite her back to our rented apartment, with its rough orange couches and the smell of our Pakistani neighbors' vindaloos and masalas pressing through the walls. Hadley Smith moved into Hokepe Woods that year. After that, when I'd see Zabet in the halls of the middle school, she was always with Hadley. At first, Zabet would wave and offer me shy hellos. But a few weeks after that, it was like we'd never known each other at all.

In the lunch line, Hadley reaches under the sneeze-guard and sets an order of fries onto her tray like nothing's wrong in the world. While she's paying, I make my way over to the ketchup station. I have no food, nothing to put ketchup on, so I fiddle with the napkin dispenser. The cashier gives Hadley her change and touches her hand briefly when she does it, saying something. Hadley nods but slides her hand out from under the cashier's fingers, hiding it behind her back. I can see it there, closed into a fist like she might, any second, sock the cashier in the mouth.

Finally, Hadley comes my way. She sets her fries under the ketchup spigot and pushes. I try to think what to say. I'd practiced earlier, testing and rejecting different sentences. *How are you doing?* I rejected because everyone was probably saying that to her already. Besides, how did they think she was doing? I also rejected *I'm sorry* because I hate when people apologize for things that aren't their fault.

I guess I'm staring at Hadley while I think about all this (I don't mean to be staring, but sometimes I do it without thinking) because she gives one last push to the ketchup dispenser, then turns and says, "What?"

"Hi," I say, which is not what I mean to say at all.

"Yeah, hi." She grabs her fries and tries to walk around me.

"Wait." I don't step in front of her, but I shift a little to keep her from getting past me. I'm surprised that I've done this, and even more surprised that Hadley actually stops at the barrier of my shoulder.

"What?" she says.

I still don't know what to say.

"What?"

I come up with "So, everyone's probably bugging you, right?"

She makes a noise that means, me—I'm the one bugging her.

"They're all talking about Zabet," I say. I want to say that they don't have the right, and I want Hadley to agree, but she only shrugs.

"They don't even know her," I say, but it comes out in a whine.

Hadley mutters something.

"What? What did you say?"

She looks at me in a way that makes me feel like I've done something unforgivably rude.

"I'm sorry. I couldn't hear you, but it's not because you talk quiet," I babble. "It's just . . . it's loud in here."

She shrugs as if to say that the noise in the room is not her fault. "I have to eat," she tells me, looking down at her tray and adding, "Everybody's real concerned about it."

"That's annoying," I say. "I mean, you'll eat when you want, right?"

She cuts around me then, and I follow. She didn't invite me, but I figure that she didn't *not* invite me either. I figure that maybe we can sit and talk. I could tell her what I saw—the body carried out of the woods—and maybe she'll touch her fingers to the back of my hand and say, *Oh, Evie. I'm so sorry.*

But then Hadley glances over her shoulder, sees me following her, and starts walking faster. And it's silly, but I start walking faster, too. We pass lunch tables where kids nudge each other so that their friends won't miss a glimpse of Hadley Smith. The talk dies as we approach and rises as we pass, dies and rises again. They're all talking about her, about Hadley. She looks back at me again, a glare. We're still walking fast, as fast as we can without running. But it's not like a chase, because there's nowhere to go really. We've already circled the cafeteria once, and now we're going around again. I feel stupid, but once you start doing something like that, it's hard to stop.

It's Hadley who finally stops, turning and letting me catch up. Her face is red all over, except for the scar on her chin, which doesn't color up with the rest of her. I wonder how she got that scar. Zabet must have known how. I used to think that maybe Hadley was so tough because of that scar, like if you have a mean-looking scar on your chin, you sort of have to act tough to live up to it.

Hadley leans in and whispers, "Stop it."

"I just wanted to say—"

"*Please*," she says, and I realize something astounding: She might cry then—she really might—and I don't know how that happened. Her chin is trembling, the scar quaking like a fault line, and she won't blink. I wanted to say something to her is all. I still do, but I realize then that there's nothing for me to say.

"I'm sorry," I say.

She doesn't even nod at this, which makes it terrible, like my apology was a coin left dropped on the floor.

When she walks away this time, she doesn't turn to see if I'm following. I'm not, though. I stay where I am. People sneak looks as she goes by. They look at her and then at each other and then back at her again. Hadley finds an empty table, pushes her tray onto it, and sits down. She leans over her fries and her hair falls around her face so I can't see her scar anymore. She starts putting food in her mouth and chewing it, and after a while people stop looking at her and they go back to their conversations. Hadley keeps chewing.

That's when I figure out what she'd said before, at the ketchup station, when I couldn't really hear her. She'd said, "You don't know her either." And she's right. I don't.

Chapter SIX

PRINCIPAL CAPP makes an announcement that we can go to the funeral on Friday as long as we sign up with our homeroom teachers in advance. I ask Mr. Denby to put me on the list; most of our class is on the list already. Even the Whisperers are going.

"It's the right thing to do," one of them says.

"Why?" I ask.

"Why what?"

"Why is it the right thing to do?"

She just looks at me.

I sit with them on the bus. They're all wearing floral dresses under their coats, but they make pretty lame flowers. I think of the talking flowers in *Alice in Wonderland*. Then I think of the garden that I hid in the morning that Jonah found the body and how, even though it was a garden, none of the flowers had bloomed yet.

Jonah was in the news on Thursday night, but not his name—just "local man," as in "the body was discovered by a local man." The number at Jefferson Wildlife Control still rings through to the answering machine. I keep thinking about last Sunday, when I ran away from Jonah and he yelled out my name. I replay it a lot in my

head, the way it sounded when he said it. *Evie*. That it—my name—
was there in his mouth. But after thinking about it a few dozen times,
it's like I've worn the memory out, and the voice yelling my name isn't
his anymore, but my own.

The bus to the funeral smells like sack lunches and teacher perfume. Everyone is dressed up, but I'm one of the only ones wearing
all black. I thought that was what you were supposed to wear to a
funeral—black. I chose my clothes the night before. I laid them on
my bed, placing the sweater above the skirt, the skirt over the tights.
There was something orderly about the way they looked set out like
that. When I was done, I didn't want to put the clothes away, so I slid
in under them and slept there, making sure not to move too much so
that they wouldn't get wrinkled.

"Have you ever been to a funeral before?" one of the Whisperers
asks the others.

A few of them nod. I don't because I haven't been to a funeral. In
fact, I've only been to church half a dozen times in my life—only when
Mom's upset about something. So I've always thought of going to
church as something you do when you're in a pinch, like eating at a restaurant because you forgot to go to the grocery store. Afterward, when
we walk out with the crowd of real churchgoers, with their brunch
plans and khaki pants, Mom always stops on the front steps and looks
up at the sky for a second, like she's going to see something up there.

"I went to my great-uncle's funeral," one Whisperer says. "A year
ago. They'd plucked out all his nose hairs. His face looked funny
without nose hairs."

"Ew," the other Whisperers say.

I pinch my nose to feel my own nose hairs bend against my skin.

"Do you think we'll see her? Zabet?" I ask. I picture Zabet's body zipped up in the bag, draped with the sheet.

"Like open face?" one of them asks.

"You mean open casket," another says. "Open face is a sandwich."

"Gross," says a third.

"Stop. Don't make me laugh."

"It won't be open."

"Open face?"

"Shut up. Open casket. It won't be."

"No way."

"No."

The Whisperers shudder and shake their heads. The bus stops and Mr. Denby tells us to rise and walk in twos. We follow him across the parking lot and into the church, which has the green piled carpet and beige popcorn ceilings of the rec rooms in the old houses Mom and I rent. The main chapel is nicer than the hall is. It has slanted ceilings and a big, plain, blond-wood cross. I've always liked crosses better when they have a Jesus on them. I like to see what people thought his face looked like.

The bus got us there early, so we're some of the only ones in the chapel. Mr. Denby has us slide into the pews in the back. Up at the front of the chapel, under the cross, is a raised area packed with as many flowers as Mr. Denby's classroom windowsill. There's a platform up there, too, draped and pinned with cloth. I guess that's where the casket will go. I look over and spot Hadley sitting in the second row, watching me watch the platform. Since our talk in the lunchroom, she's avoided me, changing direction if she sees me in the hall, ducking into a crowd or a classroom door, which is funny because usually Hadley's the one people avoid. Now in the church we lock eyes, but she looks away, and then I do, too.

That's when I start to feel a little funny, cold and sweaty both. My stomach twists and burbles. The Whisperer next to me giggles at it. "I'm hungry," I say, but I don't really feel hungry. I feel sick. I wonder what will happen if my stomach growls during the service. Will everyone pretend that they haven't heard it? Will they turn and look? If my stomach growls, is that disrespectful? I press my hands to my middle, but it gurgles again. I can hear my pulse in my ears, and as my stomach turns, its lining seems to pull away from its walls, and I realize that I actually might throw up.

"How do I look?" I say to the Whisperer next to me.

"Good," she says absently.

"No. Do I look sick?"

She turns and peers at me. "Do you feel sick?"

"I feel like I might throw up."

"You might throw up?" She says it loud, and the other Whisperers lean forward along the pew to look at me, each one bending a little farther than the last like they're taking part in some sort of ridiculous choreography. I let out a wild laugh, and they all narrow their eyes in unison. This makes me laugh again. One of them reaches out a hand and puts it on my forehead.

"Uck." She yanks it back and wipes it off on her skirt. "You're, like, wet."

All of us Chippewa students are seated now. Older people—relatives, neighbors—are filling in the front rows, wrinkles around their somber mouths. I can still see Hadley. The back of her hair has been pinned into a complicated twist. She sits next to two tall, colorless adults who lean into each other like elm trees. Hadley sits up straight, the kind of straight you have to think about. Her neck is rigid. Just in front of her is the platform.

"Do you want some water?" a Whisperer asks. "How do you feel?"

"I think I should—"

"Should you go?"

"Yeah. I think." I look to my right and left. We're in the center of the pew. I get up, pressing a hand against my stomach. The Whisperers get up, too. *She needs out! Excuse us!* They wave their hands, and I feel grateful, so grateful to them as I trip over feet and push aside knees, until I'm finally into the aisle and then out of the chapel.

Someone points me to a bathroom, which is down a dark hallway. By the time I reach it, I'm already retching. I put a hand over my mouth, not sure that I'll make it. The bathroom is empty, and I'm grateful for that, too, as I scramble down onto the pink tiles and bend over the toilet bowl. I gasp and retch, and my breath creates ripples in the water of the toilet. I spit into the bowl, and spit again, but nothing comes up—no vomit, no bile. I try for a while longer, and then the feeling passes and my breathing slows. I sit back, pressing my cheek against the cold side of the stall. The inside of my mouth tastes metallic, like I've been hiding pennies under my tongue. I wipe my lips over with toilet paper, rubbing away the last smudges of my lip gloss. Once I'm sure I can, I stand up. In the mirror, I look gray and ghostlike, but I feel better. I swish water in my mouth and go back out.

The hallway I've come down is lined with doors. I glance into each room as I pass it. There's a Sunday school room, painted yellow.

There's an office. There's a room with a chipped and dinged piano. There's a room with nothing in it but rows of folding chairs and, in one chair, a man.

I stop. He's sitting in the first row, and even though his head is bowed, for some reason it doesn't look like he's praying. It's his hands, I realize. They aren't clasped in his lap, but instead are curled around his chair, gripping the seat. He's in a dark suit. I wonder if he's here for Zabet's funeral, which must have already started by now.

I step into the room. "Hello?"

He takes a minute to look around, as if I've woken him up, and I think that maybe he was praying after all. His face is the sort that looks beaten up even though it isn't: low-slung jaw, watery eyes— a bulldog face. There's something familiar to it.

"Are you here for the funeral?" I say. "Because I think it's probably started already."

He nods. "It started a minute ago. And you?"

"Me? I was . . ." *Sick*, I was going to say, but then I realize that I wasn't. "Yes. I'm here for it."

He releases the bottom of the chair and plays with his shirt cuff. "You should go back in, then."

"Did you want to . . . ? You could . . ." I indicate the hall.

He studies me for a second, long enough for me to get self-conscious and drop my arm. He shakes his head. "I don't want to disrupt the service."

"Me neither," I say and take a chair in the back row. It's an impulsive decision, to sit down, and he watches me as I do it.

"I'm Ray," he says.

"I'm Evie."

"Evie." He inclines his head.

As soon as I give him my name, a thought crosses my mind: This man could be Zabet's killer. In the movies, they say that killers like to return to the crime scene to watch events unfold. I think that I would be one of those kind of killers, too, coming back to watch people react to what I'd done. Otherwise, what would be the point? But I'm not a killer. This man might be, though, here alone, at the funeral but not at the funeral. I look around. The room is nearly bare except for the chairs, with their feet sinking into the carpeting. A copy of the Ten Commandments curls on one wall, its tape gone dry. There are three rows of chairs between the man and me. The door to the hallway is just behind me. I could run if I needed to.

The man looks up at me then. "How did you know Elizabeth?" And so he knows her name. Would he know her name if he'd killed her? I decide that he might. It's been in all of the papers and on the programs at the door. And besides, maybe she told it to him before he killed her.

"She was my friend," I say. "My best friend." I don't even think about the lie before I tell it, so does that make it a lie?

"Are you Hadley?" he says.

"No. Evie."

"That's right. You told me that." He nods. "I'm afraid that I didn't get to meet too many of Elizabeth's friends."

This stops me, when he says this, and all of a sudden I know why he seems familiar. "Are you her—"

"Her dad." He wipes a hand over his forehead. "Did I not say that?"

"You're Mr. McCabe." I can see him now, in the photo on the sideboard in the McCabe dining room in a suit with a green tie. In all those afternoons there at Zabet's house, I'd never met him; he had always stayed late at work, never came home early, not even once. My heart starts to pound, more than it did when I thought he might be the killer. I lied to him about being his daughter's friend, and since he's her father, he must know I lied. "When I said that I was Zabet's friend—"

"I'm very sorry that I never got to meet you. There was a Hadley she talked about a lot, and"—he presses his lips together, nods— "I think an Evie, too."

"Sure," I say, wondering if he really thinks this or if he is lying in return to try to spare my feelings.

"I should have met you, both you and Hadley. You think about things after the fact, sometimes, and you . . ." He shrugs. It's a sad shrug, his shoulders ending up a notch lower than they were before.

"We've met now," I say. "I mean, here, just now, we met. You and me."

"Yes."

"And you could meet Hadley. She's right over there in the . . . she has blonde hair and a scar here. I could point her out to you, if you want."

"No. I'm going to stay here. You should go back in, though. I'm sure there are people waiting for you."

"Okay. If you want . . . ," I offer, not knowing the end of my sentence.

"I want to be alone, if . . . if you don't mind."

"Okay." I stand up and brush the wrinkles out of my skirt. I still feel like maybe I should stay, but he's an adult and he's told me to go.

"It was nice to meet you, Evie," he says. "You be good to your parents, even if—" He waves a hand in the air, and I'm not sure what he intends it to mean.

I stop in the doorway for a second, twisting my feet. "She thought that you were a good dad. Zabet did."

His hand moves to his chin, then to his lap. He looks at his lap. "You don't have to say that."

"I'm not just saying it. I'm not." I probably should listen to him and stop talking, but I don't. "She said that you guys fought sometimes, but that you were a good dad anyway."

"She said that?" He doesn't look up from his lap.

"Yeah."

"She said that to you?"

"Yeah, to me."

"She—"

"She said it, Mr. McCabe. Of course she did."

I walk back down the dark hall and pause outside the chapel next to a stack of programs and extra flower arrangements that didn't make it onto the dais. Through the doors, I can hear a man's voice, the lilt of a Bible passage being read. I can't make myself go back in, though. I'm afraid that if I open the doors, everyone will turn to stare at me, that Hadley will narrow her eyes, the Whisperers will whisper, and the minister *tsk* his disapproval into the microphone. So even though I'd left my coat in the church, I go out to the empty bus and shiver in the back until everyone files on, and the Whisperers bring me my coat and pat my arm and ask if I'm okay now, and I say that I am.

Chapter SEVEN

THE CALL COMES THE NEXT WEEK. Mom is in the kitchen, so she gets to the phone first. I hear her say, "Hello?" and then, "Yes," and then, after a pause, "Pete, is that you?" I turn the volume down on my show, though not so much that Mom will notice that I've gone quiet. Pete is my dad's name—well, Peter, really. She tries to call him Peter or "your father" when she refers to him, to show that she's mad at him, but usually she forgets and just calls him Pete. It's not him on the phone after all, though, because next Mom says, "I'm sorry. My mistake." And then a startled "*Oh*, I'm so sorry." And then, "Of course. I'll get her."

There she is in the doorway of the living room with the phone held out to me. She shakes her head a little, hitches herself up against the door frame, and stays there even after I take the phone from her.

"Hello?"

The man on the phone says, "Hello, Evie." I don't know how Mom mistook him; he doesn't sound like my dad at all. Though I'll admit that it's been years since I've talked to him. In my memory, my dad sounds like he's about to laugh, and like, if you didn't know better, you might be the joke. This man sounds like he has to try hard if he wants to laugh, and even then he might only cough.

"This is Ray McCabe," he says. "Elizabeth's father. We met at the funeral. Maybe you remember?"

I tell him, "Sure, of course." My first thought is that he found out that I had lied to him about being Zabet's friend and is calling to yell at me. So I stay quiet, which is the best thing to do if you aren't sure whether or not you're in trouble. I bite the inside of my cheek and avoid Mom's eyes.

But Mr. McCabe hasn't called to yell at me after all. At first, it seems like he's called just to ask questions. He asks me about school and my friends and my after-school activities—all the regular things adults ask about. I give my answers, and it feels boring and awkward. But then I think about how he'll never get to ask these questions to his daughter because she's dead, and so I'm nice about it and answer in an enthusiastic voice.

Then Mr. McCabe says, "I'd like to invite you and Hadley to dinner on Friday."

"At the school?" They'd had a pancake supper after those two kids died in the car crash so that they could raise money for a memorial scholarship and the twin trees.

"No," Mr. McCabe says. "No. At my house . . . well, condo, actually. Hadley will be there, and I thought we could eat and"—the cough that's been in his throat makes its way out.

"Did you ask her already?"

"Who?"

"Hadley."

"Yes. She said she could come."

"Did you tell her that I was coming?"

I try to sound casual when I say this, but Mr. McCabe must hear something in my voice because he says, "I did. Is that . . . ? She seemed to feel that was okay. Is it okay with you?"

"Yeah," I say. "Sure. Of course. Definitely."

The next day at school, when I see Hadley in the hall, she doesn't turn and dart away like usual, but instead checks her path to head right at me. Now I'm the one who wants to get lost in the crowd, and I look for some shoulders or backpacks to hide behind. But it's too late. She's right on me with her cig breath, stink eye, and the slice taken out of her chin. Her skin has gone all white along the road of that scar, like it's bone, like it's ghost.

She doesn't say hello, just sort of shrugs her shoulders instead. She yanks her ponytail around to one side and begins to rake her fingers through it, over and over. It reminds me of a movie I saw where this guy—this evil villain guy—sharpens a knife on a leather strap while he's talking to people, and he's so cool, he doesn't even have to look at it. In the scene, the knife's going on the strap, and the person the villain's talking to is staring at it (because wouldn't you?) and it's making this *whisk whisk* sound, which is almost the sound Hadley's fingers make going through her hair.

"You're going to dinner tonight?" she says.

"At the McCabes'? Yeah."

"Not McCabes." She frowns. "Just Mr. McCabe. They're divorced."

"I know," I say, though obviously I hadn't.

She screws up her mouth and gives her hair another tug. "So you're coming, then?"

"Well, yeah. He invited me, so I thought—"

"Right." She furrows her brow, like she's very worried about something, and then, swift and graceful, turns her head and blows a wad of spit onto the ground. I've never seen anyone spit like that, right out onto the floor. I stare at the glob of it, pearly, shimmering, until someone treads through it.

"Sorry. That was gross." She smiles for a second, brilliantly, but then it's gone like a camera flash.

"We met at the funeral." I speak these words in almost a whisper. "Mr. McCabe and me."

She shrugs again like she doesn't care and tosses her hair back over her shoulder, finished with it and me.

⌒

That night, I tell Mom that I'm meeting some friends at a school basketball game. She's so excited about it that her cheeks get pink without even any blush to help them along. She asks for the friends' names, so I choose three of the Whisperers' names at random. She repeats each of them like they're foreign words she must remember.

"Are you going to wear colors?" she asks.

"Colors?" I look down at my green sweater and think, *Green isn't a color?*

"Your school colors—Chippewa Braves. Let's see, you're gold and crimson, right?"

"No. We don't really do that." Though I honestly have no idea whether people do that or not. In fact, the more I think about it, the more it seems like the exact sort of thing that people at my school would do.

"We used to paint our faces"—she grazes her cheeks with her fingertips—"before games. You're going to have so much fun. You can stay out late," she says, pleased. "I won't even look at the clock."

I ride my bike to Mr. McCabe's condominium, my nose and fingertips freezing in the wind, my scarf flying out behind me. The condominium parks popped up a few years after the big neighborhoods, one across the street from each. Mr. McCabe's condo park is across from Hokepe Woods, where Mrs. McCabe still lives in the pretty house I walked to after school years ago. She must have been at the funeral. Not with Mr. McCabe, though, now that they are divorced. Maybe with a new husband? I hadn't seen her there. Of course, I'd missed the entire thing. I ride on the other side of the street from Hokepe Woods like it's cursed. I can't see much of it from the road— just a few peaked roofs and the stone sign.

I was back on my paper route last Sunday; I even went back to the place where they had brought out Zabet's body, out in front of that ancient woman's modern house. I had deliveries, after all. Turns out that even after a dead girl is carried across their lawns, people still read the newspaper. As I approached the house, I caught myself looking at my feet, at where I was going to step, like I might accidentally trample some undiscovered clue or tromp through an errant puddle of blood. Of course there was nothing like that. The neighborhood was just the neighborhood, tidy as ever.

Jonah wasn't there on Sunday. I saw his boss, Mr. Jefferson of Jefferson Wildlife Control, struggling with a trussed deer. The spring rains had begun this week, and the sled's runner was caught in a tire rut made from last night's mud. Mr. Jefferson's stomach was astounding, folded over his belt like a sack of loot. I went over and helped him right the sled, my satchel knocking into the deer's flank with a dull sound. The deer's eyes were lined in black with tiny white feathers of fur in their corners.

"Beyond the call of duty, sweetheart," Mr. Jefferson said when we were done, sticking his hands on his hips and puffing a bit.

"No problem. How's Jonah?"

"Oh, ho!" He pressed at his side. "I assume she's altruistic—that she's here to help. Now I see her true motives. She's in love with the boy!"

"We just talk," I said, hating this man, hating the whole expanse of his stomach. "Just sometimes."

"Sure, sure, honey. Sure. Jonah's on a little sabbatical, a little rest-up-and-feel-better."

"Is he okay?"

He made a great big gesture in the air like he was presenting something, a trophy maybe. "He's fine. Strong, young boy." He winked. "I'll tell him his girlfriend misses him."

Before I could help myself I said, "Tell him his girlfriend's pregnant."

Mr. Jefferson's face turned pink and his belly rippled with a fit of coughs. I only said it to punish him for what he said, but then I worried that he might flop into a faint over the dead deer, and I'd have to pull them both out to the truck. Finally his coughs slowed down, and he wiped his hands over his face and mouth. Somewhere between coughs he'd figured out that I was only joking. He offered another "Oh, ho, ho!"

"Well, I gotta deliver these," I told him and left him there, panting for breath over the dead deer.

⌒ᴐ

I turn my bike into Mr. McCabe's condo park and weave through. They've got the condos blocked out in groups of three or four, which repeat over and over like the background in old cartoons. Their porches are empty except for a plain doormat in the center of each, like a postage stamp stuck to an envelope. I aim my bike between two shiny cars. Almost all the cars are nice here, since it's mostly divorced dads in these condo parks; they get to keep the good car but not the house.

I imagine dads in condo after condo, just home from work in their rumpled suits. One wields a martini shaker; the next, a billiards cue; and the third, a high-class skin magazine. I picture Mr. McCabe cooking, an artichoke cupped in his hand. The artichoke is small, delicate, a mossy green; its leaves are wrapped tight over its middle like it's protecting something there. I wonder where my dad lives, if it's in a place like this.

I park my bike and walk up to the door. The porch light is on, even though it's not dark yet. I straighten my coat and scarf and the sweater underneath and think that maybe I should have worn a dress. I knock on the door. After a long moment, Hadley answers it, in a dress.

"Hey," I say.

She steps back, and I step in. She hunches against the wall and grimaces like I've just said something horrible.

"He's in there."

"Oh," I say. She tips her head back against the wall like she's going to tack herself up next in the line of watercolor seascapes hanging at measured intervals.

"Evie!" Mr. McCabe steps into the hallway, working a dish towel between his hands. He looks different from the way he did at the funeral, or maybe I'm just not remembering him right. His eyes are bright, almost glassy. Before I can say hello or "thanks for having me," he's closed me up in a hug. His shirt is rough on my cheek, and he smells like a lot of garlic. I don't know what to do with my hands. I end up patting him on the back until he pulls away to reveal Hadley still leaning on the wall, disgruntled and ponytailed and heaving with unaired sighs.

"Do you like pasta?" Mr. McCabe looks at me expectantly, and when I nod, he nods back so that both of us are nodding at once like we've agreed on something, and I guess what we've agreed on is that I do like pasta. "I made spaghetti, and this sauce is *not* from a jar." He wheels around and uses his dish towel to wave us on after him.

Hadley doesn't move, so I go in first. For a second, I think she might stay there, leaning and frowning, but then I hear her push off of the wall and follow me. The kitchen is small, and the appliances are three-quarter size and squeezed in. There's a little bar jutting out of the wall, and Mr. McCabe leads me to it, setting his hand just behind my shoulder and sweeping me along. There are bar stools tucked under it, so I pull one out, drape my coat and scarf over it, and then sit on it. Hadley is swept into the seat next to mine. She sits astride it like a horse, her dress falling over her knees. Her dress is splashed with yellow flowers. It has the faded fabric and moth-ball smell of a thrift store, but it's pretty, like one of the dresses my mom has on in pictures from when she was my age. It's strange to see her dressed up.

"I like your dress," I tell her.

She doesn't look at me.

Mr. McCabe leans over a tall pot on the stove. He peers into it, stirs, tastes whatever's in there. Then he's up watching us again. All of his gestures are quick, his words, too, like a timer's been set somewhere, ticking down to zero, and he's racing to beat it.

"Ten more minutes. At first, I thought that I'd make lasagna. You girls remember how Elizabeth loved lasagna."

He looks at us, and I look over at Hadley for help, but she leans on the counter, her jaw set.

"Yes," I say. "That's right." Though, truth be told, I don't. I don't know Zabet's favorite foods; I don't know her middle name; I don't know anything but what little snatches I've gotten from the hallway gossip at school and the afternoons I spent with her years ago. I can't even remember what foods Zabet liked then. Sandwiches, I think. We ate a lot of ham sandwiches and nachos made with strips of American cheese laid over tortilla chips.

Mr. McCabe is still talking. "I'd say that was her favorite food—lasagna was—and I thought that if she liked it, then probably you girls would like it, too. But then I thought maybe I shouldn't make it because she liked it so much. So I thought spaghetti. Everyone likes spaghetti. And you do? You like spaghetti?"

Hadley stares at nothing.

"Sure," I say again. "Spaghetti's great."

It's like this for the next half hour. Mr. McCabe talks about Zabet, dogging each sentence with the question "Do you remember that?" I keep nodding and saying "that's right" and "yeah, exactly," even though I don't remember any of it—how could I? Hadley sinks lower and lower, until one of her cheeks is actually resting on the counter. Mr. McCabe doesn't seem to notice her disgruntlement; he's flying around the kitchen, lining up spice jars, pouring us ginger ale, and tearing apart a head of lettuce.

"Are you okay?" I whisper to her while he's bent over the cooking pot.

"Fine," she says.

She's so listless and huffy that I'm almost surprised when she rouses herself to join us at the table for dinner. I tell myself that her mood has nothing to do with me. But as a test, I ask her to pass me the bread. She does, but when she swings the basket over to my side of the table, she lets it go before I've got my hands on it. It drops, careening off the edge of the table. Somehow I catch it before it hits the floor.

"Hey," I say softly.

"Watch out!" Mr. McCabe says in a hearty, jokey voice, oblivious to the fact that it was anything but accidental. He grabs a hunk from the basket in my hands and adds it to his plate, which is still full of food. He's moved the spaghetti around a lot, stirring and whirling it, but I haven't seen him take one bite.

Hadley says something under her breath.

"What?" I say.

"Nothing," she says, but I'm pretty sure she repeated his words: *Watch out.*

"Reflexes," Mr. McCabe tells us, making a swinging gesture as if to bat the bread across the table. "Hand-eye coordination. Do you remember when Elizabeth took tennis lessons? Her mother's idea." He pulls apart the slice.

"She threw the racket," Hadley says, then snaps her mouth shut, determined, I'm pretty sure, to say no more. She hits her fingertips against her bottom lip like she's punishing it for opening at all.

Mr. McCabe points at Hadley with his clump of bread. "That's right! She threw the racket."

Which is when Hadley turns to me and says, "So you remember that, too, Evie?" Her voice is even and sweet, like the voice boxes that they put in talking dolls. And I realize that I've been nodding all this time.

"Uh . . . I . . ." I try to stop my head from nodding, but it's still going, ticking along on the end of my neck. "I don't—"

"Last summer," Hadley prompts, and she's looking at me now, suddenly animated. "She threw the racket because . . ." She twirls her hand in the air like it's up to me to finish the sentence.

"Well," I say.

"Come on. You remember." She tugs at her hair; Mr. McCabe looks at me with his watery eyes, and I wonder if they've been this watery the whole time or if he's just now about to cry. "She threw the racket because . . ."

"Because," I repeat dumbly.

I hate Hadley then, even though she has every right to hate me back, to try to expose my lies. Even though she's the hero and I'm the villain, I hate her still, backed into my corner like I am. I stare at the scar on her chin like it's a fault line. I imagine digging into it, her face fissuring, cracking, falling to pieces on the peach condo carpet.

"Because?"

"She had a lot of spirit?" I offer, and both of us jump a little as Mr. McCabe shouts, "Yes!" His bread is now pointing at me. "Yes, that's just the right word for it."

I don't look at Hadley, but I can tell that she's still staring at me.

"Not everyone has that," Mr. McCabe says and takes a bite of the bread with each word. "Spirit. Gumption. Chutzpah."

"You tell us a memory now, Evie," Hadley says, her sentence nearly on top of his. "I'm sure you have one. About Zabet."

"Oh, well I don't want to—"

"Hmm?" She inserts the noise into my protest, and it's like that little noise pierces and paralyzes me. I stop, my mouth still partway open.

"Come on. A memory about Zabet, your friend."

I listen for the sarcasm in this, but there isn't any, not even a hint. She says it so straight that I almost believe she means it. But, of course, she doesn't. She knows that Zabet wasn't my friend. She's angry and determined to catch me out. Maybe this should make me feel guilty or apologetic or scared, and I do feel all those things, but more than any of that, I'm impressed. I'm impressed by the gentle blink of her eyes and the way that, even though she's pissed, she can make her face still and lovely like one of the yellow roses on her sleeve.

"Yes," Mr. McCabe says. Even though he's sitting down, he looks like he's standing on his tiptoes.

And I realize that this is why he invited us over. This is why he told all the Elizabeth-this and Elizabeth-that stories. He wants us to tell our stories in return. He wants what's left of her, every scrap. And I can hardly blame him.

"Go on," he tells me.

"Sure," I say. "Right." But I have nothing to say. I think of my only Zabet story, the one I won't tell—the two of us in the trees acting out my parents' fight, the ladle spinning, shining, toward her face. Mr. McCabe watches me through his watery eyes. Hadley sits back an inch, her lips tight. I try to think of the Zabet I would want to be told about, the one I've tried to imagine this past couple of weeks—fiery, beautiful, clever, and strong. The one who wasn't carried out of the woods.

"We were—"

"When?" Hadley interrupts.

"When?"

"When did this happen?"

"Last year."

"Last year?" she repeats. And it would be rude—this sentence—if it weren't for her polite voice. "So you were friends then?"

Mr. McCabe sets his hunk of bread down on his plate and cups his hands over it as if it is something he is hiding from us.

"We had a class together."

"Which class?" Hadley asks.

And this is dangerous because I don't know any of Zabet's classes, don't even know which track she was in. I think she was in the lower track, most of the bad girls are, but sometimes one of them pops up in accelerated, bringing with her a hard amusement over the fact that the rest of us expect her not to have done the assigned reading.

"Gym," I say. Everyone has to take gym.

"Gym," Hadley repeats as if the word tastes bad.

I picture the gym, its reek of salt and piss that lingers even after they've sent us all in to shower, the gritty pebbled tile of the locker room floors, the nests of hair left in the drains, the burn of chlorine that wafts up from the pool. I picture Zabet among all of this.

"She was good in gym." I feel like I'm pretty safe saying this. Zabet wasn't on any of the sports teams, but I'd bet that this was because of attitude, not ability. "Good reflexes," I add, "like you said." I see the flash of the ladle. "So she got chosen first for teams, and Coach Kenk liked her and everything."

Hadley leans over the table and makes getting another ginger ale as loud a process as possible. I wait until she sits back again, cracking the can and letting it fizz.

"But then, in April or so, there's the swim unit. It's terrible. The water's cold, and they use too much chlorine, so everyone's eyes turn pink. We have to wear the school suits, which smell like oatmeal. And, at the end of the unit, Kenk makes everyone go off the high dive."

Hadley sucks the overflow from the top of her can.

"It's the worst, right, Hadley?" I say. "Don't you think? Swim unit is the worst?"

I stare at her, and Mr. McCabe looks at her, too, so that she has to respond. Finally she nods, once, a little dip of the chin like she can hardly stand it.

"So the high dive is really tall, Mr. McCabe, and lots of kids are sort of . . . well, *scared* of it. But no one thinks Zabet will be scared, because like I said, she's been so good at gym and first pick for the teams and all that.

"Well, the thing is, I can tell that really she *is* scared of it, really scared of it—maybe more scared of it than the rest of us. She doesn't say that to me or anything, but she keeps looking at the board, like when we're doing other things, and she asks me once if I think that Kenk will make us go off it again this year."

"Zabet wasn't scared of heights," Hadley says, but the story is mine now; I'm in it, and I let it roll right over her.

"The high dive is different. Lots of people who aren't normally scared of heights are scared of a high dive. I mean, it's the difference between standing on something high and *jumping off* something high, right?" I say it simply and I picture Zabet, the board above her like a gallows, her flat freckled cheeks tipped upward. "So Friday, the last day of the unit, Zabet doesn't change into her suit. She tells Kenk she's sick, that she's got"—I glance at Mr. McCabe and feel my cheeks heat up—"her period. But, Kenk is Kenk. She says that it's not an excuse and to put on the suit. I sit with Zabet while she changes, and she's going off about Kenk and how unfair she is. I don't tell her that I know it's not really Kenk, that it's really the high dive that's got her upset, because there are some things you just might as well not say to Zabet."

I'm glad when Mr. McCabe nods at this observation of mine, because it was only a guess based on what Zabet was like when she was younger. I'm glad, too, that I know something about Zabet that is still true.

"Well, we're late because of all that, so when we come out, everyone is already around the high dive, but no one's gone off it yet. Kenk is telling us that we don't have to do a perfect dive or anything. We can cannonball or just jump or whatever we want as long as we try it. We have to try it. And we're all shivering in these oatmeal suits and hating Kenk, who's in her gross, evil sweat suit and doesn't even have to get wet, much less jump off a skyscraper. Zabet is next to me, and she's shivering more than anyone, even though she never gets cold.

"Then Kenk tells us to line up. Right away, everyone looks at Zabet. In fact, they just line up behind her. See, she's always the one to do it first, whatever it is.

"I'm trying to catch her eye, but she won't look back at me. Zabet. She just walks over to the ladder, puts her hands right on the rungs, and starts climbing up the damn thing . . . sorry . . . the thing. So we're all down there on the ground, watching her just go. You wouldn't believe it. Really, you wouldn't. She goes right up, step after step, all the way to the top. Then she walks out to the end of the board, just like that."

The crazy thing is, as I'm telling them this, I can actually see Zabet up there—the racerback of her suit, the frazzled rope of her braid—she's blurred, all the details gone because she's up so high with the fluorescent lights sending yellow down on her head. I can see all of our faces tipped up, too, all the rest of us in the class, gawking at her, waiting for her. For a second, it's all so real that I believe it might actually have happened the way I'm telling it.

Hadley sets her can down with a little clink. This time she doesn't even pretend to be polite. "And she does a perfect dive off it, right?"

This was exactly what I was going to have Zabet do in my story. I was going to have her dive off, not perfect, but a dive, all right. And it was going to make the rest of us bold enough to go up and off the board, too. A hero's ending. But I can hardly say that now, with Hadley watching me with her tight little screw of a smile like she's got it all figured out.

"No," I say. "No, she doesn't. Actually, she turns around and climbs right back down. She couldn't do it after all."

As I say it, I can still see it, Zabet's bottom, the pads of her feet pink from the rough surface of the board, the purple birthmark on the back of her right knee, all of it growing closer as she steps down the ladder rungs. And as I see it, I realize that this—*this*—is the right ending.

Hadley's mouth unscrews a turn. She fiddles at the sleeves of her dress, fussy like a cat licking its paws. "No offense, but what was the point of that story? I thought you were supposed to tell—"

She glances at Mr. McCabe and has good enough sense to stop. He holds the wrist of one of his hands between the fingers of the other, like he's taking his own pulse. He's looking across the table at me, but also *not* at me. He has a faint smile on his face like maybe he can see Zabet up on that board, too.

"Thank you," he says. "Thank you for sharing that, Evie."

Hadley pulls the sleeves of her dress over her hands and balls them in her lap, mad as hell. I wish I could tell her what I'd just figured out, what she'd helped me figure out: The point of the story isn't that Zabet triumphed. The point is that Zabet climbed down the ladder, that she survived.

Dinner ends soon after that. Hadley lets Mr. McCabe fuss over her, helping her with her coat and sending her off with a steamed-up container of leftover spaghetti. She's a different Hadley now than she was before—with a warm wick of a smile and quick, bright eyes. And if for a minute I think that she's come around, given up trying to expose my lies, maybe even making an attempt to be friends, it is only for a minute. Because if I observe closely, I can see that the edges of Hadley's smile are yanked up by force and her voice is almost tearful in its good cheer. She's putting on a face. I've seen my mother do it a million times. She's still angry; she's just decided to fake it.

Hadley dips into a darling bow when she thanks Mr. McCabe for the dinner. "Don't make spaghetti again without me," she says sweetly.

If Mr. McCabe notices the difference between the pouting Hadley of earlier in the evening and the charmer she is now, he doesn't mention it. She smacks his cheek with a kiss and slides out the door while I'm still fiddling with my shoes. When I finally get them done up, Mr. McCabe is holding out a portion of spaghetti for me.

"You, missy," he says in a way that's sad instead of playful.

"Thanks," I say, taking the container.

He sets a paw on my shoulder. "No, no. Thank *you*. It's good to know that Eliz—well, I won't talk about her anymore tonight."

"You can."

"No." He smiles under his mustache. "My battery's wound down." He looks at me for a second, steady, and I look down at my fingers crossing the top of the spaghetti container because I can hardly look back at him. "You're a good girl," he says.

I nod and shuffle my way backward until I bump into the door. "Dinner was really good. Really. And thanks for"—I lift the container—"the spaghetti."

I slip out the door with his good-byes heavy at my back and the spaghetti losing heat in my hands. Out front, Hadley's sitting on my bike, the hem of her dress floating perilously close to the grimy gears. She's like a kid once again, her forehead wrinkled up in determination. She stands up on the pedals so that the bike wavers, trying to go forward but stuck, its lock pulled taut between the pole of the carport and the back wheel. When she sees me, she steps onto the ground.

"I would have ridden it away if it weren't locked up."

"I have the key in my bag," I say dumbly, offering what? To unlock it and let her go?

She snorts. She's none of the Hadleys I've seen before—not desperate like she was in the cafeteria, not furious like she was tonight at dinner. She's something else, something a little more like I'd imagined she would be all the times I'd watched her from across the hall at school.

She eyes me. "You're hanging around because she's dead, huh? It's exciting for you?"

"No." I feel my cheeks burn up.

"Then why are you doing it?"

"Doing what?"

She gives me a look. "What you're doing."

"I'm not doing . . . I got sick at the funeral, or almost. Then I said something to him, to Mr. McCabe. I didn't know, and I didn't really mean to."

Hadley watches me sputter; she rocks my bike, going up on her tiptoes and taking it an inch forward, sliding onto her heels, taking it back. She sets her eyes on the juncture of my handlebars.

"She was beaten up. Did you know that? They didn't say it in the paper. He—whoever killed her—he beat her so bad her head was big, swollen, like . . . huge. Her nose was broken." Hadley rocks forward. "All her front teeth were broken out." Rocks back. "Her cheekbones. Her face was practically gone." She rocks once more back and forth, and then she looks up. "My parents don't think I can hear them talk when they go downstairs, but their voices come up through the vents." She gets off without bothering with the kickstand, and so the bike wheels around, hanging off the pole. "They're so stupid sometimes."

"That's awful," I say, seeing the body bag again, now seeing what was in it.

"*That's awful,*" she mimics.

"It is," I say, my voice wobbling.

Hadley looks at me for a second, sizing me up. "It is, isn't it?" She walks around the front of her car, letting her keys scratch along the hood. "You want a ride home? It's cold, and besides, I don't know how you think you're going to ride home with that thing of spaghetti."

Hadley and I barely talk on the drive back. When she pulls in front of my house, she doesn't help me get my bike out of the trunk, and she doesn't wait until I get in the house before she drives off. She winks her brake lights at the end of the street, and I tell myself that maybe she means it as a sort of good-bye.

Chapter EIGHT

ON SUNDAY, Jonah is back in Hokepe Woods. I hear the whisk of the sled runners while I'm delivering my papers, and it sounds different somehow from when Mr. Jefferson pulls the sled. I finish my route as quickly as I can—*smack, smack, smack*—and hurry back to the curb where Jonah usually parks his truck. It's there, rust creeping up on it, dusty windows, junk still mounded in the back. The mornings are getting warmer, so it's not so painful to sit on the bumper until Jonah emerges from the woods, sled slicing the muddy lawn behind him. When he sees me there on his truck, his stride falters just a little bit. I wave, but he doesn't wave back. It occurs to me that maybe he's mad because I ran away back when he found the body, maybe he even hates me now. Thinking that almost makes me hop off the truck, go back to my car, and drive away. But then I think about Jonah knowing my name, calling it, calling me, and this keeps me waving. There's a small something on his sled, and when he gets closer I can see that it's a possum, rough gray pelt, sharp snout, and bare, pink tail winding out behind.

"Hey," Jonah says when he reaches me, and it's nice the way he says it, not angry at all. I feel it in my body like a sigh, the fact that he's not angry.

"You were gone last week," I say back, and right away I wish I could unsay it because it's obvious and desperate, like something my mother would say.

"Well. Huh." He squints for a second. "Everybody needs a break sometimes."

Jonah looks a little different than how I remember him looking, as if over the past two weeks the hands of my memory had changed his face somehow, pressing on its angles and planes, plying its lips and earlobes so that the face in my memory only resembles Jonah's. My memory has spread his eyes a smidge and thickened his chin; I've made his hair a bit shaggier and messier, or maybe he's just started brushing it better than he used to. I correct the Jonah in my head so that he looks how this Jonah, the honest-to-God Jonah, does.

Then I think of my father and Zabet and other people I haven't seen for a while. It occurs to me that my memories of their faces are only memories of photographs from albums and yearbooks and fireplace mantels. And when I try to call up real memories of them, it's just the figures from these pictures that get up and walk around—same clothes, same haircuts, and same smiles—like actors dressed up for a part.

"Are you . . . how have you been?" I ask, knowing full well that this is a second stupid thing to say.

Jonah squints as if he has to think about it. "All right," he finally says. "And you?"

There's so much I want to tell him about Hadley and Mr. McCabe and Zabet, but his question seems too small to hold such a large answer, so I end up saying "all right," too.

I watch Jonah slide the possum into a garbage-type bag, though it's thicker than a garbage bag and bright blue, with a spiky contamination symbol on it. He gestures that I should get off the truck, and when I do, he swings the sled and bag into the back.

Then, without anything more than a "see you next Sunday, kiddo," he's heading to his truck like he's going to leave. I stand there for a second, stunned, because I can't believe he's leaving—after all my phone calls, after driving around trying to find him, after Zabet's body in the woods—like nothing has changed. But he's already swinging the truck door open, has his boot up in the cab.

"She's dead," I blurt out.

He stops, and turns to look at me. He doesn't have an expression on his face, though it seems like there's something working behind his eyes. Me, I'm just standing there having said what I said, my mouth still open a bit, the hatch through which the words had escaped. This is the stupidest thing I've blurted out yet; I cover my face with my hands because I can't look at Jonah anymore, and I can't stand him looking back at me.

Then suddenly Jonah's arms are around me. I'm so startled that I nearly jump right out of them; in fact, I gasp from surprise, but the arms only tighten.

Jonah is holding me. I feel the nubby fleece of his jacket sleeve against one cheek, and his actual arm is under that flannel, in that sleeve, around me. I don't know what I've done to deserve this, to prompt it. My heart is a rabbit's; my heart is on his sled, racing away through the woods. I tell myself to remember this moment—every detail of it. And one of these details is that Jonah's patting my back. And another is that he's murmuring, "It's okay. It's okay." I wish I could look out and see the world from this viewpoint from within Jonah's arms, but I can't see anything because my hands are still covering my face.

That's when I realize: My hands are covering my face, which must make Jonah think that I'm crying. He thinks I'm crying about Zabet. He thinks he's comforting me. That's why he embraced me.

And though I know it's terrible, probably my worst crime yet, there's nothing for me to do but shake in Jonah's arms and press my hands tighter to my face to make it pink, like I've actually been crying. I send a quick apology up to Zabet. (Up? Yes, up.) Then I allow myself to appreciate Jonah's sleeve, his arms beneath, his voice in my ear.

When he pulls back, I lower my hands from my face and draw a shaky breath. He looks at me with serious eyes, then he does an amazing thing, and tucks away a loose strand of my hair. I feel his fingertips run the length of my forehead and then brush, for an instant, the secret spot behind my ear.

"Okay?" he says.

No, I think. After you touched my hair like that, okay will never be a word I can use to describe my state of being again.

But I know I should nod, so I nod, and he smiles.

"Okay," he says. "We're both okay. Yeah?"

I nod again; it's all I can manage.

But Jonah, he's already back to his truck, hopping up into the cab. "See you next Sunday, kiddo," he says again.

Kiddo, my mind whispers. As soon as the truck turns, I sit down on the curb, and for some reason that I can't even begin to explain, *that's* when I start to cry.

Chapter NINE

On Monday, in the hall at school, I look over to see Hadley matching her steps to mine. I get the feeling that she might give me a shove into the bank of lockers, and I get ready to jump out of the way. But instead of shoving, she starts talking.

"So my parents are obsessed with how Mr. McCabe is. *How did he seem? How did he seem?*" she chirps in a voice that's got to be her mother's. "Like I'm a goddamned psychiatrist. What do they want me to say?"

I eye her, not sure how to respond. She doesn't seem angry with me anymore. In fact, she seems casual, like we talk every day. "That he's fine? Maybe?" I say, not sure if this answer is right.

"Maaaybe." She draws the word out. "Do yours do that? Bother you?"

"I didn't tell my mom I was going over there."

"Smart." She nods approvingly. Then after a few steps, she says, "I have calc now."

"Bio," I say.

We walk for a while without saying anything. I glimpse the kids we pass out of the corner of my eye. I wonder if they're watching us, wondering who that girl walking with Hadley Smith is, if she's tough like Hadley, if she's bad. I try desperately to think of something to say, something about Mr. McCabe, something about calculus, nothing about Zabet.

Since Hadley told me what she told me out in front of Mr. McCabe's house, I keep seeing Zabet's broken face. It squints out at me from a gnarl in a tree, from a knot of my laundry, or from an imprint in the pillowcase I've just slept on. I wonder what else Hadley knows, what other classified facts—what broken fingers, what abrasions, what bruises—are suspended like gristle in the meat of her brain.

I'm still thinking about this when we hit the fork between the math and science halls. I wonder what I should do if Hadley heads into the math hall, if I should follow her or just keep going to science without saying good-bye. But she stops at the juncture.

The crowd splits around us; aside from a few rubberneckers, people aren't staring so hard or long at Hadley anymore. Already people are letting Zabet's death fade like the facts from last week's test. A week ago, you'd hear the *zizz* of the first letter of her name, like the chatter of a new type of insect or the spun flint of a lighter. That's mostly died out now.

"He seemed okay," Hadley says, and at first I don't know who she means. "He cooked us dinner. He talked. He seemed, like, okay."

"Yeah. I mean, how is he supposed to be?"

"Exactly," she says. "Like, tap dancing?"

"With a cane and top hat."

"And those steps," Hadley adds.

"Steps?" I ask.

"You know, those stair steps. The ones they tap-dance down."

"*Those* steps. Right."

She socks me in the shoulder and marches away down the hall, boots untied, laces whipping.

～

She finds me after that, in the hall, at my locker, outside in the bus circle. Each time, I expect it to be the last time, a fluke, but then she finds me again. She slaps my backpack instead of saying good-bye and tugs at the collar of my coat when she wants to make a point. She smells like a baby, soapy and milky, but with a whiff of something sharp—ugly little shreds of tobacco—underneath.

She admits that she can't stand any of her friends, and I make mention of some of the Whisperers so that she won't know that she's my only friend, really, if I can even call her that. I've been friendless so long, I think, *Is this how it happens?* And it does just happen, without me trying to make it happen, for once. She finds me again, and she snorts pleasantly at the things I say; she knocks her shoulder into mine. One morning she tells me, "I'll see you at lunch," and she does. During passing, I catch myself scanning the crowds for the yellow cap of her hair or listening for her smoker's cough.

A couple of times I catch her looking at me slyly out from under her bangs.

Finally, I say, "What?"

She blinks and says, "What what?"

"You're staring. So, *what?*"

She reaches out and flicks me on the nose. "That's what."

I tell Hadley about Jonah, but for real, not the way I tell the Whisperers. I tell her how he was the one who had found Zabet, and she gets a look on her face like she's packing everything she owns in a suitcase, looking at each object before she drops it in. Something about the look on her face keeps me from telling her that I was there, too. And then there's the body bag; I don't want to have to mention that.

"He in college?" she asks about Jonah, and I vaguely remember some rumor about Hadley and college boys.

"He dropped out."

She sniffs. "And now he picks up dead animals . . . and dead girls."

"Geez," I say.

"Geez what? It's true. Maybe he liked finding a girl in the woods. Maybe he's creepy."

"He's not. He's okay."

"You never know about guys." She looks out from under her bangs. "You in love with him or something?"

I had thought things might change between Jonah and me after that hug. I spent the whole week wrapping my arms around myself, trying to recreate the feeling of it. But when I saw Jonah the next Sunday, we were back to our old ways, him grunting and nodding while I babbled on about animal carcasses. I stood close to him just before he got into his truck to go—as close as I dared—my body humming with the week-old ghost of his embrace. "'Scuse me, there," he said, so I moved. I don't tell Hadley about that, either.

Hadley tells me everything—things people say that are meant to be comforting but end up being terrible, more details of the autopsy that have floated up in her parents' voices through the vent in her bedroom, last night's nightmare, the whole story about how she had seen Zabet the afternoon before she died. She'd picked her up and driven over to the mall, where they'd walked the circuit from Coney Dog to Waldenbooks and back.

"What was the last thing she said to you?" I ask.

She squints at me. "What?"

"The last thing she said. Her last words."

"I don't know. I don't remember. Probably just 'bye.'"

"You don't ever think about it? Like, try to remember?"

"She said 'bye,' okay? Just 'bye,'" Hadley snaps, and I don't ask her about it again.

All of Hadley's nightmares are set in the mall. She claims that they wouldn't be scary to anyone but her. She describes them in an offhand voice between bites of French fries. Sometimes, in her dream mall, the clothes racks rattle with empty hangers; sometimes the corridors bend and twist and she can't find her way out; sometimes the stores aren't selling their normal wares, but, instead, people she knows. "My optometrist," she says, "Coach Kenk, my Aunt Beth . . . some of them are on sale, with the big red tags. Some of them are bargains. And, I always think, *Good! Sell them all.* Everyone's so stupid. Zabet, she was stupid, too, letting some guy do that to her. I hate everyone, Evie. If I'm being honest, I hate everyone most of the time. Even her. Even you."

I don't have any nightmares to tell. The body bag refuses to parade through my dreams, or if it does, it doesn't leave a print. I sleep right through the night now—ten hours, eleven—without dreams, even though sometimes I wake with the feeling that some-one has been standing right over me, breathing. Sleeping isn't hard. Lying in the dark room, waiting to sleep—that's the hard part. I call Jefferson Wildlife Control just to hear the voice on the machine, the beep, the silence that comes after.

Chapter TEN

A FEW WEEKS LATER, Hadley and I have dinner with Mr. McCabe again—our fourth dinner in as many weeks. Since our first dinner with Mr. McCabe, Hadley hasn't mentioned the fact that I lied about being friends with Zabet. In fact, now she covers for me, including my name in stories about things she and Zabet had done together. The first time that she did this, I looked up at her, startled, and she gave me a secret smile as she spoke, like saying, *Yes. This is okay.* And so now I have a whole new history, one that includes late-night calls, home-pierced ears, and summer-break doldrums with Hadley and Zabet. When Hadley tells Mr. McCabe things like, "But it was Evie who said we shouldn't miss curfew," I can almost believe it happened that way myself.

Tonight, Mr. McCabe makes the same spaghetti he always does. "I should expand my repertoire," he says. "Sorry, girls, I'm one-note."

"Don't say that," Hadley says, twirling up more on her fork. "It's really good." To prove her point, she takes a bite.

Mr. McCabe shakes his head, visibly pleased by her words. "You could ask Elizabeth—it's either this or lasagna or something out of a box. And it'll be nothing out of a box for you girls."

"It could be, like, a tradition," I say.

He sends a finger at me in a swoop. His energy is still frenetic, his gestures and cadences like a hopped-up game-show host's. I wonder if he's always this hyper; I get the feeling that it's just when we're around.

At the end of dinner, Mr. McCabe holds out his hands, each closed into a fist—one toward Hadley, one toward me. I glance at Hadley, and she's already extended her hand, palm open, under his. So I do the same. Mr. McCabe leans forward, his shoulders up around his ears, looking like he's getting ready to bound up onto the table. He opens his hands, and something light and feathery falls into mine.

I examine what I've got—a thin, tarnished chain with a glass globe strung on it, a tiny gold seed suspended in the globe's center. I remember this. I saw it hanging around Zabet's neck, but I was always too far away to see what was in the globe. Once I saw her tuck her chin under the chain and tip the globe into her mouth, pulling it out shiny with spit. I look over at Hadley. She has a necklace strung between her fingers, too. The chain is gold, and lined up along the center is a row of glass beads. She looks over at what I've got, and something moves over her face, running like a tremor through her eyes and cheeks and burying itself at her mouth, which she tightens up, forcing it into a smile.

Mr. McCabe sits back, satisfied. "I thought you girls might like those. They were Elizabeth's, and well, what would I do with them besides get them out and look at them from time to time?" And . . . though he says this lightly, it sounds like that is what he, in fact, really *does* want to do with the necklaces instead of give them to us. "They should be worn."

"Thank you," Hadley and I both say together.

"That's a mustard seed." Mr. McCabe tips his chin at me. "Elizabeth's mother wore that in the seventies. It's supposed to be good luck."

"Zabet wore it all the time," Hadley tells me, then adds. "I mean, you know that."

Mr. McCabe points to the necklace in my hand. "She wasn't wearing it when—" Mr. McCabe stops and wipes a napkin over his mouth like he's going to mop up the end of his sentence. *She wasn't wearing it when she was killed.* Is that what he means? I glance over at Hadley, but she's gazing down at her own necklace. Mr. McCabe looks at us miserably. "The police do the best they can," he says. "I know that. I have to believe that. But I had thought by now—well, I guess it was only a hope—I had *hoped* by now that they'd have found him."

Hadley and I are both still. This is new, Mr. McCabe confiding in us about the murder investigation, and I worry that if I move or speak, he might remember himself and stop talking.

Hadley, as always, is bolder. "Do they have any suspects?" she inserts smoothly, still looking down at her hands.

"Huh," Mr. McCabe huffs. "Huh. They don't call them suspects anymore. *Persons of interest,* that's what they say. And, no. None they've told me about. No persons of interest. No one's interesting. Everyone's boring." He shakes his head. "My brother keeps saying, 'Wouldn't you like ten minutes in a room alone with him? He killed your daughter. Wouldn't you like ten minutes alone with him cuffed to a chair and the police and lawyers out for a long coffee break?'" Mr. McCabe stops shaking his head and looks right at me. It takes all my will not to look away. His eyes are not angry, not sad, but startled, as if he is watching something he can't quite believe is happening. "And I would. I'd take those ten minutes. But not to hit him, not to . . . just to ask him, 'Why? Why did you? How could you?'"

I break his gaze.

"Well, it's good luck, in any case," he repeats. "The necklace is."

I bring the seed up to my eye. I wonder how long it's been suspended in the glass. I wonder if it was planted now, like, in the ground, could it still sprout? Through the glass globe, I see Hadley staring at me and the necklace.

"Do you want to switch?" I ask.

"No," she says, and I can tell she's lying. Then to Mr. McCabe, "No, I love mine." She holds it up with the clasp open. "Will you help me?"

Mr. McCabe assists each of us, his hands fumbling at the backs of our necks. The globe of my necklace fits in the divot of my collarbone, swinging forward and then bouncing back against my throat when I reach for my cup. When we leave, Mr. McCabe walks us to the door, and we can see the shadow of his face in one of the glass cutouts, watching as we pull out of the driveway and down the street.

I touch my necklace, pushing the globe deeper into my skin until it presses against my windpipe. Hadley glances over at it again.

"Do you want it? You can have it." I reach to undo the clasp. Really, I'm insincere. I want to keep the mustard seed necklace for myself, so I'm hoping that she'll say no. In fact, I've made my voice eager and my gestures quick in order to startle a no out of her, and I pause with my hands on the clasp, waiting for her to demur.

"No, no, you keep it," she finally says. After a few more miles, she says, "Zabet really liked it a lot. She believed in the luck part. Guess she was wrong, huh?"

She punches in the cigarette lighter, but when it pops back out, she doesn't take it. She raps a fist against her forehead. "I don't want to go home. Do you have to?"

I don't. Mom is on a date with a car salesman Veronica introduced her to, so she has no need for my company. On her date nights, she paints streaks of blush so high up her cheeks that the pink powder stains her hairline. Her regular poses and pauses change into something less refined, something baser and looser—a blow-up doll, a big dumb girl. Instead of *come hither*, she telegraphs *get on over here, you!*

She comes back from these dates late and tipsy. I always make sure that I'm in my room with the lights out by the time she bumps around the kitchen, knocks bottles off the shelf in the bathroom, curses when the water is too cold, and finally collapses with a sigh of bedsprings. In the morning she's pale and sweaty from last night's wine, her face like some pearly-fleshed mollusk. She presses the heel of her hand into her forehead as she sips her coffee. "Why do I do it?" she always asks. The one time I actually offered an answer to this question, she didn't speak to me for a week.

In the car, I tell Hadley, "I have some time."

We end up at a diner near the highway. I order a pop, but Hadley gets another meal: coffee and a plate of pancakes.

"I need to get the taste of spaghetti out of my mouth," she says and then looks stricken for a second. "God, I'm such a bitch," she sighs.

I don't say anything, because I know that when she calls herself a bitch, she doesn't mean it to be entirely an insult. There's a table of guys across the aisle all with coffees and no food. I don't recognize them from school, so maybe they're older. A couple of them sneak glances at Hadley, her hank of light hair, her laced-up boots, her tough-girl clothes, her sneer.

A few of Hadley's old friends are playing quarters at a booth near ours. They wave at us shyly, and Hadley returns a weary salute.

"They suck," she whispers to me, and I'm more pleased by this than I should be. Twice, kids at school have come up to me in the halls to ask if I know where Hadley is, and when she was sick one day, the guidance counselor sent the packet of her missed homework with me. We're considered best friends now; we're considered a pair.

While we're waiting for our food, we blow straw wrappers at each other and use the jam containers as bricks for a miniature pyramid. We stare out at the entrance ramp to the parking lot, which beads up with a steady string of cars. There's been an away game, and we see the school buses return, their headlights high and familiar.

"Ugh. They're coming back," Hadley says and rests her head on the tabletop, a chunk of her hair landing in something sticky, probably syrup from her pancakes. She spends the next few minutes dabbing at it with a wet napkin and picking the strands apart.

"I feel drunk," she announces a few minutes later.

"All you've had is coffee."

"And syrup."

"Wicked combo."

She snorts. "Yeah, wicked. You ever been drunk?"

"No," I say.

She studies me. "No." She agrees that I haven't. "Have you ever hitchhiked?" She nods out to the highway.

"No. You?"

She rolls her eyes. "I have a car, dummy. Have you ever—"

"I've never nothing."

"God, Evie. You're sixteen. You should do *something*." She looks around. For something for me to do, I guess. Her eyes land on the table across from ours. "Go talk to those guys."

I feel myself blush at the suggestion. The boys aren't looking at us now; they're hunched over the center of the table, doing something furtive with the sugar packets. "I don't have anything to say."

"Pick one and tell him to meet you in the parking lot to make out." She says this like it's nothing.

"Sure. Right. *Hi, stranger.*"

Hadley shrugs. "He'll come."

"No," I whisper.

"Of course he will. He's a guy." She shrugs again.

I try to keep my eyes half lidded, my voice nonchalant. "Is that something people, like, do? I mean, have you?"

"Shit!" Hadley says. "They're leaving."

She slides out of the booth and grabs my hand. It's all I can do to latch on to a sleeve of my coat and pull it after me.

"We haven't paid!" I say, but we're already out the door and in the parking lot, stamping our feet against the chill of the spring night.

The boys have already piled into their car, exhaust putting out its back. The car rolls forward a few feet and then stops. We hear a shout and see the wave of a hand out one of the windows. At us? Hadley takes a step toward it, pulling me after her. Just as she does, the car shoots forward, out of the parking lot, and down the road.

"Wait!" Hadley shouts after them. "My friend was going to give it to you!"

"Hadley!" I try to cover her mouth, but my hand is still tangled in hers. She yanks my arm, breaks free of me, and runs around the parking lot in circles.

"Come back," she cries to the boys. "My friend wants you!"

I chase after, trying to catch and shush her. It's a ghost that's taken us up; I can feel it in my chest, a high happiness that wavers, arms pinwheeling wide, on the edge of some other scarier feeling. We hop and poke at each other's sides. Hadley yodels and, when I try to cover her mouth again, blows a wet raspberry into my palm.

"Gee, thanks." I wipe my hand on my jeans.

"Aw, Evie." She takes ahold of my head and pulls it close to hers, knocking our temples together. She holds my head too hard, and when I squirm, she won't let it free. "Let's run away together."

Then she's pulling me across the parking lot and down the muddy slope of the drainage ditch, then back up the other side of it to the edge of the highway. She's singing something high and tuneless, her hair flying out behind her and into my face. I feel a syrupy strand of hair flick up beneath my eye. She's got me by the arm still, and when we get to the shoulder of the road, she forms my hand into a fist, thumb up.

"Hadley," I say, but she's jumping around me, wild, with her hair over her face so that I can't read her expression. Then she's stretching my arm out toward the road. "Hadley!" I say again, and make a swipe at her with my free arm. "Come on." I'm half laughing now, mostly because I don't know what else to do. She's pulling my arm so hard that I have to put all my weight on my heels if I don't want to tumble out into the road. "Come on. Let's get your car."

"No, Vie. We're out of here. Someone will pick us up. We'll hitch-hike to Chicago. New York!"

"Hadley. We can't. It's not . . . it's dangerous."

"*We're* dangerous!"

She lets go of my hand, and I drop the hitchhiking thumb. I present my palms to her, flat. "We're not," I say.

She reaches for my face, and I flinch, but it's only my necklace that she wants. She closes her hand around the globe. I can feel her fist, warm and hard at my throat. I swallow against it, frightened.

"I'll protect you," she says in a voice so fierce that I have the impulse to laugh at her, except then suddenly I don't feel like laughing at all. She tightens her grip on the necklace and the chain digs into the back of my neck. "You can count on it. I'd fight him. I'd—"

"Hey," I say to her, coaxing. "Hey."

She lets go of the necklace. "Let's just go, okay, Vie? We're gonna go."

"Where?"

She spins around. The intersection is dead, no cars coming or going, only the traffic light hanging from its wire, blinking red.

She sags against me. "Aw, hell," she mutters.

But then from around the corner, a car appears, as if she's called for it. And even though Hadley's no longer signaling for a ride, the car slows as it passes us, pulling to the shoulder of the road a few yards from where we're standing. Hadley's head jerks up like she's scented something on the wind. She stares at the car. It's dark blue and compact and nondescript. It looks more like a mom's car than a killer's car. Still, I'm not getting in it. Hadley, though. She's already taken a step for it.

"We can't just—" I say.

A head pops out of the passenger window, followed by shoulders and arms: one of the boys from the diner. He perches on the frame of the open window, holding the top of the car to steady himself. He's what my mother would call lanky and what I would call stringy, and his jacket is a size or two too big, making him look even stringier. His cheeks are ruddy, like he's just drunk something warm.

"Hey, ladies," he calls, and there's some noise from inside the car in response, the word *ladies* sung in a falsetto. The boy ducks back into the car for a second and then pops out again. "I apologize. My friends are losers."

At this, the car jerks forward a foot, and the boy curses and nearly falls out onto the ground. He keeps his grip on the roof, though, and swings back into the car as soon as it stops. I look over at Hadley, who's watching the car with a little grin on her face as if this is all for our amusement. In a moment, the boy is back out, though just his head this time.

"We're going to a party. Near campus."

"They're in *college*," I whisper.

Hadley ignores me. She tosses a shoulder and tilts her head at the boy as if to say, *So? What does your party have to do with me?*

"You ladies"—the car jerks forward again at *ladies*—"you wanna come?"

There's no question that Hadley will want to go, so I wait for her to answer him. But she doesn't answer him; instead she turns and watches me steadily as if waiting for something. I nod at her to mean that I agree, we can go, but she just keeps looking at me.

"What?" I whisper.

"*You* tell him," she says, tipping her head toward the guy in the car.

"Me? Tell him what?"

"That we'll go."

"Oh. Well. It really doesn't matter who tells him, does it?"

"Scared, little Vie?"

"No. It's just . . . he's mostly talking to you."

"Go on. Don't be a baby." Her voice isn't mean as she says this last bit; rather, it's indulgent, almost as if I *am* a baby.

"I don't—"

"It's not a big deal. Just say *yeah* or *okay*. Just one word."

There are other passengers in the car, their silhouettes moving behind the windows. The boy turns and says something to one of them, then sticks his head back out the window and a stringy arm along with it. He looks at us expectantly. I feel as I haven't used my voice in years, and if I open my mouth, only a sighing wheeze of ancient dust will swirl out.

"You coming?" he asks.

Hadley sneaks a hand under my coat and pinches my side.

"Yes," I whisper too soft for him, or even Hadley, to hear. But before Hadley can pinch me again, I gather my breath and say it louder—too loud really—a shout that travels past the boy and the car and all the way down the road.

Chapter ELEVEN

WE FOLLOW THE BOYS IN HADLEY'S CAR. They drive too fast and stop at stoplights too short. I ask Hadley why, after inviting us, they're trying their best to lose us, and she explains that they're not; they're just showing off. At each light, Hadley reaches over and grabs my chin, coating a section of my face, and then her own, with a different sort of makeup—blush, mascara, lipstick, even eyeliner. When she's done, I flip down the sun-visor mirror and peer at the strip of my reflection it allows. My lips look sticky, my cheeks hollow, my eyes bright mirrors set in frames of sooty black makeup.

"No one will think I really look like this," I say. "They'll think I'm wearing makeup."

"You *are* wearing makeup."

I adjust the mirror, appraising my face from different angles. We're out of Chippewa now, and the streetlights are less frequent, some burnt out. My face glides in and out of shadow. "You don't think it makes me look funny?"

"Nope." Hadley considers for a moment. "It makes you look ready." Ahead of us, the boys pull to the curb, adding their car to a long chain of parked cars that winds down the street. Hadley pulls in behind them.

"Ready for what?"

I can see the party house up ahead, all lit up, dark shapes moving together on the front lawn. I can't hear the music yet, but when I rest my fingertips on the dashboard, it hums with a shallow vibration.

"Ready for something to happen," Hadley says, getting out of the car and walking toward the boys. I hurry after her, conscious of the fact that it must look like I'm hurrying after her.

A whole group of boys have climbed out of the car, too many to safely fit in it. Some of them must have been squeezed onto the floor or piled in each other's laps. I imagine them all in there, knees pressed to their chests, one boy's breath on the back of another's neck while they waited, car idling on the shoulder of the highway, for our answer.

We fall in with them—no introductions more elaborate than a few heys—and all trudge toward the house. Hadley slips into the center of the group of boys, and it is as if she has dived into an icy-cold lake, leaving me on the shore, watching the echo of her ripples. I fall back a step. I can see only glimpses of Hadley now, past upturned jacket collars, baseball-cap brims, and overlapping shoulders. A hand shoots up from within the group, offering a flask that shines silver as a surfacing fish. I've never seen a flask before—only in movies. Then there's Hadley's familiar hand, stretching up, reaching over, and taking the flask. The shoulders part for a moment, and I see her tip her head back and drink deep. I want nothing more than to call Hadley back to me; of course, I can't, not without looking totally stupid, anyway.

"Hey," says a voice next to me, and it's the stringy boy who'd invited us along. He matches his pace with my reluctant one. "I'm Anthony don't call me Tony," he says in one breath, and then smiles like he expects me to smile back.

"Evie," I say. "And that's already a nickname."

"For what?"

"Eve," I say, bracing myself for some stupid college-boy joke about an apple and a snake.

"Aren't nicknames supposed to be shorter?"

I scuff my shoe on the ground. "Go figure."

He smiles more, and I wish he'd stop because I haven't said anything funny. It's lonely when someone thinks you've made a joke and you really haven't. Besides, I'm not sure I want this stringy college boy smiling at me. I'm not sure what it means when a college boy smiles at you—when any boy smiles at you. Sure, there's Jonah, but he's different. He's Jonah. The only thing he'll probably ever do to me is smile. And anyway, Jonah's smiles don't come as easy as this. I glance at the group of boys ahead of us and wonder if they put Tony up to talking to me so that they could vie for Hadley's attention or if it was something he actually wanted to do.

"Do you go to State?" he asks.

"No," I say, but that's all. I'm not about to tell him I go to Chippewa High School. Let him figure it out.

"Do you, like, work, then?"

"What else?"

"Well, um, where?"

"For a newspaper. In sales," I add before he can ask anything else more specific. I look down at my feet because now I *am* making a joke, but I don't want him to know it.

"That's cool. I'm thinking about majoring in communications, so that's sort of related."

He babbles on about communications classes as we come up to the house. I decide that despite the fact he's in college, Tony's not intimidating—not at all. He's too eager to be intimidating. In fact, he's a little annoying.

The party must be well attended because people have spilled out of the house and onto the lawn, many of them without coats despite the cold. *These are college kids*, I think with a little thrill. *I'm at a college party.* They're standing in clumps on the dead grass, drinking beer out of plastic cups, leaning on each other for warmth. And, yes, I know high school kids do this, too—hang out, drink beer, stand in the cold—but I've never been invited to those parties. Or any parties.

I follow Tony, which is how I can't help but think of him now, across the lawn and onto the concrete slab of porch. Hadley is up ahead of us with the boys, the silver flask changing from hand to hand. They don't knock on the front door but walk right in, and we follow them into a living room that is nearly bare of furniture and nearly full of bodies. Strange arms, legs, breasts, shoulders, and elbow push against me. There's the damp, bready smell of beer and a richer smell that I can't identify but reminds me of when the neighbors burn their raked-up leaves in the fall. A thumping, electronic music fills up the entire room, so loud that it becomes a crackling white noise blanketing every other sound.

"Cool that you came," Tony leans over and shouts, pressing his arm against mine. I'd move away if I weren't scared of losing him in the crowd.

"Yeah, well, we weren't . . ." I look around to include Hadley in my "we," but she's somehow squeezed through the entire room full of people and is disappearing into the back of the house with the rest of the boys. "Oh!" I say, despite myself. "Your friends!" I gesture after them.

"Looking for the keg," Tony says, then adds, "I'm designated," as if he's very proud of the fact.

"Designated for what?" I ask for no other reason than to be difficult. "Team mascot? Human sacrifice?"

Confusion crosses his face. "Designated *driver*," he says.

"Yeah, I know. I was just—"

"Hey!" He cranes over the crowd. "Spot!"

He pulls us through a mob of partygoers and over to a sagging couch upholstered in a mystifying print of flowers and old stains. He sinks down and seems to expect that I'll do the same. I perch on the arm instead, and he looks up at me, still smiling. He's sort of goofy— too goofy to be in college. But then that's wrong isn't it? Goofiness, awkwardness, loneliness . . . I'd been assuming that these things ended with high school. I guess they don't. I guess they can stretch on for years.

"I should find my friend," I say, edging off of the couch.

Tony grabs the hem of my coat. "She'll be back in a second." I look down at his handful of fabric and am faced with three equally ludicrous decisions: yank harder to pull my coat loose, try to pry open his hand with my own, or sit back down like he wants me to. It's silly, Tony holding on to my coat to keep me from going. I come up with a fourth option: slip out of my coat, leaving him holding an empty garment. But before I have to decide which of my options to take, Tony says, "See?" and points at someone behind me.

It's not Hadley who approaches, though, but one of the other boys in the group. He's holding three plastic cups by the rims in a way that causes his fingers to dip into their contents. He hands one to Tony and one to me before sitting on the coffee table facing us. Tony sets his cup on the table.

"None for me," he says to his friend. "Remember, I'm your ride home tonight." He glances at me as if to make sure that I'm witnessing his sacrifice.

I stare down into the beer in my cup, not wanting to drink something that has had a strange boy's fingers in it. The boys are both watching me, though, so I take a sip. I'm careful not to make a face at the taste of the beer, which I know will be bitter. Turns out that it's not that bitter, or maybe it is and I don't care. I decide to down it all just to see what the boys will do. Tony says, "Whoa!" like *Hold on!* But the boy who brought me a drink makes an impressed noise and hands me his cup. I take a healthy gulp of that, too.

"You okay?" Tony asks, releasing my coat and patting the fabric back into place.

I nod. I don't feel drunk. Am I supposed to? My cheeks feel a little warm is all, and the taste of beer sits in my mouth, dark and woodsy, like plants might start growing up out of my tongue.

"You always drink like that?" one of them asks.

But I don't answer and we sit for a while in silence. I finish Tony's beer and the boy who brought them disappears and reappears with more full cups. Tony tries to talk to me, but I pretend that the music is too loud for me to hear him. He uses this as an excuse to lean closer, but I just pull away and teeter like I might fall off the arm of the couch if he unbalances me anymore. I wonder where Hadley is, how long I'm supposed to wait for her, what I'm meant to be doing here with this boy. Finally, she passes by in the sweep of the crowd between two boys, her arms linked with theirs. They must have been drinking more from the silver flask, all three of them, because they lurch and stumble; one regains his balance only to be tripped up by the other two.

"Hadley!" I shout, but the room is loud with music and chatter and she doesn't hear me. "Hadley!" I lean forward on the edge of my couch perch, stretching to reach her arm. Tony's friend is watching me warily, like if I get any louder or weirder he might have to pretend he doesn't know me. Tony is amused, though, and calls out, "Hey! Hadley!" an echo of my shout. She hears this and makes her way over to us, towing the boys after her.

"Oh. *Hi*," she says, like we've happened to meet by accident. Her eyelids are heavy, but her eyes gazing out from beneath them gleam. She sways slightly and leans back against one of the boys who gazes down at us impassively from under the brim of his baseball cap. His hand is on her waist, and I'm startled to see his thumb rubbing up and down her side. It looks so intimate, so adult. I tell myself that I'm being silly. After all, it's just a thumb.

"What's going on?" Tony asks. And I nod in agreement with his question. *What is going on?* I want to ask Hadley. No, I don't want to ask that. I just want to say, *Stay. Stay here with me, please.*

"We're gonna check out this . . ." The boy Hadley's leaning on stops mid-sentence, takes a look around, and then finishes with "place." His voice is slurred, and he sways under Hadley's weight, as if he's barely able to hold her upright. Is he drunk? Are they both drunk? I've overheard kids at school say to each other, *I was so wasted last night.* Is this what it's like to be wasted? I've had two beers already. Is it only a matter of time before I'm wasted, too?

"Upstairs," the boy says out of nowhere. Tony laughs, and the boy looks bewildered. "What?" he says in an empty voice. "Did I say it already? We're going to go upstairs." The other boy who was with them has sat on the sticky, rickety coffee table and is staring at the palms of his hands, opening and closing one hand, then the other.

I try to catch Hadley's eye to make sure she's okay with this upstairs plan. When she sees me watching her, she pulls a face, stretching her lips in different directions and crossing her eyes. I laugh and she laughs even louder, and the boys look at us slightly startled and maybe even put out, like we're laughing at them.

Hadley tips forward, her arms outstretched as if to give me a hug. I catch her, and she clings to me, reaching up to push my hair away from my ear and whisper, "You could, too. With yours." I wonder if she can smell the beer on my breath. I can smell it on hers. *Yours?* Does she mean Tony?

"Tell him you want to see the rest of the house."

"What?" I say, though I can hear her just fine.

"Or outside. He'll know you mean . . . what you mean."

I look over at the boys. They're having their own whispered conversation. I wonder if they're saying the same thing. *Ask her if she wants to see upstairs. She'll know what you mean.* Could I make out with Tony? I imagine caressing his pink cheeks. I imagine his lips puckering and kissing just as rapidly as they talked about communications. I fight the impulse to giggle.

"Catch you later," the boy in the cap mumbles and clumsily pats at Hadley's shoulder. The boy who was with them makes no move to rise from the coffee table and join them. The other boys answer with a rote, "Catch ya."

Hadley withdraws from me with a sleepy smile. The boy's hand fumbles back down to her waist, but it is she who leads him back into the crowd. Soon there are too many people for me to see them anymore, but I keep looking after them because I'm honestly not so sure they'll be capable of climbing the stairs. Then I hear Tony say something about pills. I whip around and the boys all fall silent.

"Your friend gave Hadley pills?" I look at them sharply one after the next. I know what to do here. We had a school assembly about this. There are phone calls and speeches to be made, peer pressure to be withstood.

The boys look away from me and at each other, not-so-secret glances that translate into *Should we tell her?*

The one sitting on the coffee table finally says, "They were her pills. They were *strong*." He shakes his head, puts it in his hands, and groans.

The other boys laugh at him.

"Strength, son," the boy who brought us the beer says to his drugged friend. "Fortitude! Gumption!"

"What were they?" I ask. The boy doesn't answer, so I reach out and shake his arm, which makes his whole upper body sway.

He groans again and the boys laugh again. I don't understand why they're laughing. "Something in a prescription bottle," he mumbles.

"She wouldn't," I say with conviction, even though inside I'm certain that Hadley *would*.

I look over at the stairs, hoping to see her descending. And wouldn't you know it? Standing by the foot of the stairs is Jonah Luks. I blink but he's still there, leaning against the wall, peering down into his cup of beer. Jonah Luks, actual and verifiable. Jonah Luks, college dropout. Jonah Luks, employee of Jefferson Wildlife Control. I'm so surprised that I nearly fall off the arm of the couch and into Tony's lap, and wouldn't he like that? I keep my balance, though. And I have to admit that it's probably not the best part of me that abandons all concerns about her pill-popping friend, takes another gulp of beer, screws up her courage, and heads for Jonah Luks.

I can hear Tony calling out behind me, but I pretend I can't. I wriggle through the crowd, disrupting conversations and splashing people's beer onto the floor. I don't care, though, because when I arrive in front of Jonah, he looks at me like I'm a wonder.

"What," he says, "are you doing here?"

"Hey, Jonah!" I clink our plastic cups together. "Cheers."

"Yeah, cheers." He eyes my cup. "How much have you had?"

"I'm fine." I scowl and pretend like I'm going to turn away mad, but to my delight, Jonah catches my sleeve to keep me from going.

"Sorry. Just looking out for my Sunday-morning buddy."

Of course his apology is accepted. All is forgiven. We are 100 percent A-okay. And I'm just about to tell Jonah so when Tony appears at my side, stringy and beaming. I take another mouthful of beer and contemplate squirting it at him.

"Hey, Evie," Tony says and puts a hand on my shoulder. I resist shrugging it off. "One second you were there, and the next—"

"I saw a friend." I glance at Jonah, silently pleading that he not think that Tony and I are together. Unless that would make him jealous. I might endure the misunderstanding if I got a bit of Jonah-jealousy in return. I make introductions. "Jonah, Tony. Tony, Jonah."

Tony's smile wilts. "Actually, it's Anthony." He offers his hand. I'd forgotten that I wasn't supposed to call him *Tony*.

"Hey, man," Jonah says, and he's very generous, Jonah is, to refer to Tony as a man.

I wait for Jonah to ask if we're here together so that I can deny it. He doesn't say anything more, though, so I offer, "We're here in a group of people . . . friends . . . acquaintances, actually. Where is everyone, anyway?" I ask Tony, hoping he'll take the hint and go find them.

He doesn't move, though, just swivels his head on his skinny neck, looking around. "Your friend went upstairs with Chad. I don't know where the rest of the guys are."

His hand is still heavy on my shoulder. I can't resist anymore. I shrug my shoulder, and Tony's hand jumps. Jonah stares at it, but Tony keeps it there on my shoulder. I shrug again.

"How do you guys know each other?" Tony asks Jonah.

At this, Jonah smiles, and the fact that a question about me makes him smile stuns me for a second. Or maybe it's just that the beer is finally having its effect on me. Either way, I grin a dopey grin and don't realize that Jonah is about to reveal my age until he's already a few words into his answer.

"Oh, well, Evie and I run into each other every—"

But before Jonah has a chance to expose me, before I have a chance to interrupt and try to save my skin, a voice sails over the music. My name.

Tony turns to me. "Was that your—"

I'm already yanking my way through the crowd to the stairs and up to the second floor of the house. People look up for a second at the sound of the scream, but when there isn't a second one, they return to their flirting and bragging and guzzling. Not me. I make it to the stairs, which are clogged with people. I squeeze under a boy's arm and through a clutch of girls. It feels like I'm moving slow, too slow, and there seems to be an impossibly long stretch of time between the beats of the music. I emerge upstairs in a hallway. I spot a circle of people at its end. I barrel down the hall and break through the people to find Hadley holding on to a doorknob, leaning her full weight backward to keep the door closed.

"Hadley," I say. "Hadley?"

Slowly, as if she's afraid of what she's going to see, she opens her eyes and looks around. When she sees that it's me, she lets go of the door and collapses onto my shoulder, burrowing her face into my neck. I wonder again what she took and how long it'll take to wear off. "You heard me," she says. "You came."

One of the onlookers murmurs, "Maybe we should—"

The door behind Hadley opens and a guy emerges, the one who wanted to show her upstairs. He has a hand pressed to his left cheek and eye. The hallway is dark and his cap still pulled low, so I can't see the expression on his face, but I'm guessing that he might just possibly be angry. I hold Hadley closer and shuffle a step back toward the edge of the circle of onlookers, dragging her with me.

"Hey," The boy tries to stagger forward but thinks better of it and grabs onto the doorjamb to steady himself. "What the hell?"

Hadley's sobs quicken and she leans heavier on my shoulder. I tighten my arms around her in case the boy tries to run forward and tear Hadley from me, throwing her to the ground, kicking her— once, twice—in the stomach. When he's done with that, he might decide to punch me in the face. I've never been punched in the face before. I try to imagine what it would feel like, the dull thump of knuckle against delicate eyes, nose, teeth, cheek. I feel my bones splinter, my teeth uproot from my gums; I can see the blood pool dark in my eyes. I can't breathe, can't think; the music won't stop, either. But then Hadley sobs again, a seal of spit and breath against my neck, and I think of her words: *You heard me. You came.* And I know, suddenly and certainly, that it's my job to protect her. I take back my step backward. Instead I take a step forward, toward the guy.

"Leave her alone," I say, and my voice wobbles in a way I wish it wouldn't. "You just leave," and then I remember his name, "Chad."

"She's . . . she's fucking . . . crazy," Chad splutters and points at Hadley. His arm isn't steady, so his accusing finger swings from Hadley to me.

"Maybe you're the crazy one. You obviously did *something* to her."

"I didn't." He presses his forehead, for a second, against the doorjamb as if to collect his thoughts or temper. "I didn't do anything to—"

"Then why's she crying? And holding the door so you can't get out?" My voice is stronger, and I'm proud of it. In fact, it's nearly a miracle of nature that I can get any sound out at all, because still I can barely breathe. I hold Hadley even tighter to me, and she is like a shield; her sobs, my courage. "So she didn't want to have sex with you? So you wouldn't let her go?"

"Me? You want to see what she—?" He takes a step toward us, and I lose my nerve, gasping and dragging Hadley back until I thump up against someone at the edge of the circle. It's Tony, and he's not smiling at me anymore. In fact, he doesn't even look at me. He sidesteps Hadley and me and goes over to Chad. He speaks in a low tone, but the noise of the party has withered away, and I can hear what he says.

"They're in high school. Some guy downstairs knows her from her—get this—paper route."

"What?" Chad says, shaking his head.

"Seriously. Fifteen or sixteen or some shit."

"Sixteen?" Chad says, and his voice isn't angry but slurrily incredulous. "Shit."

I look from Chad to Tony and see an opening. I may not be able to fight my way out of here, but I can talk my way out. "Yeah. Sixteen," I say. "Which means statutory rape, and probably more. My dad's a lawyer. Don't think he won't come after you. He'll call your school and your parents and . . . the police!" I glance at the crowd around us, everyone staring, all these college kids. "Everyone saw her crying, holding the door to keep you in. You'll get kicked out of school. Jail! You'll go to jail!"

Chad takes a step back as if *I've* punched *him*. And I feel a surge of power. I want to sink more words into him, word after word, until he curls up on the ground and I stand over him, victorious.

But Hadley has finally gained her feet and stopped her crying. She tugs on my sleeve. "Let's go. Let's go," she pleads in a desperate voice. And so we leave Chad in the doorway, hand still pressed to his cheek, and Tony talking to him quietly. He doesn't come after us.

We make our way back through the house and out onto the lawn. I don't see Jonah on our way down. I wish I could've heard the rest of the conversation between him and Tony. Tony probably told him that I'd lied about my age . . . well, not lied, but *misled*. The distinction was probably lost on Tony, though. Did Jonah think I was a liar now? Would he be angry? Amused? Indifferent? Probably indifferent, I decide.

When we get to her car, Hadley scoots into the passenger seat and draws her knees to her chest, hiding her face in the crevasse. "Hadley," I say again and again. Finally I scoop my hands under her chin and pull her face up so that she's forced to look at me. "What did you take? Pills?"

She scowls, which comforts me. If she's able to be sullen, she can't be too bad off. "Fine," she says, which I take to mean both that she's fine and also fine, she admits she took the pills. "I just had a couple."

"A couple of what?" Her scowl deepens, but she doesn't resist as I search her pockets, coming up with an orange prescription bottle made out in Hadley's name. I don't recognize the name of the medication, but the label warns against taking it when drinking, driving a car, or operating heavy machinery. The date, I notice, is three days after Zabet's death. I feel a pang of sympathy. I brush Hadley's hair back from her face.

"You just had two?" I ask softly. I shake the bottle. It's nearly full, which is comforting.

Hadley nods. She seems more awake now, more alert.

"Promise?" I say.

"Promise," she answers. "I'm fine. They're already wearing off."

I drive her home, but when I offer to walk her to the door, she shrugs me off.

"I just want to sleep," she says firmly.

"But your car."

She waves a hand in the air. "Bring it back tomorrow."

"We'll talk tomorrow?"

"Yes, yes." We don't, though—not the next day and not after. When I ask about the party and what had happened in the room with Chad, Hadley gets a somber look on her face and says she doesn't remember. And I think of the date on that prescription bottle and don't press it. She's been through enough. Jonah and I don't talk about it either. The next time I see him, in Hokepe Woods, he asks if I've been to any good parties lately, and I laugh and say, "Every damn night," and we leave it at that.

Chapter TWELVE

THE REPORT COMES with the noon news the week after the party, and so, once again, I see it first, before my mother, Hadley, or Mr. McCabe does. I'm knotted up in my bedsheets, which I'd carried out to the couch that morning, my vision shining with the fever that's got me home sick, the walls of my throat aching like they want to press slick up against each other like two kids at a dance. Mom suspects strep. I have a doctor's appointment tomorrow. I almost wish she'd stayed home with me like she did when I was little.

"There's soup in the pantry," she had said with a little wave as she trotted out the door.

So there I am, possibly streppy, flipping channels between the soap opera dames and the game show dicks when Zabet's face winks out at me. At first, I think it's just something that my imagination has spit up, like her face in my laundry or in the knot of a tree, but this face isn't the bruised and beaten Zabet of Hadley's description. The image from the television is still on the backs of my eyes: Zabet's yearbook photo.

I've seen a lot of this photo lately, and it's awful—not the photo itself, which is a fine one that shows Zabet smiling like she always smiled, her eyes lost in the puff of her cheeks. What's awful is how the TV stations keep showing this picture. Yearbook photos are supposed to catch an instant in your life while you're growing up, but flashing Zabet's photo like they do just reminds everyone that she won't be growing up any more than she was already able to.

I flip back to the channel where I saw Zabet's picture. Actually, I'm not sure it's the right channel, because the picture isn't up there anymore; it's a waitress instead. She's got sharp eyes and a thick, gloss-tinged lower lip that, together, make her look like she's plotting and pouting both at the same time. She's wearing a requisition polo shirt, and her hair is done in two complicated braids that rest like badges on each side of her chest.

". . . didn't think they would find the body so soon," she's saying, nodding with each word. "I wrote it down here." She holds up her order pad. "But I would remember it even if I hadn't."

The scene switches to the news reporter standing at the edge of the parking lot with the diner where the waitress works squatting behind her. The reporter's eye shadow matches her jacket. She says some phrases that sound like they belong in the script of a cop show—"ongoing investigation" and "crucial break." She raises her eyebrows every few seconds to make sure we all understand how important she is. Then it's back to the desk anchors, who put on their concerned faces and announce that they'll report more about all this on the five-o'clock news.

Fever-dazed, I punch through the channels looking for a repeat of Zabet's face; instead I find the same polo, pout, and braids. The waitress is on one of the other news stations. At the bottom of the screen, next to the stamp of the news station are the words *Laura Grossman—Eyewitness?*

"... whispering," Laura Grossman says. "I'm not a suspicious sort of person, but they were down there hunkered over the table going back and forth about something." She inhales noisily, like each sentence takes a full breath to get out. "Then when I went over to refill, I heard one of them say, 'I didn't think they'd find the body so soon.'"

"Are those words exact?" the off-screen reporter asks. I can see only the swing of her bob, the dark bulb of her microphone.

"I wrote it down," Laura Grossman says. She holds up her order pad. "But I would've remembered it anyway."

I squint at the order pad, but the words are blotted out by the light of the camera.

The station switches to a pretty reporter with a scarf knotted neatly under her chin. From the shot of the restaurant behind her, I can tell that she's on the other side of the parking lot from where the first reporter was standing. From this angle, I recognize the diner—it's the twenty-four-hour place where Hadley and I were last weekend, which gives me a little chill. What if the killers were there that night? Two among the guys from the party? What if I'd asked one of them to meet me in the parking lot? To take me upstairs? What if it was Chad, that guy from the party who'd attacked Hadley? What if it was him and Tony? Not that I could imagine Tony killing anyone.

The new reporter explains what the other reporter must have revealed at the beginning of the segment—waitress Laura Grossman believes that she overheard two men discussing the murder of local teenager Elizabeth McCabe. I wait to see if they've caught the men, if they have descriptions or sketches, but the segment ends there, with a promise to report more later.

I click the TV off and wrap my sheets tighter around myself. It feels like there's something I should be doing. Since I saw the body bag in Hokepe Woods, it's always felt like there's something I should be doing. I consider calling Hadley, Mr. McCabe, someone. Jonah? Hadley's in school, though, and Mr. McCabe is at work. And I have neither the phone number nor the nerve to call Jonah. Besides, I figure, if the story's on the news, they'll hear about it eventually. In fact, I tell myself, they might already know now, might be thinking right this minute, *Should I call Evie?*

I consider the waitress, Laura Grossman. I admire the presence of mind it took to write down the men's words on her order pad. I'm certain that I, too, given the opportunity, would have noticed the men's suspicious behavior, would have found a way to draw close to their conversation. I imagine myself pouring them coffee, trying to keep my hand from shaking.

⁓

I fall asleep and wake up with my throat pulsing and my tongue mucus-stuck to the roof of my mouth. The light in the room has changed, and the shadows drip longer over my legs. Instead of feeling like a different hour, it feels like a different season. Beneath all of this is a ticking . . . no, a rapping. Someone is hitting the door with such evenly spaced knocks that they've become background noise—the pendulum of a clock, the drip of a faucet. I gather my bedsheets around me—being sick makes me feel that they should go where I go—and look through the peephole. Hadley stands on the porch, swinging her fist in rhythm. I unlock and open.

"Jesus," she says, taking a look at me; then she marches in. "I was going to ask you to cough on me so I could miss school, but, Jesus. I don't know if I want whatever"—she waves a hand at me—"*that* is."

"I'm sick," I offer.

"You're gross."

"Thanks." I shuffle back to the couch.

She sits carefully on a chair, first pulling a sweater from it with a thumb and forefinger.

"How was school?"

"Ugh," she says.

She sticks out her lower lip and blows upward so that her bangs rise and fall. The light from the window or maybe the muzziness of my fever blurs her hair, making it shine up off of her head like a nimbus. I don't know if she's seen the news report, don't know if I should bring it up.

"Did you—"

"Yes," she says. "About a hundred and seventeen people told me."

"Yeah?"

"They kept saying the exact same thing: They found Zabet's killer. They found Zabet's killer."

"They didn't actually find—"

"I know that."

Hadley is in one of her dangerous moods, her eyes shiny and her fingers working at the zipper of her hooded sweatshirt. I sit a little farther back in my nest, pulling the sheets up near my chin.

"Are you going to get dressed?" she says, like I've agreed to do so hours ago and she's been sitting here this entire time, waiting.

"I'm sick."

Hadley gets up and sits next to me. She lifts a hand, and I flinch, though it's just a reflex; obviously she isn't going to hit me. Hadley presses the back of her hand to my forehead. She considers for a minute and then pulls her hand away, wiping it on her jeans.

"You know what would make you feel great?" she asks. She reaches forward and gathers my hair in her hands, twisting it up off the back of my neck. "I'm going to pour you a glass of orange juice while you get dressed."

"I'm wearing my pajamas. I'm sick."

"You'll feel better when you're dressed." She smiles and nods encouragingly.

I sigh. "Where do you want me to go?"

"Come on. I'll help you get up."

"That diner, right? Where the waitress is?"

"Come on, Evie. Up and at 'em."

She offers me her hands.

The drive out to the diner is an uncomfortable one. Hadley blasts the heater in my face, promising that the air will heal me. Really, it's too warm outside for a heater, and the hot, dry air just makes my throat want to turn inside out. I cough into my hand and lean my head against the window.

"This is silly," I say. "I should be in bed."

"I know," Hadley says, soothing me. "I know."

The fields outside are flat and muddy with shoots of spring grass, the gray-green of the ground a dark band under the gray of the sky.

It's a line, I tell myself of the gray horizon. *It's a path*. Birds rise and fall in the distance like someone is pulling on their strings.

The diner is in the crotch of the highway entrance, the parking lot half full, no news vans, no police cars. Maybe they're there anyway, undercover. The blinds in the diner are pulled down to keep out the afternoon sun. We sit in the car for a while. Hadley smokes a cigarette, and I dial around the radio band until she bats my hand away. She offers me the end of her cigarette, and I take it, pulling the smoke, hot and terrible, into my ruined throat. Though I know it's bad, it feels good, like I'm purging something, some ancient medical remedy—bitter tinctures, leeches, herbs inhaled over a fire.

"Well," Hadley says finally, yanking the keys out and setting off across the parking lot. I hurry after her, the cigarette butt still in my hand. I drop it on the ground and stop, stomping a few times to grind it out. By the time I'm done, Hadley's already in the restaurant, the blinds swaying behind her. I jog to the door, picturing Hadley storming the place, shouting for Laura Grossman, taking a handful of the waitress's polo shirt and shoving her against the wall like in an old cowboy movie. When I get in there, though, Hadley is pressed against the wall herself, near the plastic ferns, looking like she's lost all her nerve.

She yanks me next to her and nods toward the host stand. "You go."

I look at the host, a youngish guy with his polo shirt undone an extra button so that the stone of his Adam's apple can slide up and down his neck with ease. "You'll come with me?" I ask.

All of Hadley's previous purpose has been sloughed off. She looks nervous, shy. And it's strange—surreal even—to see someone as formidable as Hadley look so vulnerable. I feel suddenly protective, that I will do what I can to take care of her, that I can take care of *this* for her. I loop my arm through hers and take a tottering step toward the host stand. My feet are as heavy as my head and hands. I can feel my pulse points throbbing in concert with my throat. The host guy is concerned with something hidden by the lip of the stand. He makes marks on it. After a few more jots of the pen, he looks up at me and suits up his grin.

"Hello there!" he says. "Just one today, then?"

"No, uh, two." I gesture at Hadley, who's edged herself around behind me. When he glances at her, she dips her head behind my shoulder.

"Sorry 'bout that. Two, then! Table for two!" he calls out, to whom, I don't know.

He picks out a couple of menus from the slot at the side of the stand. I look around for the woman with the braids from the news, and Hadley shifts so that she's directly behind me, her chemical breath sweeping along my right cheek.

"But . . . ," I say.

He looks up, and I catch a flash of annoyance before he fits the grin back on.

"Yes, ma'am?"

"Well, we had a really good waitress in here last time. I think her name was Laura?"

I glance at Hadley, like I'm verifying this with her. She doesn't nod like I'm hoping she will but stares back at the ferns by the door, her hair falling in front of her face. I want to pinch her. The air in the diner smells like syrup, and all of a sudden I can feel it, thick and sweet, oozing in the cracks of my itching throat.

"Yeah, Laura," I say with more certainty. "Can we have her again?"

"Aw, I'm sorry." He tilts his head. "Laura's off for the afternoon, but another of our waitresses will be happy to help you."

We follow him to a booth, and we each slide into a side.

"She's not even here," I say. "Maybe we should go."

Hadley picks at the thread that binds her menu and darts a look at the host stand.

"Were you hiding from that guy?"

"Someone else will know something," she says, and then softly adds, "You'll ask them, won't you, Evie?"

"Who would I ask?"

"Our waitress. You could ask her." She slides her hands toward mine. "You will, right?"

I sigh. My head is foggy. I blink, like that will clear the fog in my head; it does nothing, of course. "And then we'll go?"

"I'll drive you home, I'll turn down your covers, I'll make you soup and sing you lullabies. Don't you *love* me, Evie? Aren't I your *best* friend?"

I squeak my hands against the vinyl of the booth and wonder if it's the same booth the murderers sat in this morning, if they've thumbed through these sugar packets, if the French fries dropped on the floor came from one of their plates.

Our waitress is Vanessa. She has rings on all her fingers, some silver, some gold, some with jewels as big as beetles, some plain. She twists on them—from thumb to pinkie on one hand, then pinkie to thumb on the other—and doesn't even write down our order.

When she comes back with the drinks, I say, "So the TV news was here today," which is what Hadley and I have decided I should say.

Vanessa flips a look at me while still pouring my water. "Saw that, did ya?"

"Were you here?"

"Before my shift," she says tidily, pulling up on the pitcher just before the glass overflows. She scoots away.

"Try again when she comes back," Hadley says. "Once more and then we'll go. *Please.*"

When Vanessa brings the food, I waste no time and blurt out, "So do you know the waitress who saw those guys?"

"Guys?" she says, sliding a plate in front of me.

"The ones the news came about."

She leans in to set down Hadley's plate. "Not supposed to talk about it, sweetie. Police orders."

She brushes her glittery hands on her apron and is about to go. Hadley's attempting to kick at me under the table, but only getting the post. And even though her legs are trying to hurt me, her face is giving me the most pathetic look that says *please* all over again—*please, Evie.*

I draw in a breath and let my mouth start going. "It's just that we knew the girl they maybe talked about, Zabet McCabe. She was her best friend." I gesture at Hadley who grants me the nod I want this time. "And I was, well—"

"Sister," Hadley cuts in.

I glare at her, but her eyes are set on Vanessa, who's wiping her hands on her apron more slowly now.

"Sister," Vanessa repeats. "Well, you do," she says to me. "You look just like her." And then she's sliding into the booth next to me, her rings hard through my shirt as she rubs my arms up and down like I need to be warmed up. "I'm so sorry," she says. "It's just the worst thing anyone could imagine."

"Thank you," I say. "I mean, I appreciate that."

"How are your parents?"

"They're okay. Sad, of course."

"Of course." She stops rubbing and scoots back a bit to look at me. She waits until I look up into her crayon-lined eyes. When she's got my gaze, she nods once. "My favorite aunt was shot in a parking garage. Someone wanted her purse. Shot her—I shouldn't tell you girls—right in the face."

"That's terrible," I say.

"No more terrible than what happened to your sister." She starts playing with her rings again. Her eyes follow her fingers, flitting from one shiny band to the next. "I don't know what people in this world . . . I don't know who could . . . why someone would . . ."

Vanessa tells us that she knows Laura Grossman only a little bit, but that she seems like a "good girl." She doesn't know any more about what happened, except that the police were mad the news got here first and so they'd ordered all the diner employees not to say anything. Not that she knows anything, she adds.

"Two young men," she says with a sigh. "To think that there could possibly be more than one of them."

Before she goes, she rests her hand for a minute on the crook of my neck, the place where you support a baby's head so it doesn't loll backward. "Maybe your sister is somewhere with my aunt. I think that sometimes, that maybe they get sorted to a particular heaven depending on the way they went. Then they'd be together. Think about it: Them together, and me, I'm here with you."

She leans forward and kisses me on the cheek. Her hair smells like diner food, but in a good way, like it could nourish you. I make Hadley leave right after that, without us even eating anything. We leave money on the table, as much as we think the bill works out to.

Chapter THIRTEEN

"I NEED TO GET HOME," I say to Hadley. We've been sitting in her car in the parking lot for five minutes now, Hadley with her hands wrapped around the wheel but the engine left dead. She's staring at the diner blinds, and I'm afraid that any second Vanessa is going to wander out with a picture of her dead aunt for us to admire.

"Maybe you can go back and ask where Laura Grossman lives. Maybe we could go to her house or apartment or trailer or . . . whatever."

"She's not going to tell us that," I say. "Come on. Let's go."

"She might tell you. She loved you."

"She didn't love me. She felt sorry for me. Fake sorry."

"Maybe we could find a phone book." Hadley chews on the edge of one of her thumbs. "Maybe she'll come back in for her paycheck or something, if we just wait." She turns in her seat and looks around the parking lot like Laura Grossman might be there already. She stops halfway through her survey and takes her thumb from her teeth, wiping it dry on the edge of the seat. "Look there."

"Let's go."

"Look!" Hadley hisses, and so I do.

Hadley's got her eyes fixed at the opposite edge of the parking lot where a few cars are parked with spaces in between like unevenly set teeth. A man, in silhouette, stands at the foot of one of the cars. Even though his features are doused in shadow, I can tell that he's facing us.

"What? Him?"

"He's looking at us."

"He's probably waiting for somebody," I say.

"He was in the restaurant," Hadley says, and she's cranking the keys. "I saw him in there. They follow you out sometimes."

As if beckoned by her words, the shadow man takes a step toward us as if he might come over here.

Who follows you? I start to say, but I'm thrown forward against my seat belt so hard that it locks up, and my question is severed in half. Then the car's backing up and turning around, fast enough that the tires actually squeal.

Hadley's driving at the man, right at him. I think that I should tell her to stop, and then I try to, but my voice won't work. All that comes out is a huff of breath—*Hhhh*—and not the rest of her name. The scary thing is that Hadley looks just how she does when she drives anywhere, down any normal road, her face blank, the wheel steady in her hands. As we get closer, the man's details get clearer, and I realize that he's not a man at all but younger, a guy about our age.

The guy sees us coming and tries to scramble up on the trunk of his car. He perches on the edge of the trunk, teeters there a second, but then tilts off, falling onto the ground hard on his side. I close my eyes. I think, *It's going to crunch; it's going to thud.* At the moment that it must be too late to stop it from happening, Hadley hits the brake. The rubber screams, and I'm hanging from my seat belt again for the split-second that the car stops but our bodies still speed forward.

Then I'm back in my seat, and everything's still—the car, Hadley in the driver's seat, the ground in front of the car. Hadley unfastens her seat belt and leans her forehead against the wheel. She turns her head sideways, my way. I think maybe she's hurt. I reach over and brush the hair from her face; her hair is soft as nothing, and her face, when I push her hair back, is quiet like she's just been sleeping. She blinks and then looks up at me without moving her head.

"I just wanted to scare him," she says.

"I should . . ." I unfasten my own belt. My chest is sore in a stripe where the seat belt was. I reach for the door and get out. For a second, I feel like my legs are going to buckle, but then my knees catch me and I stand. I glance back at the restaurant. The blinds are still down; no one is looking out at us. I tell myself it all happened in a second, it wasn't that loud. I tell myself that nothing happened at all, not really.

But the guy is there in front of me, evidence, lying on the ground on his back. He coughs and hitches himself up on one elbow, spitting. The glob of spit dangles from his mouth by a filament. He waits for it to drop before looking up at me.

For a second, I think I know him. I think of Jonah Luks, but it's not Jonah. The guy is about Jonah's age, though. Otherwise, he's just a guy, just some guy with startled pale eyes and a hairline receding too early. He looks down at his legs, and I look, too. Hadley's car had stopped less than a foot from him. Both of us stare at the tires so close to his legs, the place they meet the ground in a crevice of rubber and pavement.

The guy looks back up at me, and it takes me a second to see that his face has fear on it. I want to say something, but I don't know what. I don't understand why Hadley had done what she did, so I don't know how to explain it to him. And an apology just doesn't seem like enough. I open my mouth, not knowing what will come out of it. But before I can even think of word one, the guy is on his feet and rushing past me in a series of scrabbling, dizzy steps.

He mumbles, "I'm sorry. I didn't know," as he goes by. And for a second again, I think that maybe I do know him. But then he's across the parking lot, pulling open the door to the restaurant, and disappearing inside.

When I get back into the car, Hadley has her forehead pressed to the steering wheel and her eyes closed.

"Hadley—"

She exhales and then lifts her head from the wheel. "We should go," she says, her voice suddenly flat and businesslike. I watch her adjust the mirrors and her seat methodically, like they make you do at the start of your driving test. I'm scared to speak. Finally, I say, "Do you think that maybe—"

"Put your seat belt on."

And I almost laugh at the absurdity of this request.

"We're going," she repeats. She turns around in her seat, pulling the nose of the car back from where it'd almost hit the guy, circling around the place where his body fell, even though she could have just as easily driven through it. She pulls out onto the road. I keep expecting to hear sirens, and I even glance over my shoulder a few times to look for the lights.

A few minutes later she finally asks, "He okay?" in a tone of voice like she's being forced to ask it.

"You didn't see? He got up okay. He ran."

"I couldn't look." She's silent for a moment, then adds, "He shouldn't have been watching us," Hadley says, turning in her seat and looking right at me. "Strange guy. Two young girls. He shouldn't be following us into the parking lot, staring at us. Someone might think . . ." She trails off, pinching her lower lip so that it folds in half against itself.

The guy's words play through my head: *I'm sorry. I didn't know.* "He was just some random guy. He probably wasn't even trying to follow us."

"I'm not apologizing," Hadley says, and, Christ, it isn't like I ever expected her to.

We're almost all the way back to my house before I relax. I'd forgotten that I was sick, but as we pull into my neighborhood, the itch grabs around my throat again. Hadley pulls to the curb, but when I try to open the door, she clicks the lock shut. I unlock it, only to have her lock it again as soon as I lift my hand.

"Cute," I say, but she's not smiling. "Hey, let me out."

She won't look at me. She's staring straight ahead, her hands tapping a rhythm on the steering wheel, the same rhythm she tapped on my door this afternoon, not whimsical but methodical, a clock ticking down. Then her hands stop.

"We have to find him," she says.

"Who? The guy you just ran over?"

"No," she says. "Him. You know: him."

"Um, the cops are—"

She looks at me with eyes that I can't really describe. Maybe I'd call them sad, or maybe angry. From the right angle, in the right light, I might even call them frightened. "We're Zabet's friends, aren't we?"

I bite down on my lip.

"Aren't we?"

I nod. I have to.

"We can find him, Evie, you and me."

She unlocks the door.

Chapter FOURTEEN

HADLEY DICTATES THE LIST, and I write the list. She can't write, she says, because no one can read it when she does. This isn't true. I've seen her handwriting—clean, thick block letters constructed like houses. I tell her that we should take turns.

"But I can't move when I write," she says. "I need to *move*. That's what's wrong with school, you know. Who can even think when you're sitting still?"

This is my first time inside Hadley's house, though I've set a rolled paper on her porch for years and have coveted it as I covet all of the houses in Hokepe Woods. The Smiths' house is a dark brick box, two stories, its porch held up with wide beams and no welcome mat set in front of the door. Its outside is lush and posh and proud. It has the look of a nurse with dry, capable hands or an old-maid aunt with her hair pulled back tight in a bun, which is why I nearly gasp when Hadley yanks me through the doorway.

A mess. Wrinkled clothes are heaped over the banister and tucked in the crevice of each stair; child-sized, pilled socks dangle from the rail like ivy; I'm not sure if this laundry is unironed or unwashed altogether, though the rank, close smell of the room hints at the latter.

The dining room has no furniture, only a tower of moving boxes in one corner and a torn-up patch of shag carpeting at the other. The kitchen counters are covered with instant-dinner boxes, microwave trays crusted with old food, and glasses striped with sticky rings of soda or juice. In the sink, a stack of dirty dishes teeters within an inch of the faucet's dripping mouth, and a jumbo pack of paper plates has been left in the drying rack, cellophane torn open, ready for use. The room smells of spoiled milk.

Hadley makes no apologies for the state of her house. She doesn't seem embarrassed at all, and I think of how ashamed I'd been to bring anyone home; at least Mom and I keep our house clean. Hadley tromps ahead of me, through the kitchen and into the living room, where three towheaded boys sit on a wraparound couch, hypnotized by a video game that makes the room whistle with laser-gun fire.

"You have brothers," I say.

One of the boys, hearing my voice, whips around, a video-game controller in the shape of gun gripped between his hands. He fixes me in his sights, and then turns back to the TV screen, as if I am only some figure from his game that must be identified, eliminated, and promptly forgotten. Hadley fishes a few pens out from a nest of newspapers and bills on an ottoman.

"Don't you dare bug us," she commands. Though her warning seems unnecessary because none of the boys turn, nor do their guns slow in firing.

Upstairs, Hadley's bedroom is from another age, one of Hadley's own earlier ages. It's startlingly girlish with a pink petal design on the bedspread and a vanity with a mirrored tray like the women in old movies have. "I mean to redecorate," she says when I first step in, waving a hand to include all of it.

Hadley doesn't have any paper handy, so we use the blank pages in the back of my science notebook, past the careful grids of my labs, which makes the list feel empirical—our own controlled experiment. Despite what Hadley said about needing to move in order to think, she doesn't. She lazes on the bed, her feet planted on the wall above the headboard. I sit on the floor against her bed, and her voice floats down to me.

"Justin Paluski," she says.

"Who's he? A senior?"

"Junior. He totally beat up this kid for getting his sleeve wet with an umbrella."

I look back at her. All I can see from where I'm sitting are her sneakers and the chewed bottoms of her jeans. "For getting his sleeve wet?"

"Rule one: People are fucked up, Vie." She steps her feet against the wall in place, like she could walk up it. "Evidently."

"P-A-luski or P-O-luski?"

"A, I think. Whatever. I'll know who it is."

I have the yearbook out next to me. I flip to last year's sophomores, the Ps. Justin Paluski smiles out at me. I recognize him as one of the boys who sits at the lunch table next to the Whisperers' table. Once when I was struggling with the top of my milk carton, he reached over my shoulder, peeled it open, and handed it to me without a word.

"Thanks. I can never do it right," I said to his back.

"No sweat." His head was shaved for swim team, and there was a little spot on the back, about the size of a fingernail, where the hair didn't grow. The skin of his scalp was a soft white-blue, like a tooth or a candle.

I'd thought about the moment for weeks after that, always with a liquid feel in my stomach and the taste of sweet milk on the back of my tongue. I'd wanted him to open my milk carton again, but I was also simultaneously afraid to order milk in case it would seem like I was trying to get him to do it again. So I bought pop after that instead, snapping the can open with a hiss that I was sure sounded over to the next table.

Back in Hadley's bedroom, I count. Justin Paluski's name is the eleventh on our list. The list of suspects was my idea for how to find Zabet's killer. Hadley's idea was for us to hang out alone in Hokepe Woods at night as bait. She even wanted us to dress like Zabet. I suggested the list as a saner alternative. I lied and said that I'd seen them make a list like this on a police show.

Hadley said that the police are no help. She should know. They came over to her house the week after Zabet's death to question her.

"Mostly they talked to my parents," she told me. "Like *they* know anything. Like *they* even exist in the, like, world." Even though she was out of sight on the bed above me, I knew she was rolling her eyes. "They asked me about two questions: Did Zabet have any enemies? Did Zabet have a secret boyfriend? It was some lady officer who asked me, like they thought I'd open up to her guidance counselor bullshit. They kept apologizing for bothering me. They're probably talking to the real killer right now without even knowing it, apologizing for bothering him."

The springs squeal up above me as Hadley lets her feet fall down from the wall.

"Write *Wendy Messinger*," she says. Wendy is one of Hadley's old friends—the tough girls. "She and Zabet didn't get along," Hadley adds. "And, God, you could probably write down the whole entire soccer team. They're always getting into fights and getting high on stuff and following girls around, flipping up the backs of their skirts."

This is news to me, and I feel both relieved and deficient that my skirt has never been flipped up, not that I even wear skirts.

"Should I write down . . . ?" I pause. "I'm not going to write them all down."

"You said anyone, no matter how unlikely."

"Okay." I write down *The Soccer Team*. "Should I specify varsity or JV?"

"Don't be a smart-ass," Hadley says, swinging around so that she is leaning over my shoulder. She reads for a minute, her hair tickling my cheek. She's so close that I can see a crumb of dried milk in the corner of her mouth. I have the strange impulse to lick it away. After a moment of thought, she says, "And this is just the high school. There's still the entire town, the college."

"Yeah, like that creep at the party, that Chad," I say carefully. We haven't talked about the party since it happened a week and a half ago. I don't know what Hadley's reaction might be. Turns out, it's not much of one.

"Who?" she says blankly, and I can't tell if she's just pretending not to know who I mean.

"That guy at the party. The one who, you know, scared you."

Hadley makes a face. "Nobody scares me. I don't even remember that night."

"But he was really—"

"Add him. Definitely," she says in a neutral voice. "And that one who you messed around with."

"Tony? I didn't mess arou—"

"I don't care, Evie. Put him down anyway."

I write down *Tony*, but then ask, "Do you think Zabet would've met them, though? I mean, we just met them that night."

Hadley sighs exasperatedly right in my ear and swings back to her original position on the bed. "Why not? Zabet and I went to parties like that all the time. What? You think those guys only invited us because you were there? You think you're so damn alluring?"

"*No*," I say, stung.

We sit in a tense silence. I press my pen into the paper; I want it to leave a dark blot of ink, but it only leaves a tiny dot.

"When you think about it, we could put down almost anyone," Hadley finally says.

"No. Not anyone," I say. "That's why we're making a list."

"But when you think of who maybe could have done it, it's anyone."

"It's not anyone," I say again.

"Who *isn't* it then?"

"There are some people who we can reasonably assume aren't capable of murder." I'm pleased with the big words marching out of my mouth.

Hadley rises up on her knees, her hands on her hips. "Like who? Who's not capable?"

"Kier Dylan." I name one of the meekest Whisperers.

To my surprise, Hadley knows who she is. "Maybe she could. Maybe we just don't know the real her."

"Right. She has wheat allergies and sociopathic tendencies."

Hadley snorts. "Who the hell is allergic to *wheat?*"

"I don't know. People."

"People." Hadley snorts. "It could be anyone."

"Even me?" I ask.

"Even me," Hadley says, grabbing the list from my hand, her eyes running down it once more.

That week that we make the list, Hadley's angry. No, it's more like she was always angry, but the incident in the diner parking lot gave her permission to stop hiding it. She's in detention nearly every day after school for mouthing off to her teachers, and her little brothers hunker down into tiny blond rocks when she storms the living room. She's starting to get paranoid, too. She's convinced that cars are following her.

"Look now!" she'll shout while we're driving, turning both her head and the steering wheel so that we nearly veer off the road. I grab the wheel and steer us back center, but by the time I've done that, she claims the mysterious car is gone.

Things get even worse when the waitress-witness, Laura Grossman, turns out to be a bust. The two guys she overheard in the restaurant turn themselves in. They're bag boys on break from the supermarket down the street, and the dead body they'd been discussing was from a movie they'd watched the night before. On the evening news, they shake their heads and open their eyes wide.

"We were just talking about movies," one of them says.

"We didn't mean to sound like we'd hurt anybody," the other adds.

"We like scary movies."

"Like anybody, right?"

"We like to be scared."

"But just pretend. We're not scary."

"No, we're not scary."

The newscasters take a moment to chuckle after the clip before dialing their facial expressions back over to serious in order to announce that the hunt still continues for the murderer of local teen Elizabeth McCabe.

"Liar," Hadley hisses over the phone. "That waitress wanted attention, that's all. Sad little waitress life. Wonder how she'd like the attention I could give her. Liar."

The next part of our plan is to look for suspicious behavior and add any instances of it to our list. We try and fail to sneak into the principal's office to see if there's any information about the students the police questioned just after Zabet's murder. The police haven't come to the school in a couple weeks, or at least the rumors about police interrogations have stopped. Hadley says this proves her point even more; we can't count on the police for anything. We have to rely on ourselves, our list.

After our first brainstorming session, our list had twenty-eight people on it, and each day, during passing or lunch, Hadley asks me to add more. You wouldn't think that people would do much that's suspicious, but you'd be wrong. When you start looking for it, everyone is suspicious almost all the time.

For example, it starts to seem creepy the way Mr. Denby is so obsessed with his plants, especially after some research into Hadley's mother's detective novels, which teach us that sociopaths often express an interest in owning flower shops. Or the way that Greg Lutz doesn't use a fork to eat his Salisbury steak, just his sloppy, gravy-covered fingers. Or how whenever anyone mentions Zabet, Wendy Messinger rolls her eyes and says, "Let the girl rest in peace."

But Hadley and I won't. In addition to the list, we launch a whisper campaign. The plan is to mention Zabet as much as possible in order to shake up the killer, whoever he or she is. We start rumors about why Zabet was in the woods that night—that she was pregnant and waiting to tell her lover, that she had a drug habit and was meeting her dealer, that she knew a secret about a teacher and was there to blackmail him. The rumors hiss through the school like wind through those old Chippewa cornfields, coming back to us during the next passing break on different lips, with different details.

After we spread a rumor, my job is twofold. I write any new details or changes from the story of our initial rumor. There might, I tell Hadley, be something true there, a clue that has worked its way into our rumor like a stray hair in your homemade pie. I use the sign-out log in the office to record anyone who goes home sick after the rumor has been spread. Just in case guilt or fear might drive the killer underground. The data is never quite right, though. For example, we spread the drug rumor just before a stomach flu outbreak, and a dozen people leave by lunch. On top of that, I worry that we're ruining Zabet's reputation with rumors about pregnancy and drugs.

"She's dead," Hadley says. "She doesn't have a reputation anymore."

Our number one suspect, however, is easy to find. He can be located in one of three places: slumped in a chair in the main office, slouched against a locker bank after being ousted from class, or hunched across the street in the smokers' field with the bright bloom of a cigarette between his hands. Suspect One resists our methods of detection and defies our data. Garrett Murray skips at least one class every single day. He doesn't, as far as we can tell, bother with gossip. Even so, gossip bothers with him. Hadley knows all the rumors.

"In seventh grade he punched a teacher."

"He started a fire in the chem lab."

"He got kicked out of his last school and the one before that, too."

"The police called him in for questioning twice."

"He's supposed to be on about five different types of medication for"—she circles her finger around her ear—"but he never takes them."

"Once, he totally beat up this kid for getting his sleeve wet with water from his umbrella."

I don't remind Hadley that this last incident was the exact same one that she'd told me about Justin Paluski.

We try to scrutinize Garrett Murray. We move in close to gather more data. Hadley posts herself in the smokers' field with full packs of cigarettes, knowing that Garrett'll almost always ask to bum one. She trades the clean, white cylinders for dirty tidbits.

"He said he wanted to kill Ms. Hauser."

"He got kicked out of gym class for swinging a softball bat into the wall."

"I memorized his shoe print. We could match it to the scene of the crime."

"I asked him if he knew who Zabet was, and he said, 'Yeah, the girl who got squelched.'" She ducks her head. "I hate him a lot."

Still, she trudges back to the field during the next passing break, and I can see her through the stalks of winter wheat, letting him light his cigarette off hers, the ember glowing between them bright enough that I can see it through the stalks, past the cars, all the way to where I'm hidden behind the school doors.

Chapter FIFTEEN

"You could get him to take you there," Hadley says.

We're in the stomping area between the two sets of doors into the school. It's been over two months since Zabet's body was pulled out of Hokepe Woods. It's a Friday morning before first period, and kids come from the bus circle in waves, chattering as they pull open the heavy doors, their zipper-pulls brushing against my back, snagging my hair for a second before pulling free.

"Who?" I say. She's prefaced this sentence with nothing, just marched up to me and spat it out.

"Jonah Luks. Sunday. Get him to take you."

She pulls her ponytail around and tugs her fingers through it. She's just come back from her morning cigarette with Garrett and the smokers. The skin around her mouth is blushed pink and her eyes cut all over the stomping area.

"Where?" I say, but there's only one *there* we ever talk about—the spot in the woods where Zabet died—so Hadley doesn't even bother to answer me. Her hand is still jerking fast through her hair. I reach out and touch the knuckles; it stops. Hadley's knuckles are hard little bumps under her skin, like pellets from a pellet gun.

"How?" I ask next. "He won't want to."

"Vie." She rotates her hand under mine so that instead of her knuckles, I'm touching her palm. She wraps her hand around two of my fingers, firm and triumphant, the way a baby grabs fingers. "He will if you ask him right."

Next Sunday, early, I wait on the porch of 2010 Buckskin Blvd. It's a big house with crumbly white bricks that are rough and sparkling and threaten to rub off on the back of my coat, like I'm leaning against a giant salt lick. I don't worry much about being found. 2010's paper service has been stopped for two weeks, probably for a vacation, probably somewhere better than here. The porch is enclosed on three sides, so I can sit in the corner of it without any of the neighbors seeing me. One of those fake brooms, the kind made from twigs and twine that isn't really meant to sweep up anything, sits in one corner. I hunker down next to it and pull my knees up to my chin. I rest my head against them and practice what I mean to say to Jonah. Finally, I hear his old engine, and the sound vibrates for a moment in my chest so that I feel rewound, spooled back to the Evie I was before all this, before I saw that body bag. I get up and scoot down the front walk like I've just delivered a paper.

Jonah's leaning over the back of his truck, pulling out his stuff and setting it on the road next to him in a line—sled, tarp, twine. I think about the trap I stole. It's in my room right now, still stowed among the shoe boxes beneath my bed like it's trying to disguise itself as benign cardboard. Sometimes when I can't sleep, I think of it down below me; I pretend that I can feel it down there, coiled and sharp.

I stop at the other side of the truck, just across the truck bed, and wait for Jonah to see me. Maybe if I sneak up on him, then he'll be startled, and if he's startled, then I can apologize for startling him and, on the heels of my apology, deliver my first line. When Jonah looks up, though, it's like he's known all along that I've been standing there.

"Running late today, kiddo." He pulls his sled up on the lawn.

"You were out late last night?" I ask—not one of my lines, but I can't help asking it. I think of him at another house party, a sleek, clever college girl wound around his body, asking if he wants to check out the rooms upstairs.

He frowns. "*Up* late at least."

"Like watching TV?" I fidget with the hem of my coat. "Or reading?" I try to picture Jonah in an armchair, a pair of reading glasses on his nose, a book in his lap, a lamp casting light across his shoulder, but I can only picture the glow of the lamp illuminating the careful rows of words.

With a wave, Jonah's off, and I have to hurry to catch up.

"I've finished delivering all my papers," I tell him. I'm back on script. This is one of the lines that Hadley and I had practiced: *I've finished delivering all my papers.* Hadley says that talking to guys is easy, that it just takes a word or a look to make them follow you around. I must have done it wrong, though, because here I am tripping after Jonah. He doesn't act like he even heard my line, so I repeat it: "I've finished delivering all my papers."

"Cool. You can knock off early," he says.

This is a much nicer response than the ones Hadley would give in our practice sessions. *Why should I care about your papers?* she'd say in her gruff voice, or, *Get out of here, little girl.*

"I thought, actually, that maybe I could walk with you," I say, my next line.

He stops, and the sled skates a few feet before stopping, too.

"For just a little while," I add.

He glances, not at me but over his shoulder like he's measuring the distance from here back to the road.

"Nah," he says. "You don't want to do that."

"Sure I do. It'll be something different, and . . . don't you want company? I've got good eyes. I can help you spot animals." I spill all the rest of my lines at once, leaving me with nothing else prepared to say.

"It's all mud out there."

"I don't mind mud."

He stares at me for a second, and I try to make myself look hardy and capable. I pull my shoulders back and widen my stance.

"I like mud," I say stupidly. "It's dirt. It's earth. It's . . . muddy."

Jonah shakes his head. "Go on home."

He starts walking again. I trip after him, bumping along next to the sled because he won't let me catch up.

"Please," I say.

"Go home, kiddo," he says, tough as Hadley.

"You know my name," I tell him, and I'm pleased to hear that my voice is tough, too.

Jonah turns around at that, the pull of the sled winding around his ankles.

"You do." I take a step back. "You said it. I heard you say it when—"

But his expression isn't angry. It's amused. He huffs out a breath and tips his head up to look at the sky like maybe he can wait me out, maybe when he looks down, I'll be gone. But I'm not.

"I know why you want to go out there."

I don't say anything.

"It's no . . . joke or something, some gossip," he says to the sky.

"She went to my school," I tell him. "I knew her, and she was . . ."

"Your friend," he finishes for me.

"No," I say. "She wasn't my friend. I just knew her, that's all."

He tips his head back down, and this is when I can tell that he's going to say yes. He surveys the backyards laid out on either side of us. They're empty, pools, swing sets, sun decks empty of pets and people. "This isn't a good time to be taking girls into the woods."

"I'm not going to get you in trouble or anything like that."

He shrugs and steps out of the tangled sled rope. "Come on, then, Evie."

$\sim$

I haven't been in these woods since I was a kid with Zabet; even then, they never seemed wild. I wanted them to be wild the way woods were in books. I used to tell Zabet stories of kids getting lost in woods and how, if their parents couldn't find them quick enough, they'd turn into whatever creature of the woods laid claim to them first—rabbit, rock, or tree. After that, Zabet would pick up stones and look for petrified faces in them or knock on tree trunks as if someone might answer.

Jonah's sled makes the same noise it does when I follow it out among the houses; of course, it's louder when I'm next to it. It makes me feel like the volume has been turned up on everything. Not just the volume, but all my senses. I can see every prick of stubble on Jonah's cheek, and when the sleeve of his shirt touches the back of my hand, I feel it like a chill all the way up my arm.

"We'll walk my route," Jonah says.

It's not nearly as muddy as Jonah made it sound. Last month's rains have mostly stopped, and the only mud that's left is in patches here and there. In fact, the woods are pretty, greening up from the May sunshine, and here I am walking through them with Jonah on a bright spring morning. It's so perfect that I can almost forget what we're walking toward.

Jonah has a piece of paper in his jacket pocket. Every once in a while, we pass a tree with a ribbon tied to its trunk and he unfolds the paper and ticks something off. Otherwise, all he does is scan the ground, kicking up a patch of leaves here and there to make sure nothing's buried underneath. Before when I pictured Jonah in the woods, I thought that maybe he'd whistle or break off a stick and hit it against the tree trunks he passes. He just walks, though, yanking on his sled if it gets caught on an old branch or rock.

I follow after him, thinking, *This is where Zabet walked. This is where the killer walked. My footsteps in theirs.* I think of Zabet as a tree, a stone, a rabbit. Jonah looks over at me a few times like he needs to verify something about me. I straighten my back and try to smile. It comes out wrong (I can feel that it does), so I try talking instead. I can always talk.

"Do you find something every time?" I ask.

"Usually," he says. "At least something small."

"How often a deer?"

He pauses, calculates. "Maybe every third time. Used to be less."

"That's so many."

"Yeah." He brushes the back of his neck with his palm, like something is tickling him. We walk on.

After a minute, he says, "I think someone's poisoning them."

"Like *poison* poison? For-real poison?"

"They've got this foam coming out of their mouths, and they didn't used to. I looked it up in one of Mr. Jefferson's books, and, well, it said maybe it could be from poison."

"Who would do that?"

He shrugs. "Someone. Anyone. People don't like them in their gardens."

"You mean, like, one of the people here? In the houses?" My voice is too loud.

He looks at me sidelong. "Don't tell anyone I said that."

"I won't," I say, trying to hide my delight over the fact that Jonah's told me a secret. I've heard people describe secrets as dropping into them like stones in a pond, but this one rises in me like bread. A secret from Jonah. I immediately promise myself that I won't tell even Hadley.

"Can you try to catch them? The poisoners?"

Jonah stops. He doesn't scan the ground this time, just fixes his eyes on a spot in front of him—a muddy space between two trees. "There," he says.

I stop, too, next to him. "There is . . . there?"

He nods and sighs and puts his weight back on his heels.

I expected it to look remarkable, the spot where Zabet died. I expected branches torn down, scratches in the dirt, and tatters of police tape, but it looks like the rest of the woods. No clues, no signs. Someone could walk right past this spot, right over it, without ever knowing what they were walking on. I take another couple of steps forward, right up to the place where Jonah is staring.

"Here?" I say. He nods.

The dirt is poked through with new shoots of green. It seems wrong that anything could grow there. But I don't know what I expected—the ground to be barren, withered? I crouch and press the palm of my hand on the spot. The earth is soft and muddy, and my hand settles into it, the dirt pressing up between my fingers.

I look around me. We're in deep enough that I can't see any houses or the road.

"How do you know where we are?" I ask Jonah.

He shrugs, taps the pocket that the paper is in. "I've walked around here a lot."

I tip my face up, like he did earlier, to the trees rising up around me. Their branches tent and intersect like fingers. *This is the last thing she saw*, I think, and then I lose my balance and find myself sitting hard right in the mud.

"Fuck," I say.

Jonah looks like he's about to laugh; then suddenly, staring down at me, his eyes change and he doesn't look like he's going to laugh at all. I wonder if it's me that's making him look this way and think frantically about what it could be about me that makes him so serious. I look down at my faded jeans, my legs splayed flat in the mud, and my knees, bony, but not disgusting—at least I don't think you'd call them disgusting. I push myself up to my feet and look down to see that now the ground is marked with me now—my hand-, foot-, and ass-prints. The seat of my jeans is damp and muddy. I try to brush it off, but my hands are muddy, too.

Jonah pulls a handkerchief out of his back pocket and offers it to me. I stare at it instead of taking it.

"You carry that?"

It's light blue shot through with white thread.

"Yeah."

"My grandpa carries those."

"Take it," he says.

I do and just hold it.

"Don't worry, it's clean," he tells me.

"I know. I don't want to get it dirty."

He laughs. "It's for getting dirty."

I'm embarrassed but pleased. I've made him laugh. I give him a shrug that says, *Okay, if you say so,* and wipe my hands carefully, one and then the other, leaving streaks of dirt on the cloth. "I . . ." I hold it out to him and then snatch it back. "I'll wash it."

His eyes have crept back to the place in the mud. I watch him watch it.

"Was it awful? Finding her?"

"Sure." He nods, scuffs a foot in the leaves.

"I mean, *duh*. Of course," I say.

Jonah sweeps his foot in an arc, back and forth on the same path, and the leaves catch and fold on his heel. Like I'm watching myself do it, I walk over to him. I stand right next to him, just at the end of the arc his foot makes, stopping it with my toes. And when he doesn't move or look up or say anything, I take his wrist—I don't dare to touch his hand, his bare skin—and lean against his upper arm. I can feel the cloth of his shirt on my cheek. I tell myself to inhale, so I do. There's no smell to him—not cigarettes like Hadley or garlic like Mr. McCabe or lotions like my mother—just the damp of the mud and the trees, which is maybe the forest and maybe him and maybe both of them together. We sway a little with the movement of his foot. I sway with him, smell his nothing smell and sway.

"Were her eyes open?" I say against his sleeve.

His foot travels half of the arc, then stops.

"Did you see her eyes?" I ask.

He steps to the side, and his wrist slips out of my hand. I close my hands like maybe I'll catch it there, but my fingertips only press against each other.

"I've got the whole rest of the woods to do," he says.

"You do?" I press my fingers into my fingers. I can still feel the cotton of his sleeve against my skin, can still feel it along all the little hairs there, a presence, an absence. "I mean, okay."

He points. "You walk that way, you'll hit houses."

"Sure. I can practically see them now." I take a couple of steps. "Thanks for—"

"Not a problem," he says. He flashes a brief, unhappy smile and looks away.

I want to apologize, but I'm sure that it'll only make things worse. I've been stupid and spoken when I should have been silent. Still, I can't completely regret the question. Even if it cost me Jonah's arm, his sway, Jonah himself, I'm not entirely sure I'd take it back. I take a few more steps before I turn back. Jonah's cut to the right of the trees and the mud where I fell—the spot, the there, the there where he came upon her, her face bashed into rocks and soil and tree roots. He steps around it now, careful not to tread on the spot. His sled drags out behind him in an arc, its runners cutting through the mud and tracing a circle around the place where she once lay.

Chapter SIXTEEN

I FIND MY WAY OUT, walking the direction Jonah had said I should. Soon the trees break off into a neat line of backyards, and I'm behind the modern house where I saw Jonah go in to call 911. I imagine the puff of his breath on the phone. How did he explain it? What words did he use? *I found a dead girl.* Or did he work up to it like I did with my lines this morning? *I was walking through the woods. . . .* I walk out of the woods between the modern house and the one next to it, passing the garden where I had hidden that morning. I glance down, into the bushes, almost expecting to see myself staring back up at me, or maybe it's Zabet who I think I'll see, but, of course, no one's there but the same string of ants, like a sentence inked on the ground.

I play over the question I had asked Jonah and cringe. *Were her eyes open?* I'd upset him. He probably doesn't like to remember it. Though I still think that he has the better half of the deal. It's better to have seen her than to have to imagine her, to have one fixed, for-sure Zabet instead of dozens of possible dead Zabets lying akimbo in your head—some with their eyes open, some with their eyes closed.

I don't go over to Hadley's like I'd promised her I would. She's probably still asleep, and besides, I just don't feel like talking to her.

This is new. Usually I make up reasons to talk to Hadley like she's some boy I have a crush on. I pass by her locker when it's not on my route or call her with homework questions I know she can't answer. I can't explain why I don't want to talk to her now, now especially, when I have a something worth telling her. She'll make me take her back there, I'm sure. But what's the matter with that? It's just a little patch of mud. What harm can Hadley cause to a little patch of mud? *She's asleep anyway*, I tell myself again. When I get home, though, Mom says that Hadley's already called twice.

"Woke me up," she says, shaking her pretty head like it's beyond belief. "Tell her not before nine." She spins a chair out from the kitchen table with a flourish. And what can you do when someone spins a chair out with a flourish but go ahead and sit in it?

"Juice?" she asks, and before I can answer, she's pouring me a glass. "I thought teenagers hated getting up early. When I was your age, you couldn't have gotten me up before noon, not with an alarm clock, not with a rooster, not with a marching band."

"Sorry," I mutter. "She usually sleeps in."

Mom's behind me; she places her hands on my shoulders and presses down a little bit, like she's pressing me into my seat.

"Do you know what she said? She said, 'Make sure she calls me.' She said it twice. 'Make sure she calls me.' And when I said of course I would, she repeated it again."

"So?"

"Does she think I wouldn't give you a phone message?"

"I don't know." I shrug my shoulders, hoping to shake off her hands, but she just squeezes harder like it's some game we're playing. "She's sort of like that."

"Like what?"

"She's been through a lot," I say, this last sentence an exact repeat of what I've heard teachers, guidance counselors, and various other adults say about Hadley in the past month.

"Oh, well!" Mom says, dismissing it with a wave of her hand. "Forgiven and forgotten. Girls your age—"

The phone rings, and she stops midsentence with a disgruntled little *huh*, like the phone has purposely interrupted her. It rings again. She doesn't move to answer it, so I duck out from under her hands to pick it up.

"Did you talk to him?" Hadley asks without even returning my hello.

"Yeah. Hold on."

"What did he—?"

I hold the phone away from my ear and glance at Mom. She picks up my glass of juice and walks into the living room, sipping it, without even asking if she can. I walk in the opposite direction, down the hall into my bedroom, and close the door.

"Where'd you go?"

"I said to hold on." I hear the annoyance in my voice along with a little thrill that I would speak to Hadley in a rude tone. How do I even dare? I wait for a reaction, but she doesn't seem to notice, or maybe she notices but doesn't care.

"You were supposed to come over."

"I had to go home."

"So, he took you there?" She barely waits for the ends of my sentences. I feel like she's dancing around me in a circle and I'm spinning to keep her in my sights.

"No." It was a while ago that I decided not to tell Hadley the truth, but I realize this only as I speak. I decided back in Hokepe, back at the bushes when I watched the line of ants. There's relief in this lie that I can't explain. The anger in Hadley's voice, the questions and accusations that are sure to come, seem tinny and small in the face of my decision to keep this knowledge from her. I picture the mud between the trees, the mud Zabet lay upon. God made people out of mud, didn't he? I feel wise.

"What? *No?* Why not?"

"He wouldn't take me."

Hadley's silent. I sit down on my bed and pinch the bedspread fabric, rubbing it between my fingers until it feels rough instead of soft.

"Sorry," I add, though I hardly feel sorry at all. It's a relief not to feel sorry. Usually I feel sorry all the time—sorry for myself, for others, for Zabet.

"Did you say it how we practiced it?" Hadley asks.

"Yeah."

"You did?" she presses.

"Word for word."

"I don't understand, then. Doesn't he care?"

"Care?"

"About us."

"I don't—"

"He's a jerk."

"I don't—"

"He's obviously a jerk—a cold-hearted, asshole jerk."

"He said that it would look bad. He said, 'It's a bad time to take girls into the woods.'"

"That's creepy."

"It's practical."

"It's creepy. I'm putting him on the list."

"He's already on it."

Hadley's silent again. I say her name. For a second, I think that she's hung up and that any second the dial tone will buzz through.

Then she says, "You'll try again next Sunday. We'll practice some more, and you'll try again." Her voice wobbles at the end of this, and I'm shaken by the idea that she's crying, so much so that I almost fess up and tell her the truth—that Jonah did show me the place, that I could take her there right now, if she wanted, which she certainly would. I keep quiet, though. I think of the muddy spot on the ground between the two trees and I feel scared, not of the spot itself but of the idea of Hadley being there. Not that she could *do* anything, I repeat in my head. It's just dirt, just mud.

"Next week," I say, "I'll try again."

"You will?"

"If you want me to."

She sighs, and this time she does hang up.

Chapter SEVENTEEN

THE NEXT DAY, before first period, Hadley doesn't meet me in the stomping area like she normally does. I wait there until past the tardy bell, thinking that maybe her morning smoke break has run long and she'll show up any second. No Hadley, though. During the next passing break, I wait at her locker, but she doesn't show up there, either. I'm thinking that maybe she's at home, sick, but on a whim, during third, I ask for the bathroom pass and walk over to the math hall and past her calculus class. I can see Hadley in there, her head bent over her math book, her hair spilling all over the place. I stand in the doorway, willing her to lift her head and look over, until Mrs. Marshall catches sight of me and makes a shooing motion. Most of the rest of the class turn in their seats to see who Marshall's waving at, but Hadley doesn't even look up.

I've got a feeling in my gut that's both giddy and terrible. Is Hadley mad at me? At lunchtime, when I can't find her in the cafeteria, the feeling grows. I save a spot for her, but when lunch is half over and she still hasn't come in, I move over to the Whisperers' table, ready to be snubbed some more. But when I stand at the head of the table for a second, the Whisperers shift to make room for me, just like

I've been eating there every lunch for the past two months. None of them ask me about Hadley; in fact, they don't ask me anything at all, not that I expect them to after I've ignored them for weeks.

But then Kier says shyly, "I like your shirt," and I realize that, instead of being mad at me, they're all assuming I've been mad at them, when the truth is I haven't thought about them at all.

"Thanks," I say, and it dawns on me—terribly, horribly—that maybe Hadley hasn't given a thought to me either.

Out past the bus circle, on the other side of the street, is one of Chippewa's only remaining crop fields. If you can make it by the jaded hall monitors and across the wide arms of the bus circle, across the pressed blacktop of the teachers' parking lot and then across the road, you've traversed an invisible border. You've stepped from one country to the next. You're off school grounds—the field grants you asylum, international waters, an embassy. And you're free—free, chiefly, to smoke. Every once in a while, the vice principal will walk out to the field and herd kids back to class, but technically he can't write them up for smoking if they're not doing it on school grounds.

Everyone knows which kids smoke. "Next?" they say to each other during class, which is short for *Next break, wanna go smoke?* They keep packs of cigarettes in their front pockets, perfect rectangles, or line up loose cigarettes in the slots of their bags that are meant for pencils. They groan during the last half of class and shift in their seats in a way that's more feisty than it is bored. They come back from break in a tribe, smelling of cold air and filthy habit, ducking into their desks just before last bell sounds. It's not the smoking so much as what the smoking implies: carelessness, hedonism, willingness to say *fuck my silky lungs*, and the promise of worse behaviors to come.

I've never been to the field to smoke. Before that party I'd never drunk alcohol; I've never kissed a boy. Sometimes I feel like I shouldn't count as a teenager at all, that I'm much younger or maybe much older than I should be.

So when I stand at the school door, peering through its scored glass window and pressing on its bar, the bus circle seems like a long distance to run without getting caught. I can see them out there, slouching figures in the winter wheat. They stand a few feet away from the stalks, bold but not too bold. I can't tell for sure if Hadley is with them. From where I am, the smokers are just muddy shadows that every few seconds shift, rustling the spears of wheat.

The bus circle is vacant, bare except for a puddle of shiny oil where one of the buses has dripped. I suck in a breath and press the bar to open the door. The bar makes a clicking sound like something being fastened into place. I push the door open and step out of the building, and then I'm walking across the bus circle.

The smell of the school is gone, its damp, rubbery carpets and pencil shavings mixed with whatever's moldering in the bottoms of our lockers. The wind hits my face, and I can feel the tiny hairs along my cheek stand up and wave. I think of days when I've left school early with a note for a doctor's appointment. Walking across the parking lot to Mom's car, with that buoyant feeling of stolen time, is like being awake in the middle of the night while everyone else is asleep. It's like everyone else has been frozen into slowness and stupidity and inattention, except for you; you are still quick, alive. You can watch them breathe. You can touch their eyelids, the fringe of their eyelashes, without waking them.

I try to walk at a brisk pace, like I have a purpose, some business to attend to in the wheat. I wait to hear a shout from one of the hall monitors or the vice principal. I don't dare look over my shoulder because I'm sure that I'll see one of them running after me, write-up slips in hand. I can glimpse pieces of the smokers now dissected by the stalks, the sleeve of a shirt, a section of a jaw, shoulders hunched over to light a cigarette in the wind. Then I'm stepping across the road and into the wheat.

The thing about standing in a wheat field is that there are rows, so you can't really gather in a group. It's like trying to hold a party in the library stacks; all your guests are forced to arrange themselves in lines. So the first person I meet up with is at the end of one of these lines, a senior boy with thick slabs of both jaw and hair. He's using the end of his cigarette to light the cigarette of a sharp-faced girl with shadowy arrows of eye makeup. I know this girl, though not her name; she's the girl who got last year's photography teacher fired after he asked her to sit on his lap. I stare at them, their faces inches apart, bridged by the slender white cigarettes. I wonder if this act means something more, like a kiss, or if it's just no big deal, the kind of thing you'd do anywhere with anyone.

Cigarette lit, the two of them turn and see me.

"Hey," the boy grunts. He flicks his cigarette to the ground, barely smoked, and snuffs it with his shoe.

"Derek," the girl complains, "that's still good."

"*That's still good,*" the boy mimics her, taking hold of a stalk of wheat and bending it to shake near her face.

"Or at least it was," she says, pushing the stalk back at him.

The ground near the base of the wheat is scattered with cigarette butts, swollen and curled like pupae that have come up from the ground with the rain.

"Is, um . . . ," I mutter. They both look at me. Derek stops shaking the wheat. "Do you know Hadley? Smith? Is she here? Like, around here?"

"Who?" The boy hunches his shoulder and cups a hand to his ear, drawing the word out.

"She said *Hadley*," the girl tells him.

"Who?" he asks again in the same clownish voice.

The girl rolls her eyes. "You know. Hadley." She flicks her eyes to the left, deeper into the wheat. "Hadley," she repeats.

"Oh, *her*." He straightens up and smiles a smile like he could chomp up half the wheat field with those teeth. "She went down on me last week."

"She did not," the girl says.

"Naw. But she could have."

I look down at my feet, but then I make myself look up again because I don't want them to know that I'm embarrassed, uncool.

"Stop," the girl orders, giving him a look that indicates me. "You're going to scare her away."

And I surprise myself by feeling angry that she would think I was so easily scared, which, I realize, is a Hadley sort of reaction to things. In fact, I hear Hadley's voice in my head: *No one can scare me.*

"Is Hadley here?"

The girl shrugs a saucy little shrug, one shoulder rising up before the other. She jerks a thumb over her shoulder. "That way, maybe."

Because of the narrow rows of wheat, I have to squeeze past them to walk the way that she's pointed. I press my back into the wheat so that I won't brush up against them. As I pass the boy, he giggles, a strangely girly sound tinkling its way out of his ten-pound mouth.

"He's an idiot," the girl says. Up close I can see how elaborate her eye makeup is, dovetailing lines of black and gray.

He plucks the cigarette from her mouth and hands it to me. "Here. A gift of apology," he says.

I take it, mostly so that I don't offend him, and walk past them farther out into the wheat.

"Light me another," I hear the girl say behind me.

The wheat grows high and thick on either side of me, and I don't know how to look for anyone out here. Sometimes I can hear conversations in the rows, but I don't hear Hadley. Finally I turn around with the idea that I'll go back to the school, that I'd tried and failed, when the wall of wheat next to me rustles. I gasp and draw my hands up to my mouth. The cigarette flips from between my fingers, arcing up over the stiff heads of wheat. I am still for a moment, and so is the wheat. But then, just as I'm about to exhale and drop my hands from my face, it rustles again.

"What the hell?" someone says from the other side of the stalks.

And then Hadley's voice, wry: "You're on fire."

The wheat shakes more, and there's a list of curses in the voice that isn't Hadley's. I place myself just on the other side of the shaking wheat. The stalks have grown so thick that I can't see through them.

"Are you even going to help me?" the voice asks.

"Hadley?" I say, and when no one answers, I stick my hands into the wheat and push it apart.

The two of them are on the ground. Hadley sits on the far side of the row, her ponytail pulled loose so that her hair is a deflated balloon against the back of her neck. The skin all around her mouth and chin is pink, like she's been scrubbed raw. When she sees me looking at her, she puts a hand up to her face as if to cover this pink. The boy is the one rustling the wheat. His shirt is unbuttoned to his waist, hanging open in a silly V. He scuttles back on his heels, batting at his back, which sends up a thread of smoke like the tiniest smoke signal. Finally satisfied that he's gotten it out, he strips off his shirt to assess the damage.

"You were gonna let me burn?" he asks, brushing at the little hole burned there.

"You handled it," Hadley says to him, though she's looking at me when she says it. I try to interpret her look. Is she angry at me, as I suspect? She seems shuttered, guarded.

The boy, distracted by his shirt, hasn't seen me yet, even though my head and hands are poking through the wheat just above him. I feel like some bizarre hunting trophy, but I can't move. If I let go of the stalks of wheat to duck back through, it'll make all sorts of noise, and he'll definitely see me. But if I stay here, he'll look up any minute and see me, too. I don't know what to do. I'm stuck. What's more, I don't know what Hadley wants me to do. She watches me steadily, her hand slides down from her chin to her neck, but she doesn't give me any direction about what to do and even still no sign about whether she's mad at me. This, I realize, is my punishment for failing her with Jonah. Hadley won't help me, won't keep me safe.

"What the hell?" the boy says as he's shrugging on his shirt, and at first I think he's talking about me, but then he bends forward to pick up something off of the ground. "Look. Someone dropped this on me." He's holding my cigarette, a whisper of smoke rising from it. Then he looks up at me, and I'm staring into the squinty, infamous face of Garrett Murray.

"What the hell?" he says again.

I make a noise that is meant to be *sorry* but isn't even close and try to disappear back through the wheat. Before I can go, he reaches up and catches my wrist, yanking the upper half of me through to their row.

"You did this?" he demands. He brings his face up close to mine, so close that I can see the squinch of sleep in the corner of his eye and the flakes of his chapped lips. He holds the cigarette up between our two faces. I'm scared, and it's all I can do not to gasp in his face. He gives my wrist another tug. The stalks of wheat are rough, even through my coat, and my body is twisted between the rows so that they poke at all the soft parts—belly and ribs.

Suddenly, Hadley is between us. She plucks my wrist out of Garrett's hand. "She came to get me before the bell," she tells him. "I asked her to."

Garrett is still for a second, then he blows his breath out into my face. I flinch. "Don't drop things on me." In a slick movement, he draws back and spins my cigarette into his mouth.

His nipples are tiny on his chest, tiny brown dots like a little boy's. I can't help looking at them. Hadley pushes me back through the wheat and steps through after me, not even saying good-bye to Garrett. We walk back toward the school, shoulder to shoulder because of the narrowness of the row. We don't walk too slow or too fast, and Hadley keeps her face forward. I want to say *Are you mad at me?* I want to say *I'm sorry.* I want to say *Thank you, oh, thank you.* But she still has her hand circling my wrist, like a handcuff or a bracelet, and I don't want to say anything that might make her pull her hand away.

So Hadley is in love with Garrett Murray. I feel stupid for not figuring it out and hurt that she didn't tell me herself. Still, her hand is around my wrist.

"Garrett seems nice," I say.

Hadley snorts, and I wonder if my words sounded sarcastic. I play them back in my head. I don't think they did.

"No. Really," I say. "He does. He was just . . . on fire."

Hadley inhales through her kiss-mashed mouth, and I think that she's gathering breath to yell at me. But instead of yelling, she starts laughing.

"Really, anyone would . . ." And, then I'm laughing, too. Hadley takes her hand from my wrist in order to slap it against her thigh. "Fire!" she gasps between laughs. We trudge forward, doubled over like the laughter is a weight on our backs. And I know that she's forgiven me.

We stop at the edge of the wheat. The guy and girl I'd met earlier are gone. All the smokers are gone. The tardy bell rings faintly from the school as if someone has trapped it under a cup.

"It was my cigarette," I whisper. "The one that set him on . . ." I can't say *fire* again.

She nods and her laughter turns into little bursts of escaping breath.

"I'm sure he's nice," I offer. "Garrett, I mean. It was just a bad way to meet."

"Don't be dumb," Hadley says, her laughter all gone.

Just then, Garrett bursts out of one of the rows near ours. Hadley and I watch in silence as he slinks back across the bus circle to the school, not running—never running. I look for the hole burned in his shirt, but I can't see it from here. When he gets close to the school, one of the hall monitors opens the door and waves him in wearily.

"I still hate him and everything," Hadley says and shrugs.

"You do?"

"Sure," she says.

A thought occurs to me. "Are you saying that he, like, made you . . . you know, in the wheat? Because if he forced—"

"No," Hadley says. "No one can make me do anything." She shrugs again, casting it off.

"But, then, if you don't like him, why would you kiss him?"

She turns and tucks my hair behind my ears on both sides like I'm a kid. "Vie," she says, "shut up."

Chapter EIGHTEEN

GARRETT MURRAY doesn't talk to Hadley in school, at least not that I see now that I'm watching. Sometimes he passes us in the hall; he's always in a hurry, turning his bone-skinny body to sidle between the bumping shoulders of the kids walking ahead of us, looking like he's stepping between the bars of a jail cell. He never even glances at us. Or Hadley at him, either. It isn't even that studied sort of *not* looking, where you can sense that the person is purposely keeping his eyes averted. It's like Hadley and Garrett are strangers to each other, or ghosts, and I'm left to gawp at the phenomenon of the two of them.

Hadley doesn't talk about Garrett again, and though I'm always thinking of ways to bring him up, I never have the nerve to actually do it. The day I found them in the field, I went to my locker and crossed out his name on our list of suspects. The scribble looked bad somehow, like uncertainty, so I rewrote the entire list, leaving him off it and stowing it back on the shelf in my locker. The next day, I saw that Hadley had added his name again in her bold block letters.

After that day in the field, Hadley stopped eating lunch with me altogether. She spends her lunches in the smokers' field now, feeding herself with cigarettes and the sticky red peppermints that she pops to cover the smell. Sometimes I sneak out of the cafeteria early and stand at the door by the bus circle, staring across at the nodding tufts of winter wheat. I lean into the door and press the bar, making it click and unclick, looking out over the field for the places in the wheat that shake. Hadley will find me after lunch, but we won't talk about where she's been or what she's been doing.

Hadley's mouth and chin are raw pink these days; her lips are rubbed down to a shine; buttons have gone missing from her shirts, their threads still hanging—tiny nooses; she sports fingertip-shaped bruises on her arms and wrists like a gray pox. I don't know if this is passion or injury. I blame Garrett, want to hurt him back for her, until one morning I see him in the hall with an angry pink scratch curling around the side of his neck, pricked with blood. I fight the urge to grab Hadley's hand and look under the fingernails for peelings of his skin.

Hadley doesn't seem any happier or sadder now that she's with Garrett. She's determined to keep our investigation going. She spends hours after school completing detailed profiles of each person on our list, which has grown to include sixty-three suspects. She dictates the information, and I take it down: age, occupation, physical description, known associates, episodes of violence, connection to the deceased, etc. She got the categories out of a chapter in one of her mother's crime novels, which stand in mildewed towers, bricking up one wall of the downstairs bathroom. Our notes have expanded way beyond the capacity of my science notebook, though our main list of suspects still lives in its back pages. We keep the rest of our investigation in file folders that Hadley steals from a stack of boxes in the dining room. Her dad's old work stuff, she explains, though not why the contents of his office are packed into boxes. She crosses out the words written on the tabs of the folders—"MediaBlitz," "Travel '88," and "Lonigan, Sheryl"—replacing them with her own labels: "Suspects, Chip. High," "Suspects, College," "Newspaper Articles," and "McCabe, Elizabeth."

I've yet to meet either of Hadley's parents, though I saw her father's silhouette once as he drove away from the house. His profile was fatherly, the face of a man who might chew on a pipe. Veronica told my mother once that both of Hadley's parents are having affairs, that each knows that the other is and doesn't care. Does that mean they love each other more than other parents or less? Hadley does nothing to explain or defend them. "They didn't want kids," she said once with a dark grin, "so they had four."

The other three, her little brothers, remain at their station in front of their video games. The detritus of the house—crumbles of food, clouds of laundry, webs of dust—sometimes recedes, only to creep forward again, like the banks of dirty snow as winter ends.

In Hadley's room—that tidy, girly island—we pile our case files around us like children building a fort. We alphabetize, sort, and label. We keep the finished files in the bottom of her sweater drawer, hidden under the scented drawer liner, until the stack grows too thick, thicker than two folded sweaters, and Hadley buys an actual file box from a store in the mall and slides it to the back of her closet. We annotate and cross-check and tend to our folders, and I promise Hadley that if we're patient, a pattern will emerge.

I tell her this not because I believe it, but to keep her from following through on one of her crazy plans. Her latest idea is to type a letter composed of only one sentence—*I know you killed her*—and send it to our top ten suspects, which include the shop teacher at school, a couple of men who loiter in a back booth at the diner, and Garrett Murphy. Hadley keeps trying to get me to walk through the woods at night dressed like Zabet.

"You could almost look like her if you put on some of her clothes," she says, studying me. "Your hair's kind of the same, and you're about the same height."

"She was prettier than me," I say, hoping just a little bit that Hadley will disagree.

"Well, yeah, but in the dark, from behind," she says and absently presses a tiny bruise on her elbow, causing it to fade and then flush back like a word written in disappearing ink.

She's still obsessed with seeing the place where Jonah found Zabet's body. And I've promised, reluctantly and falsely, that I'll try to talk to him again. The entire week, we practice what I'll say.

"Touch his hand like this," Hadley instructs, resting her fingers on the back of my hand. When I look down, her hand flits away like a moth and lands on her neck just under her jaw, the same place where Garrett's scratch was. "Now you try it on me," she says.

～

On Sunday, Jonah's not even in Hokepe Woods. Pervy Mr. Jefferson is there instead, plunked in the cab of his truck like an old beanbag, eating generic Cheerios straight out of the box. When he sees me, he raps on the window and then rolls it down to call out, "You wanna trade jobs, darlin'?" I'm tempted to grab the sled out of the back of his truck and set off for the trees just to see what he'll do.

"Where's Jonah?" I ask.

"Home sick, missing you," he says and rocks with laughter.

⌒⌒

I don't call Hadley after my paper route, and she doesn't call me either, so I tell myself that, unlikely though it seems, maybe she forgot about Jonah and the woods today. That afternoon, Mom is out at the store and I'm sitting on my bed, looking at the trap I'd stolen from Jonah's truck. I think I've figured out how to load it. I don't dare do it, though, because even touching the trap at its base with only the tip of my pinky finger calls up the feel of the metal jaws snapping shut on my wrist, biting through my skin, teeth wedging themselves in my bones.

Then I hear it from my bedroom, a sound I've listened for before, those times I've woken in the middle of the night, my dreams laid out around me, my fears there with them. It's the sound of the front door's knob turning back and forth. I consider barricading my bedroom or wriggling out the window, but in the end, like the stupid girl, the inevitable victim, I walk out to meet it. My breath is a balloon in my throat, my heart a pump. I tell myself that I've made the sound up, confused it with some other sly, metal scritching—a neighbor raking out flowerbeds, a mouse in the walls. But then I'm there in the front room, and I see it for myself, the doorknob twisting one way then the other in a frantic little shimmy. I back up toward the kitchen, toward the drawer with the knives. Before I get there, the rattling stops and someone starts knocking—rapid knocks that land not just in one place but all over the door. "Open up!" I hear Hadley call. "Open up!"

At the sound of her voice, all the fear rushes out of me in a whoosh of breath, and I run to the door and unlock it. Hadley bursts in and slams it behind her, locking it and leaning back against it. She looks silly leaning against the door like that, like she's keeping out the zombies and vampires and maniacs with chainsaws. When she's sure that the door is secure, she runs to the front window. She sweeps her gaze over the street.

"What are you doing?"

She ignores me and heads down the hall to my bedroom, peering out the window there. Then she turns and sighs with relief, tipping her head back so that it rests against the pane. I think of the blot of hair grease that she'll leave behind and how Mom will go at it with a cloud of spray and a paper towel. At Hadley's house it'd remain unnoticed for weeks, forever.

"He's gone now," Hadley says.

"Who's gone?"

"That guy. The one from the parking lot."

"What are you talking about?"

"The guy I hit with my car."

"You didn't hit him."

"Fine. The one I *almost* hit. He's following me."

I picture him, the guy in the parking lot, how I stood over him, how he had a look on his face like I might kick him, like he was *afraid* of me.

"Come on. He's not *following* you."

"I knew you'd say that, but he was outside my house today."

"What—just, like, standing in your front lawn?"

"*No*," she says as if I'm purposely being dense. "In a car, but I can tell it's him anyway."

"What car?"

"It's a rusty red thing, dark red—what do you call it? Burgundy. Maroon. A junker."

"And you think it's him?"

"I know it's him."

"In a maroon junker."

"I could see him through the window. It's him."

"You could get the license plate number," I suggest.

"Sure, why don't I do that, Evie? Why don't I lie down under his back wheels? Why don't I knock on the window and ask if I can sit in his lap?"

I'm grinning now, but Hadley's unperturbed. She scratches her elbow, certain, so certain.

"He's not following you," I say.

Hadley looks at me, her mouth screwed to one side as if I've confirmed something disappointing about myself, something that she hoped she'd be wrong about. She gives all her attention to her elbow again, scratches it.

"He could've followed Zabet just the same," she murmurs.

She rotates her arm and studies the palms of her hands as if she expects to see something there—mud? Blood? She closes it into a fist.

"Had?" I say. "Hadley?"

She looks suddenly sad, deflated of her certainty and self-righteousness. I crouch down in front of her and put a cautious hand on her arm. She mumbles something, but it's too soft, and I have to ask her to repeat it.

"Do you think I'm next?" she says.

"Next?"

"After Zabet. The next one."

"No. Oh, no." I feel a burst of sympathy and also relief. I'm shaking my head rapidly, though I don't tell her that this is the same thought that I've had a hundred times, only about myself, that *I'm* next, the next one, the next victim. I know that the Whisperers fear it, too. *I don't go outside at night anymore, not even into my backyard,* one says in the tenor of a confession, and the others nod *yes, yes.* So maybe we're all thinking it: *I'm next.* Maybe that's part now, of being . . . what? Young? A girl?

"Yeah, no," Hadley says with a phlegmy little laugh. She uncurls her fists, gives me a push, and says, "Not me."

She stares off over my shoulder. I've completely forgotten about the trap right out there on my bed in plain sight, and so for a second I don't know what's made Hadley's eyes light up the way they do. By the time I turn, she's already rushed past me and is sitting on my bed next to the trap, running her fingers along its jawline.

"What's this?" she says with a hint of glee.

"Nothing."

"You could trap a moose with this thing."

"I think it's for deer, or maybe a bear." I stand over her, an adult supervising a child. I want more than anything for her to leave it alone.

"Like this," she says. In one quick motion, Hadley yanks the jaws of the trap open, fastening the catch to hold them in place. I take a step back, as if the trap might jump up and fasten itself to my shoulder or my cheek.

"You just set it," I say in disbelief.

She shrugs.

"It could snap closed now."

"Well, yeah. It's a trap."

"How am I going to get it closed again?"

She shrugs, like *no big deal*, and reaches for it.

I start to say *Stop!* but figure that would just make her all the more determined. So instead I say, "Hey!"

She looks up at me, her hands still on the trap. And now she's not even looking at what she's doing! She disarms it anyhow by unfastening a catch on the base and folding the slack teeth closed. As soon as the trap is safe again, I reach forward and pluck her hands off of it.

"Come on." I pull her up from the bed. "I have something to show you."

"Jonah, right?" she says, her eyes bright. "He showed you the spot. He did, right?"

I lift the trap carefully, stowing it back under my bed.

"Yes," I say, nodding. "Yes, that's right."

Chapter NINETEEN

I HAVE HADLEY DRIVE US all around Hokepe Woods first to make sure that Mr. Jefferson's truck is gone. On the way over, she announces that her mysterious man is not following us, not right now anyway. She's eager in the car, punching the buttons of her stereo, digging under her seat for cassettes, flicking the windshield wipers on and off even though there's no rain.

We park where Jonah always does, and I take us in through the trees, along the same path that he had walked with me a week earlier. I find the wheel of a roller skate on the ground, ball bearings rattling inside it. Hadley plucks it out of my hand and tosses it in the air, batting it back up with her palm when it drops. She's jubilant—humming shreds of the songs that were on the radio during our drive over. She slings her arm around my shoulders and squeezes my neck, somewhere between a hug and a wrestling hold. She whips the wheel at me, and I catch it and stick it in my pocket, after which she pleads that I give it back to her. Maybe I shouldn't, but I do.

I remember the way to get to the spot by following the ribbons on the trees. There were five of them before. I count them off silently, and when we pass the fifth, I see the two trees and the patch of mud between them. I sneak a glance at Hadley. She's singing "I'm the luckiest by far . . ." while braiding a tiny braid into a strand of her hair, each V perfect. I'd expected our walk out here to be a dirge, a solemn procession, a wake, or else for Hadley to be angry (like she is so much of the time), kicking at leaves and swiping at trees. I don't know how to respond to this sudden goofiness. She acts like a child who's played a trick on her mother, peeking at me out from around the column of her braid.

"There," I say. "Right there." I point at the spot.

Hadley's song trails off into a noise that sounds like *hmmm*, as if she's considering something. She drops the braid, and the bottom of it begins to unwind, the crisscrossed strands spreading and sliding over each other, growing fat without her hand there to hold them tight.

"Where?" she says.

I point to the patch of mud, the two trees.

"Where exactly?" she asks impatiently.

I walk over and point my finger directly at the place. "Here."

She walks to me, her brows knitted, focused on where I'm pointing. She steps onto the spot with precision, lining up her toes, as though she's stepping onto the photographer's X to have her school picture taken. Then she begins to lower herself onto the ground.

"It's muddy!" I cry, but she looks at me blankly and sits. She stays there cross-legged for a moment, and then she uncrosses her legs and lowers herself flat on her back. I watch all this agog. In fact, my arm is still out, my finger pointing down, not at the ground now, but at Hadley lying beneath me.

"Get up," I say, but she ignores me.

I remember how horrified I was to slip, to plant my hand in the center of that spot, my palm sinking into the dirt where Zabet's blood had sunk, where her head had pressed into the mud as he'd hit her again and again. And now Hadley is lying exactly there.

Hadley opens her eyes and gazes up at me. She looks past me at the trees and the sky up above us. She stares for a moment, very still, as if listening for something.

"Yes," she says finally, nodding so that the leaves shift and crunch under the back of her head.

"Sit down," she tells me. I act like I haven't heard her. She half rises and grabs my hand, yanking me to the ground.

She lies back down next to where I half squat, half sit. She looks up again at the sky, the blue cut into jagged teeth by the tree branches. She seems content, peaceful, like she's cloud gazing. I wonder if she lies down like this in the smokers' field. I picture Garrett's narrow back and brown nipples, the undone sides of his shirt draping over both of them.

"This is the last thing she saw," Hadley says.

This is almost exactly what I had thought when I was here with Jonah. I wonder if this is the thought that anyone would think, lying here. I wonder if Zabet thought it, too: *This is the last thing I'll see.* I look where Hadley's looking, the underskirts of the trees.

"The last thing she saw," I repeat.

"Either this or that asshole's face."

"I'm sure it was this," I say.

"No you're not. No one knows but her. And him."

"Well, I *hope* it was this, then, okay?"

"Yeah, okay." She reaches out and gives my leg a clumsy pat.

Without thinking, I lower myself onto my back next to her. The mud is soft and wet on my neck and hands, and there's something satisfying about this, mud squished between the fingers, a long-forgotten pleasure.

"What was Zabet like?" I say. It's the first time since after Mr. McCabe's dinner that I've directly referred to what Hadley and I both know and don't talk about—that I hadn't known Zabet since we were both kids, that at the time she died, I didn't know her at all.

"She was . . . whatever." I hear the leaves stir once, twice, Hadley lifting her shoulders—up, down—in a shrug. "She was okay. She was my friend."

"But what was she *like?*"

"She was like a person, just like . . . someone. Like anybody."

I can hear the annoyance in Hadley's voice, which means that any second she might rise up and storm off. But I stumble on. "What about something, like . . . specific, like, something she liked?"

"What else did Jonah tell you?" Hadley asks, her voice daring me to accuse her of changing the subject.

"I don't know," I say, then, knowing she'll want more than this and hoping that she'll give me something of Zabet in return, "That this was the spot. That she was lying here."

"How was she lying? On her back?"

"Yeah," I say, though Jonah and I never had this conversation, not anything like it.

"And was there anything around her? Any"—Hadley bites her lip—"rope or a rock or something with maybe blood on it?"

"No. Just her."

"What about her face?"

"Her face?" I echo.

"Were her eyes closed?"

"No," I stutter.

"No?" Hadley asks sharply.

"I mean, he didn't know. Her hair was over her face, covering it. So he couldn't see."

Hadley studies me for a second out of the corner of her eye. She rolls on her side so that she's facing me. I roll on my side to face her, too, resting my cheek on both of my hands, like how little kids sleep in picture books. The mud flattens under my hands; we're going to be covered in it, our clothes, our hair, and the sides of our faces.

"She was nice," Hadley says. "She was a good person. Much better than me, anyway. And she liked"—Hadley chews on her lip—"Velcro."

"Velcro?"

"Yeah. Sneakers and stuff. And science class and loud music, and she pretended she liked coffee, but really she put a shit-ton of cream and sugar in it so it was more like coffee-flavored milk. And she was real easygoing mostly. If you wanted to do something, she'd do it with you."

I pictured it again: the ladle spinning toward Zabet's face.

"Do you think you'd know him if you saw him?"

"Who?" I say.

"Who?" she repeats. "The one who killed her. Him. Do you think you could look at him and know it was him? Say, if you saw him, like, at a gas station or the mall or something. Would you know?"

I close my eyes and think for a minute, trying to puzzle out the right answer, the answer that will make her happy. "Maybe."

"I'll know," she says and then, as if I've argued with this, "*I will.*"

⟨⟩

We walk back to the car, muddy. I brush the flakes of it off my arms, comb my fingers through the mud-glued strands of my hair, and pluck my shirt away from my back so it'll dry. But Hadley lets her mud stay, the streaks across her cheek and dark wet smudges on the back of her shirt, as if it weren't even there. She must have memorized the tree ribbons on our way in because she nods to each one we pass like she's thanking it for its guidance.

I can see the neighborhood ahead of us, the primary-colored plastics of swing sets, kiddie pools, and deck chairs; my view of them striated by the trunks of the trees. Hadley reaches the edge of the woods first and steps out into the neighborhood, but then she spins right back around and is running at me. She grabs me by the arm, pulling me away from the backyards, deeper into the trees.

"He's here," she says.

"Who?"

"Him. The car."

"Jonah's car?"

She glares at me, then jabs a finger out past the tree line. "*Look.*"

There's a car there, a junky old burgundy station wagon parked just behind Hadley's car. I think I see a shadow shift in the driver's seat, but the windows are dark, and besides, we're yards away. I can't be sure anyone's even in there.

"He followed me here," Hadley says, shaking her head like she should have known.

"Are you sure it's the same one, because—"

She looks at me levelly and, as if in punishment for my ineptitude, steps out from the trees. *She's going to walk straight to the car, open the door, and climb in the backseat,* I think. *I'll never see her again.*

"Wait!" I say, grabbing her by the arm, tethering her to me, to the trees. Her arm is covered with tiny bumps. She lets herself be pulled back to safety.

"I'm just gonna look."

"No," I tell her. And when she tries to take a step, I clutch at her arm. "Hadley, *no.*"

She sizes me up. "So you believe me now?"

"It's a possibility." I glance back out at the car, sitting there. It's too old for the cars in this neighborhood, too shabby. "Just stay here for a minute."

"It's fine," she says, prying up my fingers one by one. "It's the middle of the day in the middle of the street. Okay?" She pulls up on my hand. "Let go. Okay?"

She fixes an eye on me, steady, staring me down past the lock of hair she'd been braiding. Finally, I let go. I reach forward and comb out the remnants of her braid.

"I'll be right here," I say.

"Fine. Watch me."

She squares her shoulders and steps out into the backyard in front of us. The car is up ahead of her, parked at the curb. She takes a step toward it and then another, bringing her feet together after each step like she's marching in a wedding.

As she gets closer to the car, my heart starts to pound its blood against my neck, knees, and wrists. There's definitely someone in the driver's seat, I've decided; I can almost make out a shadow now, and the windows are streaked with his breath.

Hadley walks out between the houses with her purposeful stride. I can't stand to look anymore, so I study something in my pocket, a scrap of paper, half a note I'd written to Hadley: *After school?* I don't even remember what the complete question was, what we were supposed to do after school. I stare at this little bit of paper like it has the last paragraph of one of Hadley's mother's mystery novels scribbled on it, the solution.

I hear a creak as the door of the car opens. I look. Someone is getting out of the car. I can't see who, though, because the car is parked with the driver's side facing the street. This driver, he could grab Hadley; he could shoot her; he could stab her. I take a breath and bolt forward, out of the woods, shouting Hadley's name as I go. As I run forward, everything else runs in reverse. The car door slams shut, the driver ducking back in, and the car swings out of its spot. Hadley, who had almost reached the car, takes a couple of dancing steps back and stumbles on the curb, landing on her ass on the sidewalk. The car straightens and speeds off.

It was nowhere near hitting her, but still my heart is pounding. I'm there next to her in a second, gasping her name and *oh my God*. Instead of taking the hand I offer to help her up, she slaps my arm with a stinging clap more startling than the noise of the car engine.

"Believe me now?" she asks, and I nod and press the place where she's hit me too hard. "See? You should always believe me."

She yanks herself up roughly, but when she's gotten to her feet, she holds my hand with one of her hands and my arm with her other hand, as if I'm elderly and might fall and break something.

"I hope he comes to get me," she whispers as we walk, her mouth blowing the hair near my ear, her breath fetid. "I hope he gets close enough so I can—" She squeezes my hand tight enough so that the tendons roll over the bones, the squeeze the final word of her sentence.

Chapter TWENTY

WHEN I GET HOME, I find a note instead of my mother. *On a date,* it says with loopy flowers and a lopsided heart drawn around the message. I knew this already. A second date with that friend of Veronica's: *Rick-from-the-bank. He decides who gets loans and who doesn't.* As if this was some sort of virtue and not the perfect job description for a jerk.

Tonight is like all the other date nights. I make my own dinner and write some essay for school. I go to bed early and wake, around eleven, to voices. At first, I think it's the TV. One of the voices is familiar, the voice of a beloved actress from a sitcom now in reruns. But then, no, it's my mother's voice. The other, Rick's.

I sit up in bed, winding the covers around me into a nest, and listen to the voices go back and forth—the lilt of hers, the murmur of his. His voice is a low, nasal buzz, a marching band clarinet. I can't hear much of what they say; every once in a while, though, a word steals away to my ears—*halibut, lightweight, bingo.*

I get up off my bed and make my way down the hall, careful to place my feet where the floor meets the wall, where the floorboards, anchored, don't squeak. It isn't until I'm halfway to the living room that I think a terrible thought: *It could be you. It could be you, Rick-from-the-bank. It could be you who killed Zabet. Why not? Maybe you saw her through the tinted glass walls of your bank, Zabet on her way back from the coffee shop, a cup of milky coffee in her hand, sucking her sugar through the top?*

The scenario rolls out before me like a lie off my tongue. But it's true. Suddenly it's true, and my mother's date is no longer Rick-from-the-bank but Zabet's killer. The low buzz of his voice is the ominous music, the foggy minor chords from a slasher movie that tell the audience what the heroine should already know. *Don't walk down that hall. Don't reach for that doorknob. The electricity has been cut, the phone disconnected. The knife is glimmering in that patch of shadow over there.*

I cling to the wall of the hallway, and then, when there's a lift to the conversation, the two of them talking over each other—*restrictions*, one of them says, and the other, *Barbara Walters*—I scuttle to the room next to the living room, the half bathroom, which no one ever uses.

I slide open the shutters of the one small window and peer out at the driveway. There's Mom's car and, behind it, a car that is not burgundy, not a station wagon, not the car following Hadley. It's something beiger and newer. I sigh with relief, even as my mind says, *So what? He could have two cars.*

Stakeouts, it turns out, are more boring than you might expect. It's hard to maintain a sense of alertness, an edge of fear. I keep myself occupied sorting through old bottles in the cabinet under the sink—half-used shampoos, their bright mint dried to a swampy green, lotions that have separated into oil and fat, soaps dusted with a creeping white powder like the kind that forms on old chocolate bars. The talk in the living room rises to a peak and then suddenly hushes to nothing. After a while, I hear the rustling and ceremony of good-bye. The front door opens and closes. The headlights of Rick-from-the-bank's new beige car shine through the open slats of the bathroom shutters, locking down everything in shadowy jail bars.

I can hear Mom's bare feet padding through the kitchen and then the rush of water in the other bathroom. I silently replace all the old bottles under the sink and wait to hear if her footfalls will pause at the end of the hall as she looks in at me asleep in my bed. Or, in this case, not asleep, not in my bed. But her footsteps march straight to her bedroom, shutting its door. She didn't stop to check on me at all. It occurs to me that she never checked on me, not when she first got back, not now. I could be anywhere, gone, and she wouldn't know until morning, when I failed to emerge from my room. I don't bother tiptoeing back to my room, but if she hears my footfalls in the hallway, she doesn't call out to ask why I'm awake.

Once, sometime not so long after my father left, I yawned at the breakfast table. Mom focused on this yawn. She hadn't focused on much in those first few weeks after he was gone, despite her war stripes of blush, despite the hard tin of her laugh. But that morning, she sat down next to me and took the cereal spoon, still dripping with milk, from my hand.

"Do you stay awake listening for him to come back?"

I knew who *him* was—*him, he, his* always meant my dad. She stared at me, her pretty, pretty face naked through its makeup. I nodded, but only because I thought I should. It was a lie; I'd slept straight through the night. Suddenly, I found myself caught up in her arms, my cereal bowl pushed to the side, where it slopped milk.

"You'll stop listening for him," she said, her hand stroking my hair in the rhythm of her words, as if to hypnotize me. "You'll stop. I'll stop, too."

The funny thing was, after that, I couldn't stay awake even if I'd wanted to. I'd slept fine before, but that night, and for many nights after, I laid my head on my pillow and dropped under, straight through the mattress ticking, it felt like. After nine hours, ten hours, Mom would try to wake me up. Even in my sleep, I could feel her shaking me by the shoulders; I could smell her perfume; her voice was the voice of a cricket trapped under a drinking glass. So, for her sake, I would drag myself up from sleep. Sometimes one of my arms would actually stretch up into the air as if climbing up a rope, my little hand curled in a claw, before I even opened my eyes.

The next day at school, it's obvious that Hadley hasn't slept, not a bit. She doesn't act sleepy, though, but instead almost fevered—rings of pink around her eyes, hands batting at me to get my attention, ponytail swinging like the pendulum of an overwound clock.

"He came for me," she says.

"What? Who?"

"He drove past my house last night, twice."

"Did he stop or—"

"He drove past, but slow."

"And you're sure it was the same guy who—"

"Yes, Evie. God. It was the same car. You know, the one outside the woods that almost ran me over."

"Okay. Okay."

Hadley leans in, her eyes bright, scary. "You know what I did?"

A little minnow of fear swims up through my gut. "What?"

"After the first time he drove past, I got one of my brothers' baseball bats. I climbed out my window and waited, and when I heard him coming, I stepped out into the middle of the road. I just stood there, you know, with the bat in my hands. And when he saw me, he stopped his car. His headlights were on me. I just stood there, hitting the end of the bat against my palm like I was ready to smash something."

"What did he do?" I whisper.

"He reversed. He turned around and drove away."

Hadley's face is calm now; she's beaming. I'm not sure what I feel. I can picture her standing in the middle of the road in the boxer shorts and T-shirt she sleeps in, feet bare, face hard, the headlights setting her aglow.

"He could have run you over," I say. "He could have done . . . bad things, *terrible* things."

"But he drove away."

She puts her hand on my shoulder and leans in closer as if to tell me a secret. I can see the place around her ears where the tiny hairs grow into fuzz, almost a fur, and in the corner of her nose where her makeup is a patch of unblended mud.

"It's him, Evie. It's got to be." She takes my face in her hands and draws hers close, impossibly close, even with the dozens of kids around us. "We did it. We found him. We *got* him."

"We should make sure. Before we do anything—"

The school bell rings in its cage above us.

"It felt amazing, Vie, standing there, it felt . . . to do that, it felt . . . strong."

I can't find Hadley during next passing, and she isn't in the cafeteria. I worry about what she'll do if the burgundy junker appears again. Maybe next time, it'll run her over. Maybe the driver is the one who killed Zabet, punched her face, kicked it again and again, until she wasn't Zabet anymore. We're sixteen, I keep thinking. We're kids. What can Hadley possibly want us to do next? And, yet, even though I don't know what she wants, even though I'll probably think it's crazy, I also admit that I'll end up doing it, to do something, to do something back. And I think of what Hadley said about Zabet when we were in the woods. If you wanted to do something, she'd do it with you. Am I that way, too? And really, isn't that just another way to describe someone who's a pushover, a tagalong, weak-willed?

I go to the door by the teachers' parking lot to stare across at the wheat where Hadley is likely making out with Garrett Murray—she, digging gouges in his skin; he, pressing bruises into hers. I'm searching for their shadows in the wheat, so I don't see it right away. In fact, I'm already turning back toward the cafeteria and the Whisperers, when some tiny voice nags me to turn back. There it is: the burgundy station wagon.

At first, I think that I've conjured it up, that it's not really there at all, or if it is, that it's a different burgundy station wagon, a coincidence car, a teacher's. It's not parked in the teachers' lot, though, but along the road by the field. It's really there. And, what's more, I can see someone in it.

I consider my options: running to get Principal Capp, sneaking past the car into the field to warn Hadley. I think about calling my mother or even the police. I think about doing nothing. But in the end, I picture Hadley stepping out, barefoot, pajamaed, into the middle of the road, standing in the beam of those headlights. And it's this that makes me walk out across the parking lot, across the road, and tap on the burgundy junker's window.

The driver is pressed against the opposite window, his jacket balled under his neck, his eyes closed. There's something familiar about him in profile, the jacket covering half of his face. I've seen him before. Yes, I decide, it's him. Hadley is right. He's the guy from the parking lot, the one she almost ran over. And rather than scare me, this gives me courage. Our list worked. We caught him. I lean down and knock on the window again. He wakes, blinking at the light of the afternoon and then at me. He recognizes me and looks—it's the strangest thing—*scared*. He grabs for his keys, still in the ignition, and cranks them. The car makes a grinding noise but doesn't start. He tries again; same deal. And me, I'm still standing there knocking away. It starts to feel absurd, each of us repeating the same action— me rapping on the window, him turning the keys—without success. I decide to stop knocking, and he, in turn, stops with the keys and, with a sigh, reaches over and pops the lock.

I'm not getting in, my mind says firmly. I open the door and lean down. "I'm not getting in."

I should be scared. My blood should be howling through my veins like a tangle-haired woman through the streets. Instead I am still. The streets of my body are empty; everyone is inside, calm, lights blazing. In fact, he's the one who looks scared. He doesn't rise from his spot against the driver's side window. He doesn't make a grab for me. I don't see a weapon, a gun or knife. Though, I remind myself, Zabet's killer simply used his hands, his feet. He blinks at me a few more times, his eyes red and sore looking. He has his shoulders hunched up near his jaw, as if I might reach out and smack him.

"I didn't know," he says, and his voice is high-pitched for a guy. I wonder if he's nervous or if his voice is always that high.

"You said that before," I tell him. "At the diner, in the parking lot, you said that there."

He shakes his head—no, no, no—like I'm not understanding, and the words climb over each other as if in a rush to get out his mouth. "I want you to know. No matter what Hadley says, I didn't . . . I thought she . . . she just freaked out. She seemed fine during, but then after, she . . . If she reports me . . ." He puts his face in his hands.

"Stop following her." My voice does not boom out strong and heroic like I intend it to, but is only a whisper, a scratch, barely a breath because suddenly I'm unsure. How does he know her name? What does he mean *she freaked out after*? After what? I look down at him, his hands still pressed to the sides of his face, and he looks suddenly familiar, not from the parking lot, but from somewhere else. He lowers his shaking hands from his face. I stare at them.

"I didn't mean to scare her more. I just wanted to talk to her, to explain. But then, well, you were there and I—"

"*Me?*"

"No, no, I don't mean . . ." he splutters and makes a pleading gesture with his hands, as if he's afraid he's upset me. "You were angry for your friend, I get that. But you, at the diner, you almost hit me with the car. I know you were trying to give me a good scare, and I don't blame—"

"*Me?*" I say again. "That was Hadley. She was driving. She almost hit you."

"Oh," he says in a small voice. "You got out of the car. I thought . . ."

"You were scared of *me?*" The idea is so preposterous that I almost laugh right there in his face, the face of a killer. But he's not a killer. He's scared, scared of me. Something occurs to me. "Is that why you drove away that afternoon in Hokepe Woods? Because you saw *me?*"

"You came running and shouting and I just thought . . ." He presses his hands to his eyes, hard. "I thought if I could talk to Hadley alone, explain to her that I didn't know."

Suddenly, I'm irritated by his whiny voice, his palsy, and his pleas. *Pathetic*, I think. "Didn't know what?"

"That she's only sixteen," he says miserably.

I freeze. My irritation is replaced by a feeling of alarm rising up in me.

"She said she was in college. She *told* me that. And she seemed older. I didn't even think . . . And then she freaked out, ran out of the room. Everyone at the party saw her . . . and heard you say . . . *Jesus*. I'm twenty-two, you know? I slept with a sixteen-year-old. It's . . . it's illegal, you were right. I could get kicked out of school. My father would . . . or the police, and they'd send me to . . . aw, God, I didn't know. You've got to believe me."

That voice, the hand pressed to the side of his face, his face hidden under the cap, in the dark of the hallway: Chad, the boy from the party. I remember what I said to him. *My father's a lawyer. He'll call your parents, your school, the police.* No wonder he was scared of me. But that night, the night of the party, Hadley was sobbing in the hallway, and I was sure he'd attacked her. I'm not sure about anything anymore. I feel a terrible wrongness in the center of me. I take a step back. I let go of the car door. It swings half-closed and stops.

"I didn't hurt her," he pleads.

"I know."

He stops, blinks, cocks his head. "You . . . you do?"

"It was a misunderstanding," I say, my voice matching his in energy. It's a voice not so different from the one that I used to tell him that my father was a lawyer who'd call the police. It's the voice I use to persuade, to tell a story. "She told you she was older. You didn't know."

"Right, that's right." He nods. "She did."

"It was a misunderstanding. It wasn't . . . a crime." I take another step back. "She won't report you . . . just . . . don't follow her anymore."

He shakes his head now as rapidly as he had, just a second ago, nodded it. "I won't. Thank you. I won't." And, like an eager salesman, he leans forward with his hand out, to shake mine before closing the car door. But I can't touch him, can't even move, so I wave and he does too.

"Thank you," he says again before he drives away, but the window is rolled up, so the words sound like they are traveling to me from somewhere very far away.

"You're welcome," I answer, not sure if he can hear me through the glass.

Chapter TWENTY-ONE

I WALK BACK TO THE SCHOOL, thinking about what I'm going to say to Hadley. Should I tell her that it was Chad who was following her? Should I tell her why? Ask her what happened in that room the night of the party? Why she hit him, why she was crying? Ask her what's happening between her and Garrett Murray now—the bruises, the scratches? I'm not sure I want to know the answers, not sure I'm ready for them. My curiosity, usually so eager, is nowhere to be found. And for the space of that walk back to the school from the road, I want to be ignorant, naïve, wiped clean. I want things to be, if not easy, at least simpler. I want the past three months not to have happened, even if it means not being Hadley's best friend, even if it means being alone again. For the first time, I truly and earnestly wish for Zabet to be alive. Even so, the wish is more for myself than it is for her. I want to be the old Evie, the Evie who delivered papers and told bullshit stories to the Whisperers and avoided Zabet and Hadley when they strutted down the hall. I want to only imagine things, not know them.

Our list of suspects is in my science notebook, in my locker, up on the shelf where you're supposed to set your sack lunch. We

haven't crossed off a name before (only Garrett's and only tempo-
rarily), but now I cross off *guy from the parking lot* and *Chad from the
party*. There are so many names on that list—Chrises and Scotts
and Justins. These are the only suspects I've ever eliminated, and it's
not even two suspects really, just one. I tell myself that if the guy in
the burgundy junker isn't following her around, then maybe Hadley
will forget about him. Maybe he'll fade from her memory, and some
other name—maybe one of the other names here—will take his
place in her suspicions.

I spend the rest of my lunch hour leaning against the locker next
to mine. Lunch hour ends, and the kid who owns this locker—Bill
Grauer—returns and hovers nearby until I notice him; he's too polite
to tell me to move. Voices rise at the other end of the hall, and both
Bill and I look over. Something's causing a stir, but we can't see what
it is, because everyone's drifting to the middle of the corridor, kids
standing on tiptoe to get a better view, hands on their friends' shoulders so that they can hoist themselves up an extra inch. As whatever
it is approaches, people peel back, making way, but still lining along
the lockers so that I can't see what they're looking at until she walks
right past me.

I see her hair first—long, light hair rubbed with dirt and stuck
with arrowheads of wheat. She hops a bit, favoring one foot, like
she has a stone in her shoe. But people aren't staring at that; they're
staring at her face, which is swollen like she's been crying for hours,
except the puffiness is different somehow. It's not just around her
eyes but all over her face, a yellowish tint like she's caught an illness
from a rogue mosquito or long ocean journey. That familiar scar on
her chin has opened up into a cut, as if time has reversed itself to the

moment of the initial injury; a spot of blood has dried on her neck like a beauty mark. Hadley hasn't been crying; she's been beaten.

Principal Capp has Hadley by the arm, like he's pulling her along, except he's not. Hadley walks a step ahead, leading *him* back to the principal's office. She keeps her head up, and her eyes dart at the kids around her, landing on one bystander then skipping to the next as if she's making a list of them all in her head. The kids watch her quietly, none of them turning to nudge or whisper to their friends.

"Hadley!" I call out, but her eyes flit past me like I'm just one of them. Then she's gone, and the wall of kids closes up behind her.

Bill Grauer lets out a low whistle. "Freak," he says to the brown-paper cover of his textbook. Whenever he wants to say something to me, he addresses the cavity of his locker, his mechanical pencil, the sleeve of his winter jacket. I feel a swell of outrage against shy Bill and his stupid homemade textbook covers. I think about how I could add his name to our list if I felt like it, simple as that and he's a suspect. Simple as that, he's accused.

That afternoon, I walk past the principal's office nearly a dozen times on a dozen pretexts with half a dozen hall passes, but Hadley's not out in the waiting room or anywhere else, not in her classes or the girl's bathroom or the tiny detention room at the back of the library. Finally, following a couple of office aides down the hall, I hear one of them say to the other, "At-home suspension is all," and there's only one person they could be talking about.

By the end of the day, I don't need any sleuthing to figure out why Hadley's been suspended. Wiry, jack-o'-lantern-faced Garrett Murray's been suspended, too. It's all the smokers can talk about and, soon, all anyone can talk about. During last passing, I hear the girl with the pointed eyeliner say Hadley's name, so I inch up behind her.

"She totally attacked him," she's saying, somehow both indignant and pleased. "He *had* to hit her to get her away from him. She wouldn't stop. She bit his face! With her mouth! There was blood down his cheek and teeth marks, all that. The human bite is a dirty thing," she announces, "probably hers especially. We pulled her off, of course, but . . . goddamn." She looks down at her hands, her fingers splayed as if something has slipped through them. "Goddamn," she says.

She's impressive in her telling of the story—eyes wide with surprise and outrage, the extra line about the human bite. It makes me think about all those times that I'd tell Jonah-stories to the Whisperers—how I'd weigh a phrase or spit out a particular word like I couldn't hold it in my mouth any longer, how I'd say a sentence quietly to make them lean in, how I'd collect their wide eyes and sucks of breath like beads I could string on a bracelet.

⌒⟶

Hadley's been driving me home, but this afternoon, I'm back on the bus with the other latchkey kids, the renters, the off-branders, and the sack-lunchers. There are only about twenty of us, enough to sparsely populate an old school bus. Once I'm home, I try calling Hadley, but no one answers. No one answers the next morning, either.

Tuesday afternoon after school, I bike over to her house, her homework piled in my backpack, and knock on the door. I hear someone walking around inside, but no matter how many times I knock or press the bell, the footsteps never approach.

"Hello!" I call through the door. "Hadley?"

I end up leaving the homework on the porch under a rock stolen from the next-door neighbor's garden.

I go back again on Wednesday with more homework. The homework I'd left the day before has been taken in; either that or it's blown away across all the Hokepe lawns and into the woods. The rock sits on the porch alone, bald. I don't even wait this time but just dump the stack of papers and set the rock on them—done.

The week is a quiet one for me, though everyone else is restless with only a week left until summer break. The Whisperers continue to make room for me at their cafeteria table, and not one of them asks me about Hadley or the fight. I don't talk about it either; I just sit and listen to the crunch of their carrot sticks. I raise my hand a couple of times in class on my own, instead of listlessly providing the required answer only when called on like I'd been doing lately.

"Good job today, Evie," Mr. Denby says as I gather my things.

I feel shy. During the next class break, I push my notebook with the suspect list to the back of my locker. (I can't bring myself to throw it away.)

Just as Hadley's presence fades during the week that she's suspended, Zabet's emerges, as if they are two characters in a stage play performed by the same actress, one entering the drawing room moments after the other has left it. I start to dream about Zabet. She sits on the end of my bed in my mother's favorite hat—a green felt cloche. I beg her not to take it off, because I know that there's something wrong with her head underneath. "It itches," she tells me, scratching her scalp through the felt of the hat. I wake with my own hands tangled in my hair.

I see her face again, in the smudge on my unwashed window or the nest of hair in the shower drain, in the swirl of sugar in my cereal. I stir my cereal until she disappears. "Wash away," I tell her in the shower. The water hits her face, breaking it back into hair. I bat out the wrinkles in my bedspread shaped like the neck and shoulder of a girl resting curled on the ground.

Then, on Thursday night, I have Hadley's dream, the one where all the shops in the mall are selling people. But in my dream they're not selling a random assortment, only Zabets—tangle-haired, mud-covered, beaten-up Zabets like the one Jonah pulled out of the woods. She's piled in bargain bins in the bookstore, lined up on racks in the clothing shops, tucked onto shelves, and posed in the display windows.

I wake up Friday morning not remembering any of it, lost for a minute in the white noise from Mom showering down the hall. Then the phone rings, and the entire dream hits me all at once. My heart is already pounding before I pick it up and hear Hadley say, "Hey, Vie."

"How *are* you?" I ask, and my voice sounds cheap and false, an aunt at a birthday party.

"Mmmm," she hums, as if everything is normal. She doesn't ask me back how I am, but this isn't unusual; she never asks back. She tells me, "You're going to sleep over tonight."

"Over there?"

"Of course over here, idiot."

"I thought maybe you were grounded."

"My parents will be, most definitely, out for the evening. And also, I'm *bored*." She draws out this last word, making its one syllable into two, like how a little kid would say it.

"I'll . . . I'll have to ask my mom."

There's a pause. "Oh, yeah?" she says.

"She's been, you know, wanting me home a lot."

"Fine, but make her say yes."

"I'll try."

"Don't try, *do*," she says, mimicking Principal Capp's start-of-the-year speech.

We say our good-byes, but as I'm pulling the phone away from my ear, I hear her say, "Vie?" I waver for a moment, the receiver between my face and the cradle, not knowing whether to hang up or listen. I end up pressing it back against my ear.

"Yeah?"

"Thanks for the homework."

A few minutes later, Mom emerges from the shower, but I don't ask if I can sleep over at Hadley's. I'm not sure I want to see her, to get into all that again. So I go to school and return and don't call her back, and I don't think about it. She shows up around seven anyway. I probably should have predicted this.

Mom answers the door, thinking it's Rick-from-the-bank. She's spent the past hour scurrying from her room to the mirrored wall in the kitchen where, she says, there's the best natural light. She's appraised fluted skirts and plunging blouses; she's blended eye shadows and smeared on lip goo. She studies herself from all angles, turning her back to the mirror, even, and glancing over her shoulder as if she's accidentally caught sight of her own behind.

With all of Mom's running about, I miss the sound of the door, so the first thing I hear is her startled, "What happened to you?"

When I get out to the living room, Mom is circling Hadley with the look of disapproval she reserves for rude saleswomen and slow elevators. Hadley's got a black backpack over her shoulder, like she's the one sleeping over. Her bruises have darkened to blooms of pen ink and grass stains. Garrett Murray hit her three times that I can see: one on the eye, the other on the cheek, the third on the chin, opening up her scar. The scar has been stitched back together and is held with butterflies of tape, which have grown grimy from their tenure under Hadley's fingertips. She sees me and grins. All the old facial expressions are there, curled lip and waggling eyebrow, sly winks, rolling from one countenance to the next under her bruised skin. Looking at her makes my face hurt.

"Sorry. I forgot to call you back," I say sheepishly.

Hadley lifts one side of her mouth into a smirk that looks more like a wince. "I figured you'd call if you couldn't come."

"Couldn't come where?" Mom says, now holding Hadley lightly under the chin and turning her face this way and that, as if it's an item in a store that she's thinking about purchasing.

Before I have a chance to say anything, Hadley cuts in. "Evie's sleeping over."

Mom nods absently, her eyes still stuck on Hadley's face. I stare at Mom, willing her to look at me and understand that I don't want to go, that she should say I can't, but she's lost in the bruises.

"Gotta powder my nose," Hadley announces. "Is that all right?"

"Sure. Down the—"

"I know where," Hadley interrupts. "Powder my nose," she calls from the hallway, snickering, "Isn't it weird that I just said that?"

"What happened?" Mom whispers as soon as Hadley's out of earshot. "She said she got in a fight at school."

"Yeah. That's what happened."

"*Oh*," Mom groans. "That poor girl." Mom shakes her head, then, liking how it tosses her curls, shakes it again. "How does the other girl look?"

"I was thinking, what if I stayed?"

"Stayed where?" Mom asks her reflection.

"Well, here. Home. I mean, you're going out, and, well, no one will be here."

"The house can be empty for a night, Evie. We won't be robbed. Go to your sleepover!"

"But what if I want—"

Mom glances over at me through the mirror, and our eyes lock for a second, but we're really just looking at each other's reflections, which feels like we aren't looking at each other at all. I will her to understand me—that I want her to forbid me to go. I almost say it to her, *I don't want to go.* But then Hadley returns, her backpack still on her shoulders, and Mom breaks our gaze, reaching out toward Hadley's face.

"I could do something with makeup," she says running her fingers in the air over Hadley's cheeks as if she were blending the makeup in right that moment. "Cover the bruises."

"No, thanks. I sort of like them."

"Pardon?" Mom drops her hand, steps back, and blinks.

"I like the colors they turn."

"Well," Mom says, and nothing after that.

Chapter TWENTY-TWO

THE NIGHT AT HADLEY'S is surprisingly normal. Her parents aren't home. Are they ever home? We pop popcorn for her little brothers the old-fashioned way, with oil and a pan, and slice apples that turn yellow before we have the chance to eat them. The five of us watch a beauty pageant on TV. We pick our favorites and razz the contestants who are clearly ugly under their makeup and hairstyles.

"I should be in a pageant," Hadley announces. "Just like this!" She waves her hands around her bruised face, presenting it.

"A Halloween pageant, maybe," the oldest of her brothers says.

Hadley wolf howls, and the boys giggle, and one of them grabs her arm tight in both hands, his face contorted with painful glee. In that moment everyone loves her, including me.

Upstairs, there's Hadley's queen-sized bed, but we'll sleep on the floor. She sets up two sleeping bags at its foot. I don't say anything about this, or Garrett Murray and her suspension, or Chad in the burgundy car, and I'm relieved when Hadley doesn't mention any of these topics, either.

We lie in the dark next to each other, both on our backs. Hadley's stuck plastic glow-in-the-dark stars to her ceiling; they have dark spots in them—shadowy tumors—from the wads of poster putty that hold them aloft.

She's the one to speak. "What are people saying about me?"

I figured she'd ask this, and I have an answer ready. "That you got in a fight and that you got suspended."

"I attacked *him*," she says.

"Yeah?" I've made a promise to myself to sound casual, no matter what she tells me.

"Do people know that?"

"Maybe," I say.

"It wasn't him at all. He only hit me because I wouldn't stop. I told Capp and everything." She shrugs, and the fabric of the sleeping bag whispers under her shoulders. "I don't care anyway."

I wait for a second. "Hadley?" She doesn't answer. "Hadley? Why'd you . . . *do* that?"

Silence, then finally, "Dunno."

"Did he, you know, threaten you?"

"No."

"Did you argue?"

"No."

"You just attacked him?"

"I guess so."

Neither of us says anything after that. I'm exhausted suddenly, body tired. I'm dropping down into sleep when I think I hear Hadley say, "I wanted to know what it felt like." But by then, I'm already gone.

I have the dream about Zabet again, the one in the mall, all those identical beaten faces on sale. I wake up to find Zabet herself, sitting Indian-style at the foot of my sleeping bag. I almost say her name, but then I realize that it's not Zabet but Hadley, her face painted in a soldier's camouflage of shadows and bruises.

When she sees that I'm awake, she whispers, "Get up."

"It's still night," I mumble.

"Yeah," she agrees and rises, grabbing my wrist and half pulling me up. I stand the rest of the way and stumble after her as she gathers sweaters and sneakers.

When I see the shoes, I'm suddenly all the way awake. I shake my head. "I'm not going outside."

"Get dressed," she says. She already has her jeans on and her nightshirt tucked into the waistband.

I take a step back and grab on to the edge of her dresser. "I'm not going into the woods," I say because suddenly I realize that of course that's where she wants to go, where she's wanted to go all night, where she wanted to go when she invited me over.

She doesn't respond, just yanks a sweater over my head. I stand and endure it, feeling suddenly like a child dressed hurriedly in the dark. She lifts her backpack from the corner and shrugs it on.

"Come on," I say, sitting down. "Let's go back to sleep."

"No."

"What's the point? No one's . . . nothing's out there."

Hadley sizes me up. "So why not go, then?" she asks.

And that's how I trap myself, because the reason I don't want to go into the woods is precisely the opposite of what I've said: I'm scared that something—someone—*is* out there, which, Hadley would argue, is exactly the reason to go look. She kneels down in front of me, lifts my leg, and wrestles my foot into a shoe. I wonder if Zabet were here, alive and here, if she would go out into the woods at night if Hadley had wanted her to. My shoe draws tight against my foot as Hadley gives the laces a last yank and crosses them into a knot.

⟳

In stories the woods always look completely different at night than they do during the day, spooky and scary and oogy and boogy. But in Hokepe Woods, the trees are still trees, and the leaves are still leaves. And Hadley is still tugging me along after her, like always. She's got ahold of my wrist, and she counts off the tree ribbons as she passes them, "One, two, three . . ."

We get to the spot where I know we're headed, the muddy spot where Zabet was found. But instead of stopping there, Hadley yanks me past, a few rows of trees away, until I can't see it anymore. She stops in front of a toppled tree. Tree into log, body into corpse. Hadley sits on the log, crossing one leg over the other, and pats herself down until she realizes that she has no coat and, therefore, no cigarettes. She shrugs her backpack off and sets it on her lap to rifle through it. As she does, something in it clanks, metallic.

"What's even in there?" I ask. "Tent poles?"

She looks at me mysteriously, then reaches in and pulls out a flashlight.

"You didn't want to use that while we were walking here?" I grumble.

She shrugs. "Someone might have seen it."

"No one's out here," I say; then wish I hadn't, because it sounds like a dare.

There are night bugs shuttling along the grooves of the log, their shells silvery and bluish, their legs translucent. Hadley gives up looking for cigarettes and looks around at the forest instead, nodding like she's satisfied.

"We'll hear anyone coming from here."

I squat down in the leaves in front of the log. I touch two fingers to the ground to hold myself steady, and my fingers sink into the soft dirt. The ground is cold at its surface, warmer underneath.

"Killers return to the scene of the crime all the time."

"In the movies," I mutter.

"I wish this were a movie," Hadley says.

"Why?"

"My boobs would be bigger." She gestures at them. I smile despite myself before looking away, embarrassed.

"And if we were in danger, we could tell by the music," I offer.

"And, in the end, he'd come," Hadley says.

We both hush then, and I feel a frisson, something cold trickling at my center, drip after drip. I reach out for Hadley's arm, even though I'm angry at her for waking me, for dragging me out into the woods, for calling the killer to us with her bravado. It seems like wherever he is now, whatever pickup truck he's driving, whatever bar fight he's fighting, whichever back alley he's lurking in, his path will bend to us, curving along the line of her voice.

As I reach for Hadley, she's reaching for me, too. When we see what we're both doing, we laugh at how we've spooked ourselves, and it feels like a regular slumber party again, as if we've indulged in nothing more serious than scary stories. It would have been something if the killer had come crashing through the woods right then and there. You wouldn't believe it, not even in a story.

In reality, it takes almost an hour more before he arrives.

Chapter TWENTY-THREE

WE BOTH HEAR IT AT THE SAME TIME, and Hadley makes a sound around the thumb she's biting on, not a shushing sound but more of a hiss, which still means *quiet!* At first, I tell myself that the noise we're hearing is just one of the deer crashing through the woods, but the footfalls are even and distinctly human. It's a sound I've had hours of experience learning to recognize: a person walking through the woods. Each step—each limp turning of leaves—is a little louder than the last.

I can't see anyone through the striping of trees. So instead of looking for whoever's approaching, I watch Hadley perched up there on her log. Her pupils scan from the left to the right across the patch of woods in front of her and then skip back and slide left to right again, like she's reading lines in a book. She is still, straight as a reed, as if called to attention, and her thumb is a small pink creature caught between her teeth.

"Hadley," I whisper.

She lifts her hand from the log and brings it down palm flat, like a director on a movie—*Silence!* Her eyes dart to me, to make sure that I know she means business; then they return to the trees, scanning,

scanning. I tell myself that it must be Hadley's dad who's approaching, returned home with the taste of mistress in his mouth to find our sleeping bags empty, or her violent little blond brothers, who followed us out on a dare, or some insomniac Hokepe housewife, some dreamer, charmed by the night woods. I can feel the hollow places in my body, the arteries that flutter with the coming of my blood, the chambers of my heart that flood and void. The footsteps and my heartbeat become one plodding rhythm. And it takes me a moment to realize that the footsteps have stopped, because I'm still hearing my own pulse in my ears.

Hadley's eyes halt and lock on a spot over my shoulder and to our left, about a dozen yards away. I know that spot.

We stay still, frozen, for another minute, or maybe it isn't even a minute; it seems long, as long as a staring contest, as long as holding your breath underwater, as long as the moment before you confess to a lie. Our eyes are the only things that move, finding and holding each other's; then Hadley's eyes let go of mine, flit back to the trees, back to me, back to the trees again. I think of a statue game that Zabet and I used to play when we were little. We would finish a hand-clapping rhyme—*sunshine, sunshine, moonshine, freeze!*—and freeze, staring at each other, our palms still pressed together from the last clap, children praying, until one of us twitched and the other laughed.

Slowly, I turn my head to the spot where Hadley's looking. There's too little light, too many trees; I can't see anyone. I hear another shuffle of leaves and then a groan—a voice! Under the cover of this noise, simultaneously, as if we'd practiced it before, Hadley and I stand and step toward each other, pointing our toes along the ground so that our feet slide silently under the leaves. Hadley leaves her backpack on the log, though she pulls out the flashlight and slips it into her back pocket. I reach out for Hadley's hands, and she's reaching out for mine, too. I grab and then nearly drop them. They're hot; mine are cold, clammy. Hadley leans the front of her body against my back, urging me forward. With our hands knotted together and our bodies near joined, like some circus freak of a girl, we begin to step toward the stranger.

"Stop when I stop," Hadley whispers right into my ear. I can feel her heartbeat, echoing up through her bone, muscle, skin, and sweater, pounding against my back. Or maybe it's my own heart I hear. I nod, and she flinches as my hair brushes against her face. I can smell our sweat, not the typical muggy, locker-room perspiration, but a sharp, acrid flop-sweat brewed from adrenaline. I hear another groan, which makes me stop in my tracks, but Hadley keeps moving, pushing us forward, her toes clipping my heels. *It's nothing,* I think. *Some drunk.* But at the same time, I know what Hadley's thinking: *It's him.*

I catch a flicker of movement between the trees, and Hadley must have seen it, too, because we both stop at once. He is where we knew he'd be, near that little muddy patch where Zabet died. We stop behind a tree. When I peer out around its trunk, I can see his legs, his faded blue jeans, and a ratty pair of yellow work boots, the same brand the boys in our school wear to try to look tough. He's sitting a few feet from the mud, facing it, his legs stretched out straight in front of him. Something glimmers in his hand—a knife? a gun?— and it makes me draw back, knocking my head into Hadley's nose. It must hurt but she doesn't make a sound. I start to say *sorry,* but then, not wanting to risk the noise, squeeze her hands instead. She squeezes mine back. There's the click and gasp of a bottle cap, and I exhale as the bottle just has. The glimmer was his beer bottle, that's all.

Hadley squeezes my hand again and leans into me with one of her shoulders, and I know what she means by this. We can't really see him from here. We should move one line of trees closer. There's an oak in front of us with a wide, leathery trunk, wide enough to hide the two of us. We shuffle forward, and I worry that he'll be able to hear us, that he's already heard us and is feigning drunkenness and ignorance, that as soon as we get within striking distance, he'll turn and pounce. We reach the oak, and I let go of Hadley to touch my hands to its trunk, like it's a goalpost or a base, the object in a children's game designated safe. I rest my forehead against the tree, the rough whorls and ridges of its bark, and wait while Hadley leans around to look at him. I wonder if I'll be able to feel the knowledge enter her just by standing here next to her, like the ozone of a storm, like the crackle that comes from running my hand over a skirt full of static.

"Vie," she breathes. "It's him."

I look.

Jonah Luks is beautiful. Drunk, in the mud, in the middle of the night, he is still beautiful. He sits on the ground. He holds his bottle of beer with both hands, one gripping the neck, the other caressing the label, the base. He stares at the muddy patch of ground with no wisdom or remorse in his eyes. He is blinking, not crying, just blinking. He's staring at her, of course: Zabet. He can see her there, in his memory, clear as he saw her months ago.

Hadley tenses behind me, her hands squeezing mine, mashing my fingers together, too hard. She squeezes harder and I want to cry out, but of course I can't make a noise or Jonah will hear us. So I endure the pain, letting it rush from my hands up through my wrists and forearms, finally washing out at my elbows. And it is the same as when you tell yourself to stop fighting anything—the cold, the wet, the exhaustion, the fear—you relax into it; your body still feels it, yes, but you have given it permission to live inside you.

Then Hadley drops my hands. My fingers splay and thrum with the dull remnants of her grip. She takes a silent step back, and I turn to look at her. She has bitten in on her lower lip, her mouth an expressionless slit. Her eyes are narrow, watching, carefully watching Jonah. Her hand, mottled white and pink from gripping mine, slides around her back and into her pocket, coming out with the flashlight. She squeezes it now, its dumb metal shaft numb to the pain of her grasp. It strikes me that Hadley has never met Jonah. In her mind, he is a stranger (certainly), a drifter (perhaps), and Zabet's killer (most probably). She hits the flashlight into her palm as if it were a nightstick; its dry smack is answered by Jonah shifting in the leaves. Hadley sucks in a breath.

I have seen this look on her face before—eyeing the booths of college boys in the diner, nearly mowing down Chad in the parking lot, walking down the school hall after her fight with Garrett— a hardening of her eyes as if they are made of stone and not jelly, a thinning of her lips, and a small decisive dip of her chin. Hadley is working herself up for something, something involving Jonah and the shaft of that flashlight, something bad.

No! I want to shout at her. *That's Jonah! Jonah!* But before I can say anything, she raises the flashlight in her hand like a sword brandished in battle, her upper lip lifting in an uncertain snarl. *Hadley!*

I should shout. *Stop!* I can't speak. Hadley sucks in a breath and lifts her foot from the muck of the leaves to step forward into the attack. I'm mute. I'm cowardly. I'm weak. So I do the only thing I can think of. With a yelp, I pitch myself forward, out from the safety of the trees, out into the clearing, out toward that patch of mud, out to save Jonah Luks.

Chapter TWENTY-FOUR

I LAND ON ALL FOURS, my hands sinking into the wet, slimy ground. My hair has flipped over in front of my face, a dark, oily mass, which smells too much like my pillow at home—somehow a foreign smell, a foreign object to me now. I feel a burn in my right knee. I must have scraped it on the way down, though I don't know how because everything here is soft and wet and without edges. There's a rustle— Jonah. I don't hear anything behind me—no Hadley.

With a muddy hand, I reach up to push the hair out of my face and stand. My knee is tender, but when I look down, the fabric of my pant leg isn't torn. Jonah's in front of me, still on his ass, right where he was before. He *has* moved, though, because his beer is spilled, fizzing softly onto the ground. He's leaning back on his hands, blinking rapidly like I've just startled him from a sound sleep.

"Hey," I say. I take a short hopping step toward him, away from the tree, from Hadley, like one of those birds who pretends it's injured in order to draw prey away from its nest. "I must look a mess," I say, with my mother's words, not mine. "I mean, muddy."

Jonah's eyes narrow down to a squint. "Evie?" It's funny. When he says my name, it feels like a promise to me, an intimacy. But really it's just my name; anyone could say it.

"Yeah." I take another step toward him.

"Is it morning?" He gazes up at the sky and confirms that it's not. "Are you . . . ? What are you doing here?"

"I was at a sleepover," I say, stupidly. But Jonah, I'm noticing, is far stupider than I am right now. He shakes his head, but that's too much for him, so he raises his hands to his forehead in order to hold his head steady. *You're drunk*, I want to say, but how naïve, how lame, to point out something like that. Jonah spreads his knees, aims between them, and hurks a glob of spit onto the ground. He wipes his mouth with the back of his hand and tips his chin up so that he can peer out at me from under half-lidded eyes.

"You're hurt." Jonah points a wandering finger at my leg.

"Oh, I—my knee. I scraped it."

The truth is, it doesn't hurt much at all. But somehow, without meaning to, I've exaggerated the injury. I was hopping before, I know I was, and now I've got my leg hanging limp at my side as if it were broken. To prove that I'm okay, I sit down, right in front of him, and begin to hitch up my pant leg to get a better look. Jonah leans forward, kicking his beer bottle so that it skitters through the leaves like a little animal. He hunkers close to me, so close that I inhale the loamy smell of beer on him and see the border between his pink lip and white chin. He lays his hands—the actual palms of them—on my leg. I shiver straight through, not from fear.

Jonah inspects my knee. Mostly it's just rubbed pink, but there're a few dots of blood where the skin has been snagged. It's not much of a wound, but Jonah places his hands on either side of it, framing the scrape. I try to remember the last time someone touched my bare knee. Maybe the doctor with his practiced fingers and rubber mallet, maybe my mother, after I scraped it when I was little. She would blow on my scrapes to cool them, the wind of her breath causing the pain to dance in circles. That was years ago, though. It seems like no one's touched me in years.

"You need a Band-Aid."

"It's nothing," I say.

His hands don't move, but I can feel them all over me, like they're not just framing my knee, but framing every part of me, foot, shoulder, and chin, framing me like a painting, like a photograph, like a house, framing me like a thought, like an innocent man. Jonah stares down at my knee, at the black beads of my blood, the white lace of my scratches, and I am caught between his two hands. I don't want those hands to move, not ever, but finally they lift away. I can feel where they were, though, just for a second, the way you can feel the spit from someone's kiss evaporate off of your cheek.

Jonah stares down at his knees, like my knees made him wonder about his own. Then, without a word to announce it, he lumbers up, kicking grass and leaves and twigs, brutish, clumsy. So I stand, too. He is drunk and, therefore, unsteady on his feet, swaying so slightly that looking at him makes me a little dizzy. He crosses one foot in front of the other, as if he has decided to turn and walk to one side of the clearing; then his knees buckle. I gasp, but he catches himself before falling, only to rise again and take two tripping steps forward, almost staggering into me, his toes digging furrows in the ground. I scuffle away from him but realize at the last second that I'm about to tread straight through Zabet's patch of mud. I halt at its edge, teetering, trying to catch my balance, as if it were not simply the edge of a mud puddle I'm standing on but the edge of a cliff. Jonah brings himself to a stop, too, his forward momentum still caught in his frozen posture so that he leans up and over me. I imagine what we must look like to Hadley: Jonah towering, leering, me cringing away.

The tableau holds for a quivering second and then it breaks as, with a sigh, Jonah lets his legs give way, and he slumps against me, nearly taking me to the ground with him. I make a noise—"Oomf!"—and try to shore up under him. He's impossibly heavy. But the cotton of his shirt is soft on my cheek; his breath is warm on my neck. If he were sober right now, maybe he'd whisper something against my skin. I strain under his weight and somehow, miraculously, hold him up.

"Right there," Jonah says. His head is hanging over my shoulder right over the patch of mud. "She was *there*." He mutters something else.

"Can you walk? *Jonah*. Can you—?"

In answer, he shuffles one of his feet forward, and I shore up under him so that his arm is around my shoulders and my hand is bracing his waist. I steer him back toward the street; it takes all the strength my arms have in them. His head lolls to the side, his cheek coming to rest on top of my head.

"Your hair tickles," he slurs.

"Step," I order Jonah. "Step." He lifts his yellow boots and obeys.

I think of the Whisperers right then, their pale, eager faces. It's almost like they're sitting up there in the trees, bony legs dangling like creepers, watching us. I imagine telling this story to them in the cafeteria on Monday, their gasps, their coos. This time, I wouldn't have to make up a single thing.

We limp out of the woods, Jonah and I, and I don't look back at the tree where Hadley's hiding. I keep my face forward, my eyes on the path in front of me. I picture her peeking out from behind the trunk, watching me walk away, like all the times I've watched her.

∼

When we reach the car, Jonah rouses himself a little. He manages to yank a set of keys out of his pocket and to hoist himself up into the driver's seat before passing out again, this time with his cheek against the wheel. I stare at him helplessly. I could leave him here. But then I picture the jogging divorcees surrounding his car the next morning like a forensics team, running in place as they peer in at Jonah's slumped body, jogging back to their pastel kitchens and pastel phones, and lodging their complaints. He'll get fired if I leave him.

The neighborhood is dark around me, even darker than on winter mornings when I can empty my entire satchel before the sun comes up. All the lights are out in the Hokepe houses, except for one yellow window far down the street.

I climb up into the truck next to Jonah. The floor is infested with beer cans that crinkle and squeak when I step on them, like they're mice or bugs. It's almost as grimy in here as it is in the back of the truck. Even in the dark, I can see a sanding of dirt and crumbs on the dash and in the folds of the seats. And there are more than just cans on the floor—wadded-up papers, yellowing T-shirts, fast-food wrappers shining with old grease, and a lone sneaker with quarter-size holes in its uppers like something was trapped and had gnawed its way out.

"Jonah." I shake his shoulder. "Jonah, hey." He groans. He's turned the other way, huddled against the side window, so all I can see is the back of his head, his soft, unwashed hair. I can't even see if his eyes are open or closed. "Hey!" I smack his shoulder and, when I get no reaction, punch it with a thud. Nothing.

I get out and go around to the driver's side of the cab, pushing Jonah across the bench seat and out of my way. He flops over, grumbling nonsense, but then relents, curling into a ball against the passenger door. His car keys glimmer in the sea of junk on the floor; I pluck them up and buckle myself in. I don't bother with Jonah's seat belt. He's begun to snore.

I drive us out of Hokepe Woods and then farther. We pass by my house just before we cross out of Chippewa. I spot a beige car in the driveway, Rick-from-the-bank's. Windows dark, lights out in the house. My mother's own sleepover. I imagine another Evie awake in her bed, hearing Rick-from-the-bank and her mother's noises through the wall, thinking of her father, wherever he is, knowing he wouldn't care. Or maybe that other Evie is not awake, not listening, but is asleep, wrapped in her sheets. Me, someone else, drives by in this stranger's car, no more than a passenger through the night of her world.

❧

I don't know where Jonah lives exactly, so I pull into one of the neighborhoods near the college. Mom and I have rented houses out here before. The rentals are, for the most part, shoddy and ill-used due to a seasonal rotation of college kids who burn ramen noodles on top of the stove, who coat the floors with sticky beer and the windowsills with mystic pools of candle wax, who stack intricate structures of lawn furniture and leave them to crack, oxidize, and glimmer in a cocoon of spiderwebs, who adopt pets only to abandon them when summer comes, so that armies of semiferal cats yowl, vomit mouse bones, and die under the grooved wheels of cars that don't even bother to stop.

I choose a street at random, a little piece of free curb. Jonah is still asleep when I pull over and cut the engine. I can look at him openly while he sleeps, without fear of discovery. There's a crust of wax in the curve of his ear and the rosy bloom of a coming pimple in the fold of his nose. But I forgive him these imperfections immediately and without negotiation. He is Jonah, beautiful Jonah. And I feel that I understand him, and that he would understand me if we knew each other even a little. I reach forward and touch his shoulder. My fingers rise and fall with his sleeping breath. Beneath them is the cotton of his shirt, beneath that his skin, his fat, his muscle, his bone, his marrow . . . and, is there a center? A core? Something essential? Or do the layers just fan out again: marrow, bone, muscle, fat, skin, cotton, air?

I watch my hand as it moves from Jonah's shoulder to his cheek. A muscle in his face jumps under my fingers and I gasp, startled, but I don't pull my hand away. Instead I lean forward; closer, until I can see the smudge of his beard; closer, the pores speckling his nose; closer, the threads of vein in his eyelids; closer, the pumice of his chapped lips. His breath wends from his mouth, rotten with beer and sleep. And, if he were perfect—his lips supple, his breath sweet—I wouldn't have been able to do it. I wouldn't have felt that I had the right to lean even closer, that extra fragment of an inch, and press my lips against his.

Kissing Jonah isn't how I had imagined it would be. It isn't how I would tell it, if I were telling someone the story of it. His lips are parched, flaking, paralyzed by sleep. My lips, his lips. I register this not with excitement or nervousness but with a disinterested curiosity. I release my lips and then press them to his again, just to see, once more, how it might feel.

Is this how it is for Hadley when Garrett smashes his mouth into hers? Or my mother when Rick-from-the-bank smears the perfect crayon lines of her lipstick? Is this the secret of a kiss: not that you feel something but that you feel nothing? I pull away and take a deep breath and then have to pause and fight a giddy peal of laughter that tickles the back of my throat. *One more try*, I tell myself. And this time when I lean down to kiss Jonah, he kisses me back.

Then we are kissing. Jonah's hand fumbles along my waist. His lips move under mine like blind things, newborn things searching for light. And all at once, the startling, wet muscle of his tongue is there in my mouth. All my questions about kissing are answered at once, the sum of my hypotheses exposed as false, boxes ticked with checkmarks right down the line. I don't have to think or worry or be afraid; for once, there is none of that. There is only the ferment of Jonah's breath, the grit of crumbs under my palms as I lean across the seat, and finally me, perfect me, wondrous me, pushing closer to Jonah, kissing Jonah, when he wakes and opens his eyes.

"Oh," he says when he sees me there at the other end of his lips.

It is not the *oh* of being presented with a surprise gift, nor is it the *oh* of finding a spider in the shower; rather, it is the tiny syllable mouthed during the pause in someone's tedious story, an inoffensive and noncommittal *oh*, its only purpose to show that, yes, you have been listening to whatever the speaker droned on about. *Oh.* It says everything.

I wilt back across the seat, my retreat ending only because I'm stopped by the truck door. I slip my hand behind my back, groping for the door handle. Shame creeps from its secret hovels in my throat and eye sockets. This shame presses against me, doubling, tripling, expanding until I might explode into ribbons or confetti. And I will allow it; I will let myself explode, just as soon as I find the goddamn door handle.

Jonah wipes the back of his hand across his mouth. I stare at it. *What repugnant cells have you wiped away?* I want to say. *What slimes have you gotten rid of?* Jonah sees the look on my face and drops the hand into his lap, where it twitches. I know he wants to dry it against his jeans; I can as good as see him resist the impulse.

"Oh," he says again.

I am silent. I am disgusting. I am terrible.

"Weird," he says next. He fidgets, but sleepily, scratches at an elbow in slow motion. His words are still slurry. "Weird . . . night."

He waits for a reply, but I don't have one to offer. I watch him, my hand creeping behind my back secretly, like I'm going for my weapon, the firm, cold handle of the door.

"Back there . . . you fell out of . . . *trees*." He manages to lift his heavy eyelids a bit wider and speaks like this was wondrous, not to be believed. "There you were."

This conversation feels familiar, but I can't say exactly how. My hand continues its crawl across the truck door, moving over the window crank, the too-small armrest, the tiny metal ashtray, before finally closing around the door handle itself, right at the middle of my back. And just as I take that lever in my hand, it hits me: This conversation is familiar because it's like every conversation that Jonah and I have had, *only backward*. This time, instead of me trying to charm and cajole, it is Jonah. Instead of Jonah being wordless and searching for escape, it is me. I pause with my hand on the lever, fascinated, waiting to see what Jonah will say next.

He's looking at me through his sacrificial-cow lashes, his dumb blink. It's the kindest look he's ever given me, right now, when he is rejecting me. A tiny smile touches his lips, and he looks down and back up again, as if preparing to tell me something he shouldn't.

"I thought you were her," he slurs. "But that couldn't . . . *you* couldn't . . . you weren't her. You were . . . you. I just, for a second, in the trees, I *thought*—"

"Her?" I croak. I press back against the door, the window, on the nape of my neck, damp from the condensation of our kisses. My kisses.

"Her," he says. His chin begins to drop down to his chest like he might pass out again.

"Who?" I ask. His head dips and then jerks up again. He mutters something, his eyes closed. "Jonah, who did you think I was? Jonah!"

He lifts his head, opens his eyes and says, as clear as can be, "That dead girl."

And, with that, I lift the door handle and fall backward into the night.

⟶

The landing hurts. I hit the road on my back and knock my head against the pavement. I bite down on my lip, through it, actually. When I open my mouth, I can feel my tooth slide up and out of where it was buried in my skin, slippery and metallic with blood. The breath has been knocked out of me. I gasp for air, suck at it, but my rib cage won't expand and my lungs won't fill, as if the rules have changed and I'm no longer allowed to breathe. Jonah is saying my name in a tone of dumb wonder, and I can hear him crawling across the seat. It is this—the idea of his pitying drunk face—that makes me stand and then makes me run.

I run until I can breathe again, until I can't breathe because the breath isn't enough and my sides are going to pull apart, sinew from rib bone. I cut through yards and dodge headlights, running until I have to stop and cough great gusts of lost breath down at the ground. I spend ten minutes crouched in the corner of someone's backyard until I'm sure Jonah's given up, if he even looked for me at all, that is. *The dead girl.* That's what he said. I thought he knew her name.

I emerge blocks away from where I started and walk down the road. I blot the blood on my lip and chin with one of my sleeves. Still, I am a zombie, a muddy fright. Despite this, or maybe because of it, I manage to flag down a car, a group of college students—glittered, tipsy—coming back from a party.

"Are you okay?" the girl in the passenger seat asks. "How old are you?"

I know the answer to this one. "Eighteen. Can I get a ride?"

"I'm not taking her anywhere weird," the kid who's driving says.

"Please," I say. "I just want to go home." So he agrees. And when I get out of the car, the college kids call after me to "be good" and to "sleep it off." They think I'm drunk, and what else would I be, wandering around in my pajama bottoms and Hadley's sweater, bloody-lipped, streaks of leaf mulch down my front, mud painting my face, and the scent of Jonah's spilled beer still clinging to my skin? Which is just how Mr. McCabe finds me when he answers his door.

Chapter TWENTY-FIVE

HE'S ALREADY AWAKE. The lights are on behind him, and there's the buzz of the TV. A box of voices. What did haunted people do before TV? Radio. What did haunted people do before radio? Talk to ghosts, maybe. He's dressed neatly in old-fashioned pajamas—the kind that button up—and a robe, slippers, even.

"Evie!" he says, though I haven't seen him for weeks. He takes in my muddy sweater and bloody lip in a glance. *Are you all right?* I expect him to ask, alarmed, and I'll say, *Yeah, I just bit my lip. I fell. I got lost is all. I didn't know where else to go.* I have the answer folded up in my mouth. But Mr. McCabe doesn't ask me if I'm all right, that most basic of parental questions. Instead, he smiles and waves me in.

I follow him to the living room. The TV is set to an infomercial; a pair of manicured hands slices vegetables into slivers, fruit into pulpy, shining wedges. He has a snack set up on the side table, mindful squares of crackers and cheese, one half eaten, made into a rectangle by his bite.

"Why don't you sit down?" he says. The couch pillows are set at right angles. "Would you like something? Food? A beverage?"

I'm suddenly aware of my state of dress, more so than if he'd said something about it. I tug at the sides of Hadley's sweater, pulling them down. My lip hurts; it feels huge. I'm shivering, I realize, even though it's warm that night, warm in Mr. McCabe's living room. I have shivers running a loop through me, again and again. *Calm down,* I tell my body. *You calm down now.* And my body obeys enough to stop shivering. "I'm not hungry."

"Something to drink, maybe?"

"That's okay."

"I was having a snack," he says, indicating the plate.

He sits in the chair across from me, and behind him, the pretty hands on the television chop something slick and oceanic, luminous and white.

"Sometimes I like food in the night," he says.

I glance down at my own muddy front. I have the story ready—why I'm muddy, why I'm injured, why I'm here—so why won't he ask me? Mom would blanch at the sight of me, tell me to change my clothes, wash my face, run a comb through my hair, and put something on my lip so it won't swell with infection. *Tripped and fell?* she'd say. *Well, you've never been graceful.* Then she'd tip her head to the side and add, *Once that lip scabs over, you can wear a nice bright gloss. Trust me. No one will even notice.*

But Mr. McCabe. I'd expected him to wrap me in a hug at first sight and, at the slightest shiver, wrap a blanket right around my shoulders. To sit me down and listen soberly, to keep asking if I was all right, if I was *sure* I was all right. And to give me the respect of not believing me when I said that I was.

I try to make the shivers start up again so that he'll be forced to take some interest, but the shivers won't come. I try to fake them, but it just looks like I'm restless.

"It tastes different, when you eat at night," I offer, and he nods vigorously and smiles.

"A secret meal."

We sit in silence. He crosses his legs and touches his lip self-consciously as if feeling for his own injury. But then he jerks his hand away from his lip, as if he's committed a faux pas, and slides it into his robe pocket.

"How are you, Evie?" he says at the same moment that I say, "You're probably wondering why I'm here."

"No." He shakes his head and sits back as if to get a few inches farther away from my question. "You're welcome here. Anytime. You can just show up. A friend of Elizabeth's—" He stops, not finishing with *is a friend of mine*. I forgot, somehow, that he calls her Elizabeth, and it takes me a moment to place the name, to remember that he's talking about his daughter, about Zabet. "You don't have to say anything," he says, "explain anything."

With that, my story shrivels up inside me, and, as if it were the only thing keeping me upright, I exhale and sink back into the couch. I'm so tired.

"Let me get you something to eat . . . or cocoa," he mumbles, standing and fussing with the fall of his robe.

"No," I tell him. He sits down immediately, even though I've said it neither loudly nor harshly. "I don't . . . Really, I'm not hungry."

"Would you like"—he touches his lip again but doesn't seem to realize this time that he's doing it. "Would you like a ride home? Probably you would. I'll go crank up the car."

"Actually." I twist in the chair, glance at my own muddy hands and then the manicured hands on the TV screen. "I thought I could maybe stay here tonight?"

"Of course," he says, in a falling tone, as if relieved. And I realize what it was before—his nerves, his fussiness, his insistence that he wouldn't ask me questions. It wasn't that he didn't care. It was that he was afraid that he might scare me away; one careless word or sharp movement and I'd be gone.

"You're . . . are you tired?" Mr. McCabe half rises, his arms out as if I were a small child fallen asleep whom he'd scoop up and carry to bed. "It's late."

I am tired. Bone tired. Marrow tired. It settles on me like a sheet lifted and laid over my face. I nearly lean my head back and fall asleep right there on the couch.

"Yeah," I sigh. "I'm . . . yeah."

Mr. McCabe is on his feet, waving me along, up the narrow, carpeted stairs and down the hall into a small bedroom. The bed is covered with a rumpled comforter, hunched up at the foot as if a person is crouched beneath it. The dresser drawers are each half open, loosing a spray of shirts and cords and leggings. I recognize one of the shirts, a burgundy plaid. Zabet used to wear that nearly every day. The sleeves were too long for her, so only the tips of her fingers showed, as if the shirt were slowly digesting her, savoring the last bits before it swallowed her whole. A few trinkets stand in a line along the dresser and desk—three wan shells, the slim circle of an enamel bracelet, and a music box, its ceramic flowers like frosting on a fancy cake. A drinking glass, an orphan from the set downstairs, sits at the edge of the nightstand, the water long evaporated from it.

"You can sleep here," Mr. McCabe says as he walks past me into the room. "There are pajamas." He indicates the drawer stuffed with a wad of pilled cotton. He looks around as if he's forgotten something, though everything is here, clearly memorized and untouched, made sacred by his reverent neglect. "I'm down the hall. The bathroom, too, down the hall. There's ointment, iodine, if you need to—"

"Are you sure it's okay?" I say.

"The room is yours," he says. "Sleep. Sleep tight. Don't let the— no, never mind." He touches a hand to his mouth and mutters, "Nothing will bite."

"Thanks."

We stand there for a moment amid Zabet's belongings and then, on impulse, I step forward, wrap my arms around his neck, and give him a hug. He stays very still in the loop of my arms, and I feel suddenly strong, as if I have the power to hurt him, large and solid as he is. Then he reaches up and pats my head—once, twice, fatherly—his hand lingering for a moment before lifting up and away. Finally he leaves, closing the door behind him, but I hear him pause just on the other side of it, the slight creak of the door as he lays his hand on it. "Good night," he says one more time, waiting until I say good night back before he steps away, as if he needs to reassure himself that I'm still there.

Once he's gone, I'm alone, finally, with Zabet. I rub the nap of her hoodies and the wale of the corduroys; I put finger marks in the dust on the dresser, some of it her shed skin, right? Isn't that what dust is made of? I pick up each object—those three shells from some trip to the beach; a half-squeezed tube of hand lotion that smells like a fancy department store; a movie ticket stub—a comedy—a line of bottle caps, their crimped lips pulled open. She liked to save things, I guess. I open the jewelry box to find it filled with cookie fortunes—*A feather in the hand is better than a bird in the air. Courtesy is contagious. You will travel far and wide, for both pleasure and business. Lucky numbers: 4, 39, 74.*

I slide my hands between the mattress and the box spring, managing to lift the mattress part way up before letting it go, but Zabet didn't hide anything there. I crawl into the closet and push past old dress shoes. In the back of the closet, high up on the shelf, I find her hiding place—a dinged lighter and a pack of stale cigarettes, one half smoked, marked with her peach lip gloss. There's a notebook up there, too, filled with sketches of a houseplant, a teetering line of condominiums, and what must have been Zabet's own feet. I wonder if she had secretly wanted to be an artist. Maybe this should make me sad, but instead I think at least she'll never find out that she wasn't good enough.

I pull open the dresser drawers, and the clothes that hung out collapse back into the drawer or spill out onto the carpet. I shuck off Hadley's muddy sweater, my sneakers, and pajama pants. I find a threadbare T-shirt and a pair of men's boxer shorts. I stand naked in the center of the room before I put them on, my skin goose-pimpled. I stare at myself in the mirror nailed to the closet door. I press my fingers to my knee. The beads of blood have hardened and darkened like the carapaces of insects. The worse injury is my mouth, the wound black, velvety in the dim light. I finger the cut, and it fires back at me in pain. There's a smudge of dried blood on my chin. I lick my hand and rub until it's gone.

I dress in Zabet's clothes—the shirt and boxer shorts. The fabric feels strange against my skin, too rough in some places, too worn in others, and then, suddenly, it feels fine, like these clothes have been worn by no other body but my own.

I turn in a slow circle. Zabet is everywhere in this room, her touch on everything. But of her death? There are no clues, no illumination, no solutions. For the first time, I consider that maybe there's nothing to find. Maybe there's no story to Zabet's murder. Maybe the story is simply that she's dead. Just dead.

I imagine Mr. McCabe coming into this room every night, every morning, standing at its center unable to bring himself to move anything, not to straighten the comforter nor tuck away a pair of shoes, for fear that he might wear out the last bit of her. After all, it is his Elizabeth who chewed that pen cap and then cast it into the corner. It is she who wadded her clothes into drawers, she who hid the pack of cigarettes. She, whose teeth no longer chew, whose body withers in her last outfit, whose lungs have no breath to give cigarettes.

And me, I'm looking for scraps of Zabet in this room because I didn't even know her. She was this little girl from a little corner of my childhood. She was a stranger, really, and I have no claim on her. This whole time—lying to Mr. McCabe, befriending Hadley, looking for Zabet's killer—it hasn't been about Zabet at all. It's been about me, my curiosity, my loneliness, my fear. In a way, I've been using Zabet, her memory, to get what I need. And maybe, in that same way, I'm just as bad as her killer. After all, isn't that what he did? Made her into something less than a girl, something less than a person, to get what he needed?

I make a decision. I begin to clean.

I open each of the drawers all the way, unearthing the clothes in armfuls. I heap them on top of the dresser, disturbing the dust, and then I fold them one by one, stacking them in a gradation of colors like cereal boxes on a grocery-store shelf. I lift up the comforter and let it float in the air as it falls; whatever secret loitering scent there was of her is chased away. I reach up and fish the cigarettes out of the back of the closet. I position a cigarette in the uninjured side of my mouth and smoke it halfway down, sitting there on the bed, the covers pulled up to my lap. I drop the end in the empty drinking glass where it curls into a worm of ash. I slide under the blankets, lay the weight of my head on the pillow (*Her head lay here*, I think), and fall right asleep.

You'd think that maybe I'd dream Zabet's dreams. But I sleep without dreaming. I wake early and change back into my pajama pants and Hadley's sweater, though they feel like a stranger's clothes now. I fold the T-shirt and boxer shorts, adding them to one of my tidy stacks in the dresser drawer. The wound on my lip is still open, hasn't even scabbed; I glance at it in the mirror and wonder, briefly, if it'll need stitches. I'm sort of grateful for it—my bitten lip—as proof that something happened last night, something I didn't create in my head. Last thing, I make the bed, smoothing the wrinkles with an arm, brushing away any marks my body might have left. I look around at the work I've done. It's just an empty room now.

I tiptoe down to the living room, where Mr. McCabe has fallen asleep in his chair with the TV still on. I move past the gentle buzz of his snore and turn the knob slowly, and then take care that the front door opens and closes without waking him. I step out onto the porch. I'm gone. I was never there.

Chapter TWENTY-SIX

I WALK BACK ACROSS THE STREET, running my hand along the stately brick of the Hokepe Woods sign as I pass it, and then on to Hadley's house. Hadley's car is parked out front. I slip into the house through the patio door, which is still unlocked, so I figure that maybe Hadley left it open for me. Even though it's late morning, with the sun already an egg yolk in the windows, everyone in Hadley's house seems to be asleep. Her parents' cars are in the garage now—shiny, capable machines that look like they must be driven by shiny, capable people. If one of them finds me here, I'll be a stranger, some girl who breached their home, who broke in and entered. I pass through empty rooms and hallways, stepping over cracked video-game cartridges and balled-up socks, fraying stacks of newspapers and plates crusted with food, one with a string of ants trailing from it. It's a domestic apocalypse, and I'm the last survivor.

I pause outside Hadley's bedroom. She has a placard on her door left over from childhood, wooden letters that spell out her name, each painted using a different pattern—stripes, polka-dots, tiny flowers. I tell myself to open her door, but don't. Tell myself to knock, but can't do that either. She'll ask about Jonah; of course she will. And what will I tell her? About kissing him while he was sleeping? About him opening his eyes to see me hovering over him? About his disappointed *oh?* Each twist in the story is answered by an equal twist in my gut. I can't talk about any of it.

But when I open the door and peer in, I find that Hadley's not in her room, not in the bathroom either. I check what I can of the rest of the house—a puppy-pile of blond brothers in their bedroom; a bathroom rug foggy with mold; the Smiths' closed bedroom door— no Hadley. Could she still be in the woods, pressed against that tree, shivering with morning dew, waiting for my return? *No,* I tell myself. *Silly. Impossible.* Still, I figure I'd better check. But as I retrace my steps back out to the driveway, another idea occurs to me, and I go to the curb and peer through the windows of Hadley's car. There. She's asleep in the backseat. I open the car door, and her sneakered feet unfold toward the ground. One sneaker has a plug of pink gum on its bottom, made flat and slick from time and walking. Hadley opens her eyes and smiles up at me as if she'd been waiting for me to wake her.

"You're not dead," she says sleepily. And then, just as sleepily, "Fuck you."

"I'm so sorry, Had. But that guy? That was Jonah. Jonah Luks? He was drunk, you know, and I had to drive him home. But he wasn't . . . I know you might have thought he was. But he was just Jonah."

Her answer is to sit up and slide over, pressing her knees into the seat in front of her, wedging herself in. I climb in next to her. It feels familiar sitting in the backseat of an empty car, like when I was a kid, buckled in, waiting for my parents to gather their belongings so we could go for a ride. We just sit there for a second, Hadley and

I, staring out the windshield as if the car were actually moving, the scenery passing us by.

"I don't really *care*," she finally says. "I mean, it's not a big deal or anything. You went off with a guy you liked." She shrugs as if to say, *Who hasn't?* Then she turns and sizes me up. "So." She smirks. "How was it?"

"It?"

"Yeah, *it*." She looks at me levelly.

"Oh," I gasp like a little girl and then wish I could pop it back into my mouth. "It was . . . we didn't—"

"You didn't what?"

"I mean, we kissed."

She snorts. "And he chewed half your lip off?" She touches her lower lip, and I touch mine, wince as my fingers brush the wound.

"That wasn't . . . no, I fell and bit that."

"How'd you fall inside a car?" Hadley raises her eyebrows.

"No, not inside. Out of the car. Onto the street."

"Must have been some kissing."

She's still looking at me steadily, but there's something just behind her eyes, some tick of Hadley clockwork. Forget geometry and algebra, precalc, and all that. There should be a math class that teaches you how to plot out a face, determine the angle when a squint of an eye becomes a glare, the arc of a lip that makes a smirk into a sneer. Because, judging by her face, it looks like maybe Hadley's mad at me after all.

"I didn't fall because of kissing. That . . . how could . . . ? We stopped kissing by then and—"

"Why?"

"Why did we stop kissing? Because, well, he said—"

I hear it again in my head. *Oh.* The way Jonah said it. *Oh.* Like he'd bumped into me and said "pardon," like he'd stepped on my foot and said, "my mistake."

"I reminded him of Zabet," I finish. *And it's true*, I think. *He did say that.* "He said, 'that dead girl,' he called her that, which is so . . . I mean, of course, I had to leave after that."

Hadley is still looking at me, her head cocked, her smirk winched, her face dappled with bruises. She hasn't moved at all, hasn't even twitched, and yet everything feels suddenly different, as if the car has started speeding forward and neither of us has noticed that we are speeding along inside it, being taken to our destination.

"*That dead girl?*" Hadley repeats. "He called her that?"

Oh, I hear Jonah say again, and I wish that I could take all of it back. "Well, yeah, but I think he just—"

"Fuck you," Hadley says in a quiet voice. "Really."

"Hadley?"

"I waited for you alone in the goddamn woods. I thought you'd come back, but you didn't. So then I drove over and waited outside your house, then here. I said to myself that if you weren't back by morning, I'd tell someone, call the police or someone."

"I'm sorry I scared you."

Hadley sits up straight with the feeling of a spring tightening, an arm pulled back, something loaded and ready to snap. "I wasn't *scared*. Don't think I was *scared*. So you're some dumb girl, dumb enough to follow some strange guy to his car in the middle of the night, dumb enough to drive off alone with him. Why should I be scared over you?"

"I'm sorry."

"I don't care," Hadley says, the words all mixed up with her breath. "I don't care about you. Go off with Jonah Luks, let him call you dead girl and bust your lip. I don't care." She turns away then and stares out the windshield at the empty road in front of us. "It's not like you're my friend or anything."

I'm not? I want to say. I'll admit, I feel like crying, so much so that I can't even ask that tiny two-word question because I know that I'll actually start crying if I do, so I say the other two-word sentence, the one that doesn't mean anything.

"I'm sorry."

"Get out of my car, please," Hadley says, her voice straining under its own politeness. And when, after a moment, I don't get out, she starts yelling, really yelling, her mouth so wide that I can see the dark, wet inside of her throat, her face pink, creeping up on red, lighting up the bruises. "Get out! Get out! Get the fuck out!"

So I do.

As I'm walking away from the car, the front door of the house across the street opens up, and a Hokepe divorcee steps out, blinking in the sun with a look of faint alarm. She scans the street, right then left, searching for whatever is the matter.

~

Rick-from-the-bank is gone when I get home, leaving no toothbrush balanced on the sink, no limp sock under the bed, no cheap jacket that he'll have to come back for later. His only souvenir is my mother's smiles, less frequent, more relaxed when they do come, as if she doesn't need them so much anymore. She's in the kitchen making a second breakfast and pretending it's her first. She's fully dressed—shirt to shoes—as if her bathrobe would be an admission of guilt.

"Morning," she says, not even turning around. "How was your slumber party? Did you watch movies? Paint toenails?"

I'm annoyed at her chipper voice, her breezy manner. More than annoyed. Furious, in fact. "Nope. Just busted my lip open," I say to punish her.

She turns around at this, her eyebrows raised in neat little points. "Ooooh!" she says when she sees my lip. She reaches out to touch it, and I squirm away. "You should put some ointment on that so it doesn't get infected. You don't want to have a fat lip for weeks."

And of course that's all she cares about, not if I was in danger, not if I was scared or rejected and embarrassed and ashamed, not if it hurts even, just whether it'll leave a mark.

"Don't you even care how I got it?" I say, and I'm glad to find that the tears that I had held back with Hadley are ready for me now. They spill down my cheeks. I let my bag drop to the floor, and my hand fumbles on the table across the dishes she's laid out for breakfast. If I had a colander or a ladle, I'd throw it at her now. I pick up a fork, which is too ridiculous a missile to actually express my anger. And this makes me even angrier. A fork.

Mom looks startled. She puts her hands prettily to her chest like, *Who, me?*

"Don't you care if some guy beat your daughter in the face?"

"Evie!"

I lower my head. "That's not what happened," I mutter. I let the fork drop back onto the table.

"Evie," she says again, taking a step forward and reaching out a hand but not touching me, like a statue in the park.

"I just said that's not what happened. I fell is all. I was clumsy, and I fell. But you could've asked. If you even cared, if you even . . . you could have asked."

I spin on my heel and leave her there, frozen in her pose.

I spend the day in my room. I do this. I do that. Mom knocks on the door a couple of times, but when I don't answer, she gives up. I'm half glad, but only half. We don't argue much, Mom and I. I'm not sure why I got so angry there in the kitchen. If I'm honest, my anger wasn't just for her but for Hadley and Jonah and myself. I came home wanting someone to comfort me, to put a plate of hot food in front of me and offer sensible advice. I wanted a parent. I wish suddenly, desperately for my father. But I don't know him any more than I know Zabet. He doesn't even exist, not really. I emerge from my room after she's gone to sleep. I have to use the bathroom, and I'm starved. I realize, when I sneak out into the kitchen, that Mom did have a plate of hot food for me this morning. I long for some of her eggs, but they've been scraped into the trash. I find some cold cuts in the fridge. I eat them on plain bread, too weary to bother with condiments. I make a little extra noise with the fridge door and my plate, hoping, I guess, that Mom will come out and check on me. She must be sleeping deeply; either that or she's mad at me, too. After I eat, I go to bed, dream my dreams.

⟶

The next morning, I drive into Hokepe Woods like I do every Sunday. But this time someone's sitting on the curb where I park, legs stretched out, drumming a neat little rhythm, which is swallowed up by the concrete. She has a sweatshirt on, hood up, as if to hide her face. Still, I know that it's Hadley even before she yanks the hood down.

"Surprise!" she says cheerily, as I get out of the car.

"Hi." I search her face for signs of our fight, but she returns my *hi* with another *Surprise!* and no hint that it ever happened.

"What are you doing here?"

"Helping." She brushes past me and drags my satchel out of the backseat. "Everyone needs a little help once in a while, Vie," she says in her ironic voice. And this sentence seems rehearsed, like she has stood off a little way to watch herself speak so that she can assess her performance of the memorized line.

I don't argue, though. I'm relieved, I guess, that someone isn't mad at me. After all, Mr. McCabe probably is, Mom definitely is, and maybe Jonah, too. Hadley and I deliver my papers together. I run up to the doors, while Hadley lingers at the curbs, as if she isn't allowed near the houses. We don't talk about the fight. *It was a mistake*, I think. *Never happened.* For once, we don't talk about Zabet or murders or the suspect list either. We play stupid games to pass the time, and this is fun: me at the door of the house and Hadley lobbing the paper from the curb, trying to throw it so that it will spin in the air like a baton. Whenever I hear a car coming, I take a few extra seconds on the porch in case it's Jonah and I need to hide. Hadley waits for me patiently, and I suspect that she knows what I'm up to. She doesn't mention Jonah, though, and I don't either.

Driving over, I'd had a plan: get to Hokepe extra early, finish my deliveries before Jonah arrived, and leave. Hadley slows me down, though. She lingers over the satchel as if pondering which of the identical rolled papers to choose. She stops me in front of this house or that to chatter on about the tortured house pets or cross-dressing husbands within. She whines until I agree to go back to my car to get her a stick of chewing gum. Her shoes refuse to stay tied. Consequently, my satchel is still half full when morning breaks.

Which leaves us partway up Comanche Circle, with the paper that Hadley has just thrown still spinning in the air, when Jonah's truck turns the corner. I freeze. The newspaper lands at my feet like a bird shot out of the sky. But Jonah drives past without slowing. I glimpse his profile, the profile of a man on a coin, his elbow resting on the truck's windowsill.

I look to Hadley for sympathy and find her wearing this tiny smile as if to say, *Do you dare me?* But before I can say, *Stop, don't, I don't dare you, no,* she whips around and races after the truck, waving her arms and shouting Jonah's name. I follow at a distance and tell myself that he doesn't know her, that he won't stop for some crazy girl, some strange, bruised girl. But Hadley waves and hollers and makes such a fuss that about halfway down the block, his truck drifts to the curb, and the cloud of exhaust dissipates to a puff and then a wisp as he cuts the engine.

Now, I'm well aware of the fact that a smarter Evie would turn around and plod on with the rest of her deliveries. A smarter Evie would double back to her car; she'd go home, apologize to her mother, eat breakfast, watch TV, and do homework. But me, the less-smart Evie, I run after them.

When I get to the truck, Hadley's leaning on it, her elbows hitched over the rolled-down window. She kicks her legs off the ground and tips partway into the truck, dangles, half in, half out, the beaming magician's assistant about to be sliced in half.

"I don't think so," Jonah's saying. He's not looking at her, maybe because of her bruises. He's not about to look at me either, but I can see the blush dashing up his neck as I step into view.

"Come on," Hadley says. "We just wanna see. Right, Evie?" She doesn't turn to make sure that I'm behind her. She knows I will be.

"Sure," I say, though I have no idea what I'm agreeing to.

Jonah looks past Hadley at me. The night before is there between us, and we're both careful to keep our gaze just above it, like not looking at the unfortunate purple birthmark on someone's cheek. Jonah gives me a curt nod. I make myself nod back. Down, up with the chin.

Hadley begins to deliver a little speech that I already know by heart: "Come on. We finished our deliveries early. It'll be something different, and . . . don't you want company? We've got good eyes. We can help you find animals."

A walk. So this is what Hadley has suggested. I feel relieved, considering all the other things she could have requested.

If Jonah recognizes Hadley's speech as the one I delivered a few weeks earlier, he doesn't mention it. He keeps making quiet excuses as he unloads his sled and tarp, but Hadley is unstoppable. Whatever small flirtations I've committed, she's a million times more obvious. She plays with his collar and laughs braying laughs and canters off for the woods in front of him even after he's already told her no a dozen different ways. I trudge a few feet behind them, behind the sled.

Last night seems made up. Except there's Jonah's averted gaze, his awkward half sentences, his too-long stride like if he walks fast enough, he'll outpace us. I stare at the back of Jonah's neck—the stain of sunburn, the fork of sinew, and the knob of bone that marks the top of his spine. I picture that neck bent over Zabet's body, bent over me when I was spilled out on the pavement the night before. My heart starts to thrum, and I can feel its tension echoed in

Hadley. Her shoulder-bumps become rougher, making Jonah lose his footing for a second, and her laughter doubles and redoubles into a cackle.

"You gonna cut out on us?" Hadley asks, nodding at the car keys still clutched in Jonah's hand.

"Nope." He doesn't put the keys away though, just keeps holding on to them.

"Good, because we'd be lost in the woods. Lost! We'd never find our way home. Right, Evie?"

I shrug, but she keeps staring at me, waiting for an answer. "I guess," I finally say.

"It's not really a woods," he tells her. "Just a few trees."

"Just a few trees. A few trees. That's all," she repeats and then laughs wildly and alone. I feel Jonah glance back at me, but I avoid his eyes. "So, you like animals?" she says to him. "You have dreams of being a pet-shop owner? A vet-er-i-narian?"

Jonah looks bewildered, even from behind.

"She's kidding," I say.

"No. I'm serious," she grouses. "I'm totally serious. You could own a pet shop. Just think: All the little kitties mewing."

"I like animals fine."

"You must," she says. "You're, like, their undertaker or funeral director or something. Do you bury them?"

"I just haul them away."

"Where do you take them?"

Jonah doesn't answer. The sled bumps along in front of me. I watch the kick of its red plastic surface and bite down on my back teeth, worried about where this conversation is headed.

"Did you ever find one that was still partly alive? Like it was injured but still alive?" Hadley's not pretending to laugh now, not careening into him. She walks with her head turned sideways and her eyes locked on Jonah, studying him.

Knock it off, I almost say, but I don't. I can't stand up to Hadley, so I say nothing, just keep trudging forward. *I'll get through this,* I think. *If I just stay quiet and walk, we'll come out the other side of the trees and be done.*

"And if you did find one still a *little* bit alive, would you kill it? Would you kill it right then? Like, stomp it with your boot? Or maybe you'd take out a hunting knife—do you have one of those?— take it out and slice it. Or maybe you could beat it until it's dead."

Jonah halts and turns on her. His brow is wrinkled and his mouth is screwed to the side like he's got something ready to spit. Hadley takes a step back and an expression flashes across her face, so quick that I'm the only one who can see it. So quick, I'm not sure I can read the emotion written there. Then, in one swift move, she reaches out, yanks the keys from Jonah's hand, and tosses them in the air. The keys spin and fan out like the legs of dancing girls. When they come down, she catches them, and, with a tip of her head, as if doffing a hat, takes off into the trees.

Jonah is dumbfounded. He looks from me to the sled to the direction where Hadley's run and then back to the sled again. "Christ," he mutters. "Can you watch this?"

I can't speak, so I nod, and Jonah jogs off after Hadley. Left alone, I stare down at the sled. I've taken a step too far forward and am now half standing in it. I lift my foot up and out. How long until they return, Jonah with the keys? I lean into the tree next to me. My cheek presses against something slick and synthetic. It's one of the tree ribbons, those bright orange markers. I study it while, in my head, I count back along the path of our walk. It's the fourth one we've passed, I decide. Four ribbons out of five. I picture Hadley, dancing ahead of us, flirting . . . distracting, it occurs to me, *leading* us in this direction.

I squint into the mess of trees ahead, searching for a glimpse of hair or jacket, some sign of life, but there's nothing. I tug on the tree ribbon, pulling its end like I could undo all of this if I could just undo its knot. I feel suddenly sick, sick with suspicion. *You're getting carried away,* I tell myself. *Don't be silly. You're making it all up.*

"Hadley!" I call out weakly. "Jonah!"

Silence.

I take two stumbling steps after them but stop, unable to follow. I'm ridiculous. I'm a liar. I'm a coward. I bend over with my hands on my knees, my knees shaking. Prickles run up and down my legs and in patches on my cheeks as if my body is falling asleep piece by piece. I breathe. I try to breathe. I'll go after them in a minute; I'll straighten up and go after them. In the trees ahead, someone cries out—a loud yelp of rage or pain—there and then gone again, without even an echo. I don't wait to hear if there'll be another cry. I turn and run the other way.

Chapter TWENTY-SEVEN

AT FIRST, I don't think I'll be able to find my way out of the woods. I hear Hadley's voice in my head: *Lost! We'll be lost!* Even though I know the woods is small, all I see are trees, and I worry that, in my panic, I've run in the wrong direction. But then up ahead I see the spikes of a fence and the bright paint of a swing set. I emerge in someone's backyard, right in the middle of the yellow, tamped-down circle of grass where they must set their kiddie pool. I run out to the sidewalk, smacking into the middle of a pride of jogging divorcees. They pause their rhythmic breaths and stare at me, their makeup like masks. I mutter an apology and stumble on, finally clutching the bricked back of the Hokepe Woods sign.

By the time I reach Mr. McCabe's condominium, I'm gasping. I pound on the door and then double over, spitting into the shrubbery next to the porch. When Mr. McCabe opens the door, I don't even give him a chance to say my name. "Come," I gasp. "You've got to come."

He doesn't ask where. He doesn't ask why I disappeared yesterday morning. He's wearing the same robe and pajamas he was then, and I wonder if he's been wearing them this entire time. Zabet's tidy bedroom, the bedroom I ruined, flashes in my mind, but he doesn't say anything about that, either.

"My shoes," is all he says. He goes back to collect them and then asks, "Do we need to drive?"

I shake my head, and as I do, a tear shakes off my cheek, and I realize that I've been crying, but I don't know when I started. It's not the kind of crying that you force up and out of your throat but the kind of crying where the tears slip out your eyes and down your cheeks, dissolving into one another at your chin in a stealthy escape.

Mr. McCabe runs alongside me. Even though he is large and soft in the belly, he runs fast, faster than me. He still doesn't ask why we're running, and maybe it's his faith in me that's made me cry. He grabs my arm and urges me on. We run without slowing, all the way back across the road and into his old neighborhood, between the two houses where I'd emerged minutes before. When we reach the edge of the trees, he stops.

"There?" he says and nothing else. He stands at the border between lawn and trees, not looking in, looking only at me. His daughter's body was found in there, right in there. I didn't think of that.

"I'm sorry," I say. "I'm sorry. I didn't know who else to get."

"What's going on here?" he finally asks, his voice deep, firm, a father's.

"Hadley." I put my hands over my mouth as I say it. He hasn't heard me, and I have to repeat it. "Hadley's in there."

He's still for a moment, completely so. His face white—worse, gray. "We should call the police," he finally says, like a line from a play. "We'll borrow someone's phone."

"Oh, no. She's not dead. She's not"—I ball a bit of my shirt up in my hand. "She did something. I'm not sure. I'm not . . . I think she might have done something. Help," I whisper, ashamed of the word and its drama. "Please, help."

Mr. McCabe runs a hand over his face. "Okay," he says.

⌒⌒

There are things I've imagined—gruesome things—Zabet dying over and over, beaten until her nose cracks, until her cheeks shatter, until her eyes swell shut.

There are things I've seen now. There are things I don't want to tell.

We find them by the fifth tree ribbon, by the muddy patch, the place where Zabet lay dead. Hadley is curled on the ground across the clearing from Jonah with her knees up to her chest. Her clothes are soaked. At first I think she must've been spattered with some clear fluid from Jonah's wounds, but then I realize that it is her own sweat and maybe her urine. She is clean of blood, anyway. But this cleanliness is worse, appalling even, because it means she didn't go to him; she didn't try to stop his bleeding.

Mr. McCabe walks straight to Jonah, shedding his robe as he goes. He pulls the belt out of its terry-cloth loops, feeds it under Jonah's thigh, and ties it around his leg. He wads the rest of his robe over the wound and the jaws of the trap. He glances over at me as he does this, and I wonder if he's trying to stanch the blood or simply hide the sight of Jonah's leg from my view. *Too late*, I want to say. *You're too late. I've already seen it. Can't unsee it now.*

Jonah doesn't move or make a noise as Mr. McCabe attends to him. He lies flat on his back, passed out. Or maybe he's dead, I don't know. I know that I should go to him, kneel down in the mud, hold his hand. Instead, I find myself moving toward Hadley.

She is suddenly small and fragile, young, a young girl, much younger than me. When I touch her arm, it's rough with goose bumps. She looks at me, frozen, no expression on her expressive face, and then her mouth twists into a grimace and she starts to sob. I put my arms around her, and she lets me, shaking in the circle of them so violently that I start to shake, too. She's saying something, but her hair is in her face, in her mouth. I bend my face down near hers, and the smell of her is pure and gamey, like animal piss. *Fear*, I think. I can see her hands down through the well of her body, lying still in her lap. And this is more frightening somehow—these still hands— than if she'd been balling them, working them over each other, using them to rend her clothes or skin. Guilty hands. Dead hands.

"Evie?" she whispers.

"What?"

"It was me."

I try to say *it's okay*, but this feels wrong, like forgiveness that I'm not fit to give. So I say *I know*, instead. In the kindest, quietest voice I can muster, I say, "I know."

I tell her, "Mr. McCabe's here, see? It's going to be okay, see? Do you see that, Hadley? Do you see?"

I say this and a bunch of other nonsense—coos and shushes and promises that I don't have the power to keep—while Hadley shakes in the loop of my arms and murmurs things into her hair.

It isn't until after Mr. McCabe has called me over and instructed me to press my hands against Jonah's leg, the arc of the trap's jaw under the robe like the spine of an old cat under its fur—"Keep pressing, and if he wakes up, make him lie still," Mr. McCabe tells me—it isn't until after Mr. McCabe's footfalls have crashed away, until after I've stared for minutes and minutes at the soft stretch of skin under Jonah's jaw, hoping for a flutter, a catch, a swallow; it isn't until after all this that Hadley's words make sense, echoing back from seconds before like the delay in a long-distance call.

"It was me," she'd said again and again. "It was me."

I look up and she's watching me across the clearing, her eyes huge and dark in her face, her lips the same color as her skin, as if I have stumbled upon some wild creature who waits, alert, to see if I will raise my arm and scare it away.

"It was me," she says again in a strange, flat voice.

And even though part of me feels like I shouldn't, like it'd be better not to ask, in the end, I always want to know, whatever ugliness, whatever harsh truth, whatever secret. I need to see it; I need to understand. So I say, "What was you?"

"Zabet," she says, and at first I think she's gotten confused, that she's calling me Zabet, but then she says, "Zabet's dead, and it was me. My fault."

Oh, I think. *Oh, Hadley.* "It wasn't you."

"No. It was. I want to say . . . tell. . . . There was a list, another list." The words are high on her breath as if she's not speaking them but exhaling them. Her eyes are locked on mine; her lip curls up in what could be a snarl, what could be disgust. "We met guys and added them to it. They'd meet us places, and the day after, we . . . we'd add them."

"I don't really—"

"Anywhere. Gas stations, diners, bars that let us in, on the street, the food court at the mall, we met them and added them."

"But how does that . . . You mean Zabet met someone? For the list? You think that last night, the night she . . . died, she met him for your list?"

Hadley shakes her head and lifts her dead hands, holding them cupped just under her face as if she is begging for something to fill them up, water, coins, tears. "I don't know."

"But if you knew who it might—"

"No," Hadley moans. "We met them once and then never again. Even if they wanted to. We gave fake names, numbers. It was a joke or game or . . . I don't know what it was."

"But the list! If you show them the list, the police could—"

She breathes in like this is the question she has been steeling herself for. "I burned it. I was scared."

"Oh, Hadley."

"It was my idea. She just went along with it. Just like you." She drops her face into her hands and starts to cry.

Another list. A first list. The real list of suspects, burned, gone. And then there's Hadley's and my list, the second list, the names on it in my writing. My idea. Jonah's name is on it. I press down on Mr. McCabe's robe, and through it, I can feel the hard fact of the trap, the soft flesh of Jonah's leg. Under my hands, he is still.

Chapter TWENTY-EIGHT

THE MEDICS CUT SILENTLY through the trees, like deer. There are
four of them, two stretchers. I wonder if they are the same ones who
were here before to collect Zabet. I can't recall the faces of those
other ones, if they are the same faces as these, peering down at us
firm and grim. Two of them head for Jonah and me. They set the
stretcher in the leaves, and one of the medics kneels next to me,
pressing his hands, which have been snapped into hospital gloves, on
either side of mine.

"Lift your hands for me now," he says. "Lift your hands and
sit back."

I stare at my hands. They're clean and pink. There is so much
blood here; it seems like my hands should be dipped in it. When I
lift them, I feel a surge of panic. I'm not touching Jonah anymore.
He'll die, I think wildly, *all the blood will rush from him. He'll die*. But the
medic's hands are on Jonah's leg now, pressing steadily.

"Good girl," he says. "You did good."

He begins to lift the robe from Jonah's leg, stops, glances at me,
just like Mr. McCabe did, like maybe he shouldn't do it with me
right there, but he goes ahead and lifts the robe anyway. I see a flash

of metal, the angle of the trap grinning around Jonah's leg, like a mouth grinning around a chicken drumstick.

Then Mr. McCabe is there, his hands on my shoulders, plucking me up from the ground and leading me away. "Come on, now," he says. "Come with me over here."

He's still in his pajamas. No one's given him a coat or anything. I wonder if he's embarrassed, a grown man wearing pajamas outside in the daytime with all these people around. Or maybe the pajamas make him feel like he's sleepwalking or dreaming.

"He moved a little while you were gone," I tell Mr. McCabe.

"Good," he says. "You did good."

I wish people would stop saying this, because I haven't done anything good; I've done no good at all.

We stop across the clearing, a little way away from Hadley. The other two ambulance workers crouch near her, wrapping a tinfoil blanket over her shoulders. She doesn't move as they do this, just stares out into the trees, her pupils huge as if we are all in a dark room. Her hands peep out from the blanket where she holds it closed at her neck. She shivers, and the whole blanket shivers, too.

The medics have both Jonah and Hadley strapped to the stretchers now. One of them waves Mr. McCabe over and speaks briefly to him before turning back to the stretcher and, with his partner, hoisting it up, carrying it out.

Mr. McCabe returns to me, puts a hand on my shoulder, patting it once. "We're going to follow them to the hospital, all right?"

We walk back to Mr. McCabe's condominium in silence, and I wait downstairs while he changes out of his pajamas. He makes a phone call. I can't hear most of it, but I catch the phrase "don't worry" a few times, and so I assume the call is to either Hadley's mother or mine.

We continue our silence on the drive over. Mr. McCabe doesn't ask me what happened, and I thank him for that over and over again in my head. The same few thoughts play in a loop and nothing else. Hadley's confession, about Zabet and the other list, is there in my head, too, and I know I should tell him about this. I tell myself that I'll talk to Hadley first. Really, I'm a coward.

We reach the hospital, its identical windows like pixels. I walk a step behind Mr. McCabe, who leads us through corridors to one counter and then through more corridors to another. I stand back against the wall as he talks to the women at the counters. I don't want to hear what they have to say. After the second counter, Mr. McCabe leads us to a waiting area. The chair I sit in squeaks when I move, as if to protest my fidgeting. The chairs are arranged in a circle, though we are the only ones sitting in this circle.

"Evie," Mr. McCabe says, and I look at him because he has used my name. *Now*, I think, *now is when the punishment comes*. "They need to know what happened. Do you think you can tell them?"

I look around to see who "they" is, but there is no one here. Even the nurse at the counter has disappeared.

"Do you think you can tell them?" Mr. McCabe asks again because I haven't answered.

"The police?" I say, still looking for them.

"Not the police." Mr. McCabe frowns. "There aren't any police here."

"Who, then?"

"The EMTs." And, as if he has called her, one of the medics from the woods rounds the corner with the nurse who was at the counter.

I look for bloodstains on her dark uniform, but there are none. She was one of the medics attending to Hadley, not Jonah. She takes the chair across from mine, flips a few pages on her clipboard, smoothes one out, and clicks her pen, all before acknowledging us, which she does with a crisp smile.

"I have some questions for you," she says; she doesn't even offer her name. *EMT*, Mr. McCabe had said. I try to remember what that stands for: *Emergency*, something, and something else.

I nod.

"You witnessed the accident?" she asks.

"Yes," I tell her, so startled by the word *accident* that I answer without thinking.

She ticks something off on her clipboard. "I need your name and your phone number."

I recite both, but the information seems separate from me, non-sensical even.

"Can you describe what happened?"

It was Hadley! I imagine myself saying. *She's the one! Murderer!* my mind shouts. *Murderer!* Though no one has died, at least not yet. But in the suggestion of this imaginary accusation, I realize something that almost makes me gasp. What I realize is this: Hadley had planned everything.

She'd stolen the trap from my room when she came to pick me up for our sleepover, stowed it in her stupid black backpack. *She'd* brought it out to the woods and hidden it there. *She'd* snatched Jonah's keys, made him chase her. And when she got to the clearing, to the patch of mud, strewn with the branches *she'd* used to hide the trap, *she* jumped over it, timed her feet to hit the ground before and after the open jaws, Jonah just behind her, following her path. Did she turn at the snap of the trap, the snap of bone? Or did she hit the ground and run on, heedless of the leaves and branches whipping her face? And when she did eventually return to the clearing, did she stand over him, a conqueror, believing that she'd finally avenged Zabet's death? Avenged the stupid cut on my lip? I think of Hadley that night before the party, out on the shoulder of the vacant highway, no cars to bear us away. *I'll protect you*, she'd told me.

"It was an accident," I hear myself saying, repeating the EMT's own word. "We didn't know the trap was there. We didn't know what would happen."

She doesn't nod or frown or make any sort of expression, simply writes on her clipboard in deft, swift strokes.

"We were just keeping him company. Hadley grabbed his keys as a joke. You can ask Jonah." I swallow. "I mean, you can ask him later. When he's better."

But the woman doesn't seem to care much about any of this. She's already stopped writing and moved her pen down an inch to fill in the next question on the form. "The trap was located where, would you say?"

It goes on like this for a dozen questions more. I answer them all, making my best guesses for the things I'm not sure about, making up my best stories for the things I'm lying about. Mr. McCabe sits next to me, alert, his big hand on my arm, squeezing reassuringly when my voice gets tense from some lie I'm telling. Both adults soften visibly when this happens, the EMT waving us on to the next question. They're worried that I'm upset.

"That'll do it," the EMT finally says. She smiles at me, the motherly smile of sated bureaucracy. "Thank you, honey," she murmurs. "You did good."

Mr. McCabe and I wait for another I-don't-know-how-long. The clock on the wall is dead, though it takes me a while to realize this. At first I think that it's the same minute, stretching on improbably long. I stare at my clasped hands, which aren't praying, only holding on to each other. I want to read one of the magazines on the end table, but I worry that it would seem rude if I did. Finally, Mr. McCabe picks one up, glancing at me and smiling under his mustache. He pushes another one toward me. I slide it into my lap and open it. The fashion models look exhausted, ready to collapse. Patients appear and are swept into one of the real areas of the hospital, where bone saws smoke and scalpels snag skin, where the white blossoms in your throat are scraped, your jagged wounds pulled tight with thread, your festering organs cut free.

My mother arrives and throws her arms around me in the perfect embrace of parental concern. I don't even care if she's thinking about how she looks while hugging me; I sink into her arms anyway. When she pulls away, her face is pale and young, her eyes lashless, her lips a bare pink, nearly the same color as the skin around them.

I reach out and touch her cheek. "You aren't wearing makeup," I say with wonder. Usually she puts it on before breakfast and leaves it on until bedtime. I've definitely never seen her leave the house without it. This is more extraordinary than Mr. McCabe wandering around in his pajamas.

"Oh, well." She touches her face, too, lays her fingers over mine in fact. "I was in a hurry." She peers at my face, naked concern on her naked face. "You're all right," she finally says, her tone halfway between question and pronouncement. "Sweetheart, you're really all right?"

"Yeah, I'm"—and then, before I can help it, I've started to cry. I stumble toward her. "Mom," I say into her sweater.

"I was so worried," she tells me.

"I'm sorry," I sob. "I'm so sorry."

She hushes me and strokes my hair, holding me again, even tighter, just like a mother should.

Eventually, my name is called. I am ushered through those doors by an eager young nurse who repeatedly assures me that my friend will be fine. "She was just in shock," she keeps saying. "A little shock, that's all." She repeats this three or four times, and I start to wonder if she thinks I am in shock, too.

It is good that I'm here, she tells me, so good because it was a little difficult to get ahold of my friend's parents, but this intrepid nurse, a few minutes ago, prevailed. They're on their way.

"Cheer her up now," the nurse demands of me and pauses as if waiting for a response. Her scrubs are covered with tiny gamboling lambs. Their cheerful cartoon faces make me yearn for wool coats.

I nod. "Okay."

"Nothing like a visit from a friend," she says, guiding me into a small exam room where Hadley sits up on the table in a pair of green hospital scrubs. Her hair has been combed out and her face washed; new butterfly bandages were applied to her cut so that their wings are a pristine white. *No, not butterfly bandages*, I think. *Moths.*

"Could I pass as a doctor, or what?" she says, running her hands over the scrubs.

"I guess."

"Think they'd let me do a surgery?" She grins, but it fades when I don't grin back.

"How are you feeling?" I ask.

She rolls her eyes at me as if to say, *This? This is what you want to talk about?* "They say I was in shock." She shrugs. "Now I'm not."

I've started to hate these shrugs, these twitches of indifference. I want to press my hands on Hadley's shoulders and hold them down. She makes a fist and bops her own knee, like the doctor's reflex test; her leg kicks up in response. I back up into one of the chairs, which squeaks at me in sympathy. Hadley bops her knee again. Her leg kicks out.

"Stop that," I say.

She looks at me. "Make me."

"Come on. Please."

She bops it again.

"Please don't be funny right now."

She watches me for a moment, carefully, and then, with an air of deference to me, like it's the biggest favor in the world, unclenches her fist and sets her palm, flat, at her side. Her leg rests back against the side of the exam table, still and perfect and whole.

She frowns. "What's the matter with you?"

I don't know how to answer this impossible question, so I stare at her blankly, until she shrugs once more and looks down at her hand. Her demeanor changes, that shift in the weather that I've become expert at forecasting. I'm a goddamn Hadley meteorologist.

"My parents are coming," she says in a tone that suggests I've argued that they're not. "They're on their way."

We sit for a moment without speaking. Hadley begins to rock, making the paper on either side of her whisper. I wonder how long

I have to sit there, when it's polite enough for me to get up and go, what Hadley will do if I try to leave. Finally, she stops rocking, and the last whispers of the paper smooth out into silence.

"About what I said before. You remember?" she says.

"Yeah."

"I was thinking . . ." And I think she's going to say, *Don't tell anyone* or *Don't blame me* or *I feel so guilty.* But instead she says, "It could have been him."

"It couldn't," I say. I mean my voice to be firm, but it is a trembling whine, weak and thin.

Hadley smiles down at me from the table as if she pities me. "You don't get it."

"What?"

"Guys. They'd follow us over nothing, a question, a smile, a stupid hello. Do you know how many names were on that list? Zabet's and my list?"

"Jonah's wasn't."

She shrugs. "He followed you out of the woods same as any of them, took you back to his car."

"He was drunk. I was—"

"Kissed you."

I shake my head stupidly. "It wasn't him."

She smiles and shakes her head back at me, a slow, bemused *no, no, no,* like she won't let me get away with this. "You *told* me it was him."

"I never said that!"

"He hit you."

I touch my lip, scabbed over now. "I never—"

"'I fell'? Come on. I knew what you were saying."

And there it is.

Hadley looks down at her hands again. She nods tiny nods, as if she's agreeing with what she's just said. And maybe she believes it. And maybe it's true. Maybe I did know what I was doing, did it as punishment for Jonah, since he rejected me. There could be that kind of spider in me, that scuttling gray weaver, that whisper of ill intent, that evil. You would call that evil, right? That's what evil is.

"You said it," Hadley repeats, always knowing when she has the advantage, knowing when to press it. *"That dead girl.* You told me that."

I stand up, allowing my chair one final squeak of protest, and walk to the door of the exam room, reaching out for the doorknob with a quivering hand, worried for a moment that my fingers won't be able to reach it, worried that my hand will pass right through.

"If they ask," I say, my voice shaking, "I told them it was an accident."

"Yeah," Hadley says with a bored little sigh. "I knew you would."

⟋⟍⟋

The hospital hallway is empty; the lamb-covered nurse has trotted off somewhere with her pocketful of tongue depressors. I try to follow the route back to the waiting area, but every hallway, every bend, every door looks the same, a labyrinth. I make a wrong turn and find myself in a corridor of patient rooms. I walk its length, telling myself not to look in, but it's hard not to even glance as I go by. I see a kid with covers up to his chin and a knit hat on his head, lots of sleeping lumps, lots more people watching TV, their expressions stolen by the flickering light of the screen. In one room there are two men playing cards, one in bed, the other attended by the metal scarecrow of his IV pole. In another, an ancient woman in a ruffled pink nightgown stands next to her bed doing calisthenics, the loose skin hanging under her arms like the starts of wings. She catches me watching her through the glass in the door, and I dart away just as she's beginning to smile.

If I'm looking for Jonah, I don't find him. He's probably in surgery, maybe dying or already dead. I keep walking because if I stop I might start crying, or worse, I might not be able to cry. I feel hollow, like everything has been scooped out of me, all the seeds and pulp, the edge of the spoon cutting into the pith. And it's worse *not* to be able to cry. Inhuman. Serves me right.

I must look like I know where I'm going, because no one stops me, none of the cardboard doctors or paper nurses, and finally I have to stop myself because I've reached the dead end of a corridor. There's nothing to do but turn around and go back. But I just stand there at the end of the hall. To my right is the emergency staircase, to my left, a door to a room. I peer in: a private room, dimmed by the hospital blues, the curtain drawn all the way around the bed in the center, hiding it. I go in.

The curtain is long and faint blue, clipped to a track in the ceiling, a modest shroud for the bed it covers. There's a sliver of room left outside of it, a little strip of free tile, space enough for a sink and a chair. This is where I stand. I listen for a sound behind the curtain, the stir of sheets, the falling grace note of a snore, but there is nothing, no shadow that I can discern through the folds of fabric, no blip of machinery, no scratch or cough, no rustle. I step closer to the curtain, so close that I can feel the space between the cloth and my skin. I imagine someone sitting on the edge of the bed, some patient, leaning ever so slightly forward, head cocked and eyes sweetly closed, waiting, breath bated, to hear what I will say.

I think of all that's happened, what I've seen and what I've done. I think of all the ways I could explain it, the justifications and apologies, the digressions and embellishments. I open my mouth to form the first sentence. *I was in Hokepe Woods,* I could say, *like I am every Sunday.* I could explain everything from the start so that he would understand, from that morning crouching in the garden with the sirens wailing around me to here, now, in this hospital room, the bed curtain brushing my face. And when I'm done, the last sentence shaped and spoken, I'll be at peace.

I open my mouth and look for a word. I take a breath. But then, I don't. I back out of the room, leaving the curtain in place. I retrace my path through the corridors, back to the waiting area. Mr. McCabe is still there in the circle of chairs. My mother is, too. When my mother sees me, she leans forward worriedly and says, "Evie?" But I walk past her and over to Mr. McCabe, who's watching me like he's been expecting this all along. I stand in front of his chair, make myself meet his eyes, and say, "I have something to tell you."

Chapter TWENTY-NINE

JONAH LOST HIS LEG. They took it at the knee. It's gone now, that piece of him. The doctors were able to save his thigh and the joint of his knee, but everything below that was unsalvageable.

I don't think about Jonah's leg, the chewed beam of his calf, whatever ribbons of tendon, the marbled nub of knee bone, round and white as a blind eye. I don't think about it being chucked into the hospital incinerator, a sizzle as the leg hairs go up, skin peeling and curling like burnt slips of paper, the limb withered, desiccated to a bent branch of ash. I don't think about any of that.

I didn't visit Jonah in the hospital. A few months earlier, I would've looked for any excuse to see him. I can picture myself standing next to his bed, arms bursting with carnations, candy boxes, and board games, balloons bopping along behind me. But that's a different girl—the one in my mind, who asks brightly for a vase and shifts her weight from one foot to the other, searching for any excuse to touch Jonah's arm or cheek, trying her hardest not to glance at the place where the covers sag, the leg gone from beneath them. I should've visited him anyway—me, this Evie—no matter how it would've been.

Jonah didn't return to his job in Hokepe Woods or to Chippewa at all. Instead, he went to live with his brother in South Carolina while he recovered. I think there was some physical therapy he had to do, but I'm not sure because I wasn't there for any of that, either. He has a fake leg now, made out of something fancy, and he gets around okay, I hear.

I returned to Chippewa High the Monday after the accident. Once again, the residents of Hokepe Woods had been called by the ambulance sirens to gather behind their window treatments and watch the purposeful blades of the stretchers thresh their radiant Sunday morning. They had seen Hadley carried back out on one of those stretchers, trembling in her silver blanket, a foreign princess brought forth on a litter. At school that Monday after, there were rumors that Hadley had tried to burn down the woods, rumors that she had killed a man, killed herself, killed Zabet. But somehow my name was never whispered, as if I were a ghost, an escapee, the space between the trees, the page on which a story is written.

Hadley never came back to Chippewa High. She stayed home that final week of school, self-sequestered, spent the summer traveling with an aunt I didn't know she had, and then the next fall, she transferred to a private school upstate. The day before she left, she showed up at my house. Mom was there, and we were all stiff with each other, polite and talking around things. Though probably we'd have been that way, Hadley and me, even by ourselves. When Hadley hugged me good-bye that day, though, she held me tight and buried her nose in my neck, and when I tried to pull away, she wouldn't let me. She decided when she would let me go. And when she finally did, she was all grins and swagger again. "Be good, kiddo," she said and chucked me on the head. "Walk when carrying scissors. Look both ways. Don't talk to strangers." She said this last without any trace of irony. Then she drove away, my only friend.

There was never any inquiry into what happened to Jonah, at least none that I ever heard of. That no one would be curious about this second act of violence on the same ground as the first seemed unbelievable. For months and months, I waited for the police car to pull up in front of my house or uniformed officers to march into my English class. But no one came. No one suspected. In the end, I guess they figured that we were only girls teasing a boy in the woods, playing that old game of chase and catch, that it was an accident—some idiot poacher loaded a bear trap in a woods without bears, and some kids were unlucky enough to stumble into it. And Jonah, as far as I know, believed the same. So that's how Hadley and I got away with it, disappearing among the trees, the meanest of criminals.

I told Mom and Mr. McCabe part of things that day in the hospital waiting room. I told them about the guys that Hadley and Zabet used to meet, that first burned-up list. Mr. McCabe started to cry halfway through, which was pretty awful, and I almost stopped talking then and there. But Mom looked at me levelly and said, "Go on, Evie," and that made me able to. I know Mr. McCabe told the police about the first list and all that, and the police questioned Hadley again, but it didn't help them catch him.

In the end, they caught him by chance. In August, he killed another girl in Illinois. The police didn't catch him for that either, though; they pulled him over in a stolen car. Then they found traces of blood in the car that matched the Illinois girl's and, down in the bottom of his rucksack, a sweater that had been Zabet's. He claims that he's innocent, won't say a word other than that. His name is Ben Truax, a name that was never on Hadley's and my suspect list. How could it have been? He was a drifter, gone by the time we'd started looking.

And so there it is, the answer. It doesn't feel like how I thought it would at all. I don't feel the urge to gasp or say *aha!* I am not wiser or safer. The world is not set to rights. It is a small, sad, messy world, and I am a small, sad, messy girl. I didn't understand that having a story changes you. You have to have gone through something, after all, to have something to say. Now I have my story. But I can't bear to speak a word of it.

Except this: One night this spring, about a year now after Zabet's death, I went over to have spaghetti with Mr. McCabe. I never could admit to him that it was partly my fault that Jonah lost his leg. This time, though, I tried to tell him. I sputtered out a few miserable words, and Mr. McCabe rapped his knuckles on the table to quiet me.

"You know, Evie," he said, "sometimes, not often, but sometimes, there is a terrible thing."

He looked at me hard, like he was waiting for an answer.

"Yeah," I said. "I know that. Of course."

"What can you say to a terrible thing? Not *boo*. Not anything. Can't reason with it, can't tighten its screws, can't move it from one side of the room to the other. Can't know anything about it—why it's terrible, why it even happened—can't know anything more than the fact of it."

He lowered his hand, the back of it touching his knee, the palm making the shape of a cup. "I'm glad you came and got me that morning. I don't know what made you run all the way over here. I know there were people, phones, closer, and it's selfish for me to say this, but I'm glad you got *me*. Because"—he lifted his hand and ran it over his mustache—"I was able to help. I could hold my hand on that boy's leg, and that was something I could do."

After dinner, Mr. McCabe fell asleep in his chair, his soft chin nodding with the rise and fall of his chest, and I padded up the stairs and down the hall to Zabet's room. At first I thought I'd turned the wrong way, gotten the wrong door, because the room was cleared out. The bed had been stripped down to the daisy print of its mattress. The dresser drawers were empty, the closet, too—even the pack of cigarettes gone from the top shelf. The air carried the inoffensive smell of lemon soap, and the carpet was striped with vacuum lines. I stood in the middle of the room, the buzz of Mr. McCabe's snore ascending the stairs, following the familiar curves of the hall until it reached me here. She was gone, every hint of her, and yet it seemed as if the room itself was breathing the breath of shallow sleep, waiting for someone to call it to wake. *Rest in peace*, that's what we say when we speak to the dead, and then we hold our breath and wait for them to whisper the same words back to us.

Acknowledgments

Deep thanks to my parents, Beth and Frank Williams, for their love and support and for never once suggesting that I might just be sensible and go to law school. Thanks, too, to Laura Furman for her friendship and mentorship and for the phone call she made over her summer break telling me to write this novel.

I am near worshipful of my agent, Judy Heiblum, for her candor, strength, and smarts, and of my editors, Julie Romeis and Mary Colgan, brave warriors of the writing process. These three made this book better than it was.

Thanks to the Michener Center for Writers for their support and to my teachers—Michael Adams, Laura Furman, and Elizabeth Harris—for their guidance.

I have had help from friends along the way. Thanks to Dr. Matthew Wemple for lending me his expertise. My gratitude to Riley Hoffman, Morgan Johnson, and my San Francisco workshop group for the early reads and to Kris Bronstad, James Hannaham, and Susie Meserve for the later reads. My gratitude for their friendship, too.

Finally, special thanks to Ulysses Loken for walking me around the block when I get muddled and all the rest of it.

KATIE WILLIAMS is a graduate of the MFA program at the University of Texas in Austin and has published numerous short stories for adults. She lives in San Francisco, where she currently teaches writing at the Academy of Art. This is her first novel.